THE DARK
THAT DOESN'T
SLEEP

THE DARK
THAT DOESN'T
SLEEP

A NOVEL

SIMON MOCKLER

PEGASUS CRIME

NEW YORK LONDON

THE DARK THAT DOESN'T SLEEP

Pegasus Crime is an imprint of
Pegasus Books, Ltd.
148 West 37th Street, 13th Floor
New York, NY 10018

First Pegasus Books cloth edition June 2023

ISBN: 978-1-63936-425-1

10 9 8 7 6 5 4 3 2 1

Printed in the United States of America
Distributed by Simon & Schuster
www.pegasusbooks.com

For Louis and Penelope

1

Walter Reed Army Medical Center, Washington, DC
December 27, 1967, 2:00 A.M.

The room was brightly lit. Pale blue walls shone white and the black floor tiles shimmered and rippled like water. Paper chains and tired snowflakes hung from the ceiling and a Christmas tree sat unhappily in the corner, leaning forward but somehow not tipping. In the middle of the room was a flimsy Formica table and on either side sat two men, neither of whom wanted to be there.

Jack Miller was relaxed but wary, his eyes alert and clear despite the hour. His clothes well cut. He clenched and unclenched his right fist, which was large and heavy and stiffened with arthritis. The weight of it made the table look flimsier still. He rubbed his knuckles to ease the pain then looked from the blank piece of paper in front of him to the man opposite.

Private Connor Murphy. His face and hands were covered in bandages and the parts of his scalp that showed through were either pink and raw or black and charred. It made you hurt just to look at him, Jack thought. Poor bastard. The nurses said feeding him was like weaning a baby.

"How's the pain?" Jack asked.

Connor shrugged.

"How does it look?" he whispered.

"It looks like goddamn agony," Jack replied. "Drink?" He took a hip flask from his pocket and waved it at Connor. Connor shook his head. "Guess it wouldn't be a good idea to mix with your meds. Suppose a smoke's out of the question too. Mind if I do?"

"Go ahead," Connor replied. Jack tapped a packet of Lucky Strikes on the table and flicked one up to his mouth. Then he looked at Connor and changed his mind. Replaced the cigarette and dropped the packet back in his pocket.

"Why don't we start at the beginning?" he said.

"I don't remember the beginning. I told them already."

"Why don't we start somewhere else then? Further back. Another beginning."

"Another beginning?"

"Sure. Like when you got there. You were there for twelve months before the accident."

"Not much to tell," Connor said.

Jack cleared his throat. *Not much to tell.* They'd insisted he come from New York to DC that night to talk to a man who couldn't remember anything about what they wanted to talk about, and didn't want to talk about anything he could remember.

"What was it like, so far from home?" Jack asked.

Connor sighed. "White. Land is flat. And the cold. It cuts you."

"Tough posting."

"Yeah," Connor muttered, shaking his head, his eyes flicking from one bandaged hand to the other. Jack picked up a pen and held it over the pad. *White*, he wrote after a few moments of thought. Three lines in. Connor's eyes rested on the pad. Jack underlined it and put the pen down.

"No night in summer. No day in winter that far north. Must have taken a while to get used to."

Connor shrugged. "We were mostly underground. In winter we only went out to check the vents. Scrape the ice off. Same for the antennas."

"And you did . . . construction? Maintenance?"

"I did whatever the sergeant said."

"So you're running maintenance on the base. Middle of the day and it's pitch black. No sunset and no dawn. And the job. Long hours. A lot of pressure to get out before the ice moved. No time. No sleep. Must have been hard."

Connor winced.

"I don't remember," he said.

"You're an outdoors kind of guy, aren't you? From Wyoming." Jack smiled. Connor didn't answer. Jack leaned forward.

"Growing up on a farm. Fixing stuff. Running round outdoors. Long summers. And here you are working under the ice. In the middle of a night that lasts three months. Must have been tough."

Connor shrugged. "Wyoming gets awful cold in winter too."

"True. And your record is, what's the word? *Exemplary.* You know what *exemplary* means?"

"Of course I know. I'm not an idiot."

"Sure, sorry. Listen, we need to understand more about the fire. Two guys dead. Only you left standing. And they suffered something terrible. I mean, you did too. You know how it must have felt, but they . . . they couldn't get out. They would have cooked in that room. I can't imagine it. Don't want to."

Connor stared at the table, but his eyes were far away. He coughed. His body shook.

"I tried to help," he whispered.

"I thought you couldn't remember?"

"Look at me," he held up his hands. "I must have. I must have tried."

"No one's blaming you. It was a tough posting. I'm here to help you, help you remember the accident. Help you work things out. Help you adjust."

Connor sniffed and looked away.

"Bullshit," he muttered. "You need a scapegoat for your report. You're not even military, are you? Not in those clothes. Who do you work for?"

Jack leaned back in his chair. "I'm here to help you with your recovery. Like they told you. Tell me what you remember," he said gently.

"I told you I can't remember." He scratched at his arm with a bandaged hand. "Nurse! Can I get a nurse? Nurse! I want some meds. *Jesus.*"

Jack turned his head. The door opened and a woman came in. She poured a yellow liquid into a paper cup. She was about to lift it for him but he shooed her away and picked it up carefully between his bandaged hands, tipping it gently between his lips. Some of the liquid dribbled onto the white bandage wrapped around his chin.

"I want to sleep now," Connor said. "I need to sleep. I need to close my eyes."

2

Langley, Block B
December 27, 4:00 A.M.

Jack poured himself a cup of coffee and glanced around the deputy director's office. It was the same as he remembered, only this time more of a mess. Files were stacked on bookcases and piled up on cabinets. They'd gathered on the desk, too, leaving only the smallest square of workspace. On the wall was the obligatory army photograph that all the Agency seniors had to prove they'd actually fired a gun at someone once. Jack knew half the people in the photo. He'd been in the same platoon in the war, and he knew the man sitting behind the desk: Paul Coty, twenty years older and a lot more than twenty pounds heavier than he was in the picture.

"What do you think?" Coty said. "You believe him?"

"He's lying," Jack replied, adding enough milk to cool the coffee and draining it in one swallow.

"How do you know?"

"Two reasons. Firstly, he's the only one left alive, and secondly, he's the only one left alive."

"Ha. Don't be cute. You're too old," Coty said.

"I spend most of each day listening to people tell lies. A lot of the time they don't even know they're lies. They're just telling me the things they want to be true. In their head it's the same thing. No one starts with the truth when they're talking to a psychiatrist. He's no different. The question is: Why is he lying? You got a plan of the base?" Jack asked. "I'd like to see the layout."

Coty nodded, opened one of the files, and cleared some space on the desk. He unfolded it carefully, like a linen tablecloth, flattening out the creases.

"Big site," Jack said, flicking old cigarette ash off the paper and frowning as it left a charcoal smudge.

"Average," Coty replied. "The military has got bigger bases in West Germany. And in the Pacific."

"But those aren't underground. Must be over twenty miles of tunnels."

"Sounds about right. They started digging summer of '59. Moved in before winter and kept digging right up till '66, when they figured out the ice was too unstable."

"When did they put the reactor in?"

"About a year in."

"Project *Iceworm*," Jack read the text stamped on the side. "Who comes up with these names? Our boy with the burns on his hands and face was just low-level engineering and maintenance, right?"

"That's right. Not missile crew or research."

"Huh," Jack said, rubbing his chin. "These sections here the living quarters?" His stubby forefinger hovered over the plan. Coty nodded.

"And it happened here?" Jack said, pointing to the section labelled "generator" that was close to the center of the network of tunnels.

"That's where they found the bodies. He was outside in the tunnel. Only the three of them were left. Everyone else had been evacuated.

You've got the mess hall over there. Recreation rooms here. Showers, chapel, theater, whatever else they put in to keep themselves comfortable. Same as any regular base."

"But under the ice," Jack said.

"Exactly."

"Ice that moves."

"Yeah."

"You'd think they'd have known."

"They did. They thought they had an acceptable level of tolerance. But no one's ever done anything like this before," Coty said.

Jack frowned and rubbed his knuckles.

"*An acceptable level of tolerance.* I think my wife used to write me something like that on our anniversary. I'm surprised they managed to keep it a secret."

Coty looked at him sardonically.

"Ok, I'm surprised they managed to keep it a secret for so long," Jack added.

Coty drummed his fingers on his desk, then said, "They did a whole public relations piece when they built the place, research on the ice-core. They *were* doing research. NCO called Owen Stiglitz ran the program. He's one of your bodies. They also had short- and long-range ballistic missiles ready for deployment over Russia. The movement of the ice stopped all that. The tunnels weren't stable. You want to go in for another round with Connor? I need to brief the chief at midday."

"The man's had his morphine, he's out for a few hours."

"Don't leave it too long before you go back to him. If he's not up by nine A.M. then get the nurse to give him something to bring him round. Here, take these." He took a stack of files off his desk and passed them to Jack. "Flight logs in and out of the base going back twelve months. Radio transmissions and weather reports. Photographs of the fire damage. The accident report. And pictures of Connor, Stiglitz, and the other victim. Guy called Henry Carvell. It's all we could pull together on short notice. I'll give you detailed backgrounds once they come in."

Jack took the files. "Where am I staying?"

"The Willard. But you're not going there yet. I've got you a room here. In the basement. I'm keeping this out of sight."

3

Langley, Block B basement
December 27, 6:00 A.M.

J ack left Coty's office and waited for the elevator. The lights in the corridor gave off an eerie electric hum, the way they do in an office when they think no one's around. Coty had called him at his apartment in New York the previous evening. Asked him . . . no, *told* him he had a job for him. A different kind of job. Not the usual psych assessments he did for the Agency.

Jack was curious. The clients at his private clinic were a mix of paranoid old-money, referrals from New York State Hospital, and one or two actors who weren't getting the roles they used to. The work he did for Coty was different. He reviewed reports on field agents and analysts and predicted future behaviors. Their weaknesses and strengths. Their susceptibility to blackmail, coercion, to control.

He'd known Coty for over twenty years. The bond forged as they fought their way across the Pacific had stuck through their different careers. Over time it had morphed from friendship into a kind of weary codependence. Jack appreciated the work Coty sent his way, enjoyed it more than he cared to admit; he liked to be needed, especially since his wife died. Coty found it hard to trust anyone's opinion other than his own, but he trusted Jack. Jack understood what his agents might have to go through, or had been through. How it could affect them. He knew what combat felt like, not just the noise and the danger but the hours of endless waiting and watching. He knew what it felt like to pull the trigger and see a man fall. He knew how to live alongside the memories and not drown in them. At least most of the time. Jack had always run toward the fight, not away from it. It was his instinct, and Coty respected him for it.

The reports Jack drafted went to Coty, not the agent, and from Coty they went God knew where. A committee meeting. A disciplinary hearing. A locked filing cabinet in a basement room somewhere in Langley, probably not far from the room Coty had put him in to prep for his next meeting with Connor.

Jack looked over his shoulder. He nodded as two men walked by, a hushed seriousness to their conversation. The dull pad of their shoes swallowed up in the endless corridor.

The elevator came. Down he went. His makeshift office had a desk and a chair and not much else. He switched on the light. The single bulb hanging from the ceiling didn't make much difference to the gloom but it did make the room smell of burnt dust. He turned on the desk lamp too. A circle of damp yellow light spread over the dark wood. He put the files next to the lamp and hung his jacket on the back of the chair. Unbuttoned his cuffs and rolled up his sleeves. The skin on his left arm was smooth and raw-looking. There was little sensation. A skin graft. It was needed after a car accident, back in '52. The crash that took his wife. He thought about Connor, lying in the hospital, and remembered the slow cycle of operations that cut skin from his thigh and grafted it onto his arm. Sleeping on his side. How the morphine numbed the pain but made his mind loose and warm. How underneath that, insistent and needle-sharp, was the knowledge that the person who mattered most to him was gone.

He had some idea of what Connor had been through, and what he'd still have to go through. He took out his hip flask and cigarettes and fished about in the drawers for an ashtray. Once he'd found one he lit a cigarette, then carefully took off his watch, a battered Grand Seiko his wife had given him as a wedding present. He ran his thumb over the inscription on the back and felt the shallow indentation of the kanji characters. The Japanese saying was "Dumplings before flowers." Put what you need ahead of what you want. She'd changed it to "Dumplings and flowers." They'd met in Tokyo after the Japanese surrender. Even when a city is starving you need to feed the soul, she'd told him. You need hope.

It was a useful lesson. Connor would need to learn it if he was going to survive. And he was going to need to learn to tell the truth. To trust Jack. He placed the watch on the desk and opened the files. Flight logs. Manifests. Weather reports. He skimmed through them, looking for the accident report. It was brief. No more than a summary:

The fire took hold in generator cabin (a) in tunnel 7. Incendiary cause unknown, suspected fault with the generator and subsequent ignition of fuel stores. Initial consideration suggests extremely fast spread due to presence of accelerants, denying the two men time to escape. Possible failure of the lock mechanism of the door. Significant damage to the wooden structure of the cabin. The ice walls and floor of the surrounding tunnel also suffered major heat damage, causing partial collapse of the tunnel roof. The low ambient temperatures and isolation of the unit prevented the fire spreading beyond the cabin.

Estimated date of fire is December 2. The three men had been trapped at the base for seven days. When the rescue team arrived, it was still smoldering. On examination of their ID tags the two bodies were identified as Dr. Owen Stiglitz, chief scientific officer, and Sergeant Henry Carvell. Cause of death likely to be a combination of asphyxiation/high-intensity burns. Private Connor Murphy was found outside the cabin with significant injuries to hands and face in a serious but not critical condition. He was evacuated to the American air base at Thule, 140 miles west, then flown to Walter Reed Hospital in Washington, DC.

The fire site was unsafe and the bodies removed immediately. A photograph of the cabin with the two victims in situ is included. Owen Stiglitz was found nearest to the generator, Henry Carvell by the door.

Jack stared at the remains of the burnt-out cabin. The scene was lit with a surreal brightness, the ice walls of the tunnel had intensified the flash. What was left of the cabin walls and floor was black with soot. Owen Stiglitz's body was twisted and contorted, like some dreadful bug on its back, skin blackened, legs in the air, unable to right itself. Jack had come upon bodies like this in the war. This was how people ended up when you sent the flamethrowers in first. Muscles retracted as the body dried up in the heat. He'd worn the pack during one of the campaigns, when they were clearing out the island of Iwo Jima. The memories surfaced like an unwelcome guest, the bitter smell of gasoline and burnt skin. He took a swig from the hip flask to sink it back down.

Henry Carvell was little more than a pile of ash and bones and teeth, barely distinguishable from the soot-black floor. He put the photograph to one side and looked for the photos of the three of them before they were stationed in Greenland, then laid them out on the desk. Tried to get a sense of who they were.

Stiglitz was standing on the steps of a university building. Another man beside him was identified as Peter Mendelson on the back of the photo. There was a stiffness in Stiglitz's pose, head raised so he looked down at the camera; there was something disapproving, condescending even, in his expression. Deep-set eyes and a hairline that was already receding. He looked as if he was about to tell the photographer how to frame a better shot.

He picked up the photograph of Henry Carvell. Held it at a distance so he could focus better. Henry was in gym clothes, muscled, proud, squinting into the sun and holding a football as if he wanted to crush the life out of it. Late twenties, dominant. He had the unmistakable look of privilege, but there was something to his smile, a certain goofiness, that undercut the arrogance.

The third picture showed Connor. The survivor. Full dress uniform at a military dance. He was medium height, same as Stiglitz, similar build. But that was where the similarity ended. He had a high forehead and strong jaw. A wave of thick black hair and prominent cheekbones. Handsome, strikingly so, with a broad smile. The smile was directed at the girl on his arm. She was pretty. You got the impression she'd rather be dancing than posing for photographs. Jack looked closely. There was an engagement ring on her finger.

He wondered if the army had told her what had happened to her fiancé, if she'd been able to see him yet. He wondered what she'd think when she did see him. Connor wouldn't look the way he did in the photograph.

Jack leaned back in his chair. The cigarette in the ashtray had burned itself out. He looked at the hip flask. Decided to leave it alone. The problem with photographs, he reflected, was that they told you everything and nothing at the same time.

You could see a moment, and you could see everything in that moment, but you didn't know how that moment fit into every other moment. It was dangerous to make too many assumptions about someone based on a fraction of a second.

He opened the flight log for the base. Started making notes to help him structure his conversation with Connor. The next thing he knew it was 8:45 A.M. and he had a crick in his neck and a tongue that felt like a dead mouse. He put on his jacket, fiddled awkwardly with his watch strap, grabbed the notepad.

Seven days of arctic storm. The three of them trapped at the base. Two dead. Connor survives but says he can't remember what happened. Has to be lying, Jack thought.

4

Walter Reed Army Medical Center
December 27, 9:30 A.M.

M anage to get some sleep?" Jack asked cheerfully as he entered the room.

"If you can call it sleep," Connor replied.

"What would you call it?"

"Being drugged."

"Sounds like a blast."

"It ain't." The nurses had changed Connor's bandages and dressings so they were fresh and white, but the wounds underneath were already leaking red-brown stains.

"Takes away the pain though, doesn't it? Mind if I eat this while we talk?" Jack gestured at the bacon sandwich he'd picked up on the way in.

"Knock yourself out," Connor said.

Jack took a bite.

"I want to talk about Owen Stiglitz and Henry Carvell," he said. "You remember much about them?"

"Course I remember them. We were at the base together for twelve months."

"So it's only the days leading up to the accident where you have a blank?"

"I guess."

"Ok. Let's start with Owen Stiglitz. You like him?"

Connor shrugged.

"Stiglitz was ok."

"Ok good or ok bad?"

"I didn't see much of him. He was chief scientist. He was busy. He was distant."

"So you didn't get on with him?"

"We got on fine when we spoke, which was about twice."

"What about Henry?"

"Stiglitz and Henry or me and Henry?"

"Stiglitz and Henry," Jack replied.

"They had some issues. An argument in January last year. It festered. Things do when you're all stuck in one place."

"Do you know what it was about?"

"Could have been something Stiglitz said. He was sarcastic, especially around people he thought weren't as smart as him. Which was pretty much everyone. And Henry, well, he wasn't as smart as anyone. I mean, he had all the right words. He went to military school, family tradition—they have money. But boy, was he slow. You had to go over everything at least three times before he got it. Henry-Three-Times, we called him. Told him it was because he was such a stud, he left the ladies wanting more." Connor sniffed. He shrank back in his chair. "He was a good person. I'm sorry for him. And his family. He had a big family. Liked to talk about them."

"You don't feel bad for Stiglitz?"

"Course I do. But I liked Henry. I hardly knew Stiglitz. It's different."

Jack wrote quickly in shorthand on his pad. "Mind if I ask you about the days leading up to the fire?"

"I don't remember them."

"Not so much what you remember. Just what you think might have happened. This is what I've got so far from the files." He took another bite of the sandwich and drank some coffee. "The army decided to leave the base in September because the ice was too unstable. The reactor had been taken away the year before. Dragged back over the ice to the military base at Thule. One hundred and forty miles west. Missiles removed throughout October. All the heavy work done before the winter night sets in at the end of November. Sound about right?"

"I guess."

"According to the files there were about fifteen people left once that was done. A skeleton crew, including you, Henry, and Stiglitz."

"Yeah, we were on clean-up duty."

"A twin-engined Cessna had three scheduled trips on November 25. It made the first two. You, Stiglitz, and Henry were due to leave on the last trip but it couldn't land. Winds were too strong. Then the storm came and you guys had to hunker down." He paused and looked at Connor.

Connor stared at the table. His placed his bandaged hands in front of him. His right hand shook. He put his left hand on top of it.

"Winter storms were pretty bad, they could last for days," he said softly.

"It's just you, Stiglitz, and Henry for the next week. Has anyone told you where the accident happened?"

"The cabin with the generator."

"That's right. You fixed up an old diesel generator to keep the power on, to keep you warm while you waited for them to come back," Jack continued. "They're thirsty machines. Maybe it ran out of fuel or maybe there was a mechanical problem. Stiglitz and Henry must have decided to go check it out. They head down the tunnel to the cabin with the generator. I had a look at the plans. It's about a ten-minute walk from the living quarters."

"I guess."

"Through the ice tunnels that link the cabins. We've got Stiglitz and Henry walking through the dark with their flashlights. Off to the cabin with the generator to try to fix it. Now," Jack held the pen above the pad, "my first question: How come you didn't go? You're the mechanic. Stiglitz, he's a scientist, not a dirty hands kind of guy. Henry, he couldn't fix a grilled cheese sandwich. You can fix anything. So why didn't you go?"

Connor stared at him.

"I don't know. I don't remember."

"Why do think you didn't go?"

"I didn't go because that obviously isn't what happened. If the generator had been broken then, yeah, I guess you're right. I would have gone to fix it. Maybe it just needed more fuel."

"And anyone could refuel?"

"Exactly. Anyone could. Well, two-man job really. The barrels need to be moved and they're heavy."

"But you didn't go."

"No. I don't know. I guess not. Or I'd be dead."

"Why?"

"Why what?"

"Why weren't you the one caught in the fire?"

Connor frowned. "I don't know. I don't remember. Whatever happened, we would have been working together. I would have been doing something else. They were taking care of the generator, I would be taking care of something else. That's how it works. One guy starts bossing the others around, not doing his fair share, then it all goes to shit."

"Is that what happened? It all went to shit?"

"No! You're twisting my words. That isn't what happened."

"So you know what happened?"

"No. I don't know. And neither do you," Connor kicked out with his leg and his foot caught the table. The cup of coffee bumped onto its side and rolled onto the floor. It cracked like a bad egg, spilling black liquid.

The door opened.

"Everything ok?" A doctor walked into the room, stood between Connor and Jack. Arms folded.

"We're good, Doc," Jack replied. "Just a little spirited debate. Trying to jog the memory. Knocked over my cup of coffee. No big deal. You can go."

The doctor gave him a cold stare. "I'm the senior medical officer and this man's my patient. You don't tell me what to do." He turned to Connor. "If you need a break you just say so."

"He's good," Jack said, getting up out of the chair and taking the doctor by the elbow. The doctor looked at Jack, surprised at the strength in his grip.

"I'm fine, you can go," Connor said. Jack escorted the doctor out of the room and closed the door. He sat down heavily, bent over and picked up the pieces of broken crockery, mopped up most of the coffee with his napkin—leaving a little pool by his right shoe which he didn't notice. He looked at his notes.

"We've got Henry and Stiglitz on their way to fill up the tank. Walking through the tunnels. Flashlights on. They get to the generator cabin. There's been a build-up of a gas. A leak somewhere. Something sparks. Maybe a switch, maybe dim old Henry-Three-Times tried to light a cigarette. Who knows. Flames burst out. The door jams and they can't get out. Sound plausible to you?"

"Maybe. The doors get stuck because of the cold. Metal contracts. Maybe they got it open ok but it stuck shut."

"That's good. Thank you." Jack tapped his pen on the pad. "And all the while you're somewhere else. Taking care of some other problem. Because you guys were a team and that's how you survive in that kind of environment. What do you think you might have been doing?"

"Anything. Checking the supplies. Checking the vents on the outside weren't frozen over. You check everything all the time out there. It's like being on a ship. If the cold gets in the whole base seizes up. And so do you."

Jack nodded, making more notes.

"This is good, Connor, you're doing great. They tell you where you were found?" he asked.

"In the tunnel outside the cabin with the generator."

"That's right. You had an ice pick next to you. Door had been broken open, they tell you that?"

"No," Connor replied quietly. "So, I did go to help? I did try?" His voice caught in his throat.

"Looks that way. You remembering doing that?"

"No. I don't know, I remember something. Maybe something like that. It makes sense."

"Ok," Jack replied, in a noncommittal way. "Do you remember what made you check on them? They were a long way away, in the tunnels."

Connor frowned and shook his head. "If there was an explosion it would've shaken the whole base. I would've heard it. If I was outside, I would've felt it. I would've run to them. That must be why I was lying there." His hands were shaking.

Jack got up and placed a hand gently on his shoulder.

"Take a break, get some rest. You did what you could. You did good. You're doing good. I'll be back later. We're getting there. And when we get there I can write up my report and then I'll be gone and you can get some proper rest. Maybe even see that fiancée of yours."

Connor looked up sharply, raising his hands to his face, his eyes filled with a mixture of shame and horror.

"Is she here?" he asked, his voice no more than a whisper.

"She's not," Jack said. "No rush. No rush for any of this. Get some rest. These things work themselves out. Just takes time."

Jack returned to his basement room at Langley to write up his report. It was a low blow to mention Connor's fiancée, he knew that. But he wanted to apply pressure. A cold splash of truth. Connor was eager to go along with whatever he suggested. He didn't question it. He'd seemed almost relieved. Relieved not to have to explain what had happened. To just let Dr. Miller come up with his theories and keep nodding along.

Jack opened the files and scanned the list of everyone stationed at the base in the previous twelve months. There were about twenty support staff, fifteen research scientists, then the missile crews. All in all, around one hundred people at any one time.

It would be helpful to talk to some of them. Find out how other people described Stiglitz and Henry. Find out how they described Connor. More than helpful. It was necessary to understand the dynamic between the three of them, to work out what might have happened in the run-up to the accident. And the incident earlier in the year, back in January. Connor hadn't wanted to talk about it but it was obvious there was bad blood between Henry and Stiglitz.

He circled some of the names, then took his jacket off, rolled up his sleeves, and took off his watch. He ran his thumb over the inscription on the back, placed it on the desk in front of him, and threaded a sheet of paper into the typewriter. He hammered away with thick fingers, wishing he could pick up a phone and dictate his report to one of the secretaries.

When he was done he bundled the files together, slipped them into his briefcase along with his report, and went to meet Coty's boss.

5

Langley, Block B
December 27, 3:00 P.M.

E dward Gill's office was a larger version of Coty's but with a more traditional approach to filing, in that his files were actually filed away out of sight. Gill reached up from behind his desk and grabbed Jack's hand. He was tall and broad with fine gray hair cropped close and bright blue eyes. He exuded the kind of energy that could power a small suburb. Or blow it up.

"Good to meet you in person at last. Seen your name on a lot of reports over the years. Coty says you're a human lie detector. Better in fact, those machines have a pretty wide margin for error."

"Coty exaggerates," Jack replied.

"Well, we're grateful. I hope your patients will forgive us stealing you away from New York for a few days. Sit." He pointed at one of the chairs. Jack sat, feeling like a well-behaved beagle.

"Coty give you the accident report and flight logs for the base?" he asked, the smile still there but the eyes clinical and focused.

"He did."

"Good. Did he tell you what's not in the files?"

Jack looked across at Coty.

"Not yet," Coty replied. He cleared his throat, then said, "I wanted to get Jack's take on Connor first. See what impression he got before we get into the details."

"Sure. Makes sense. There's more to this than the fire," Gill said. "I'm guessing you've worked out that we wouldn't have brought you here just to help write an accident report. The Agency wouldn't be involved if it was just a fire, regardless of how strange it looked."

"Right," Jack said, a little wearily. "What's the thing you can't put in the file?"

"Oh, we can put it in a file. One of our files. We just can't put it in the military files," Coty said. "Not yet anyway. Signal engineers started picking up radio transmissions from outside the base in June. Not a military channel. It was broadcast on long wave. Weather reports. A code."

"How often?" Jack said.

"Maybe once or twice a month." Gill paused. His secretary set out a coffee pot and cups on his desk then left.

"And you didn't put an Agency man in there to investigate?"

Coty and Gill exchanged a look.

"It's sensitive. This was an army project. We don't think they knew about this. We'd prefer to keep it that way, otherwise investigations get messy. There are a lot of vested interests. Makes it harder to get things done."

"Ok." Jack digested this. "Did the broadcasts continue when it was just Connor, Stiglitz, and Henry?" he asked.

"Once," Coty said.

"So one of the three went out into the storm to play disc jockey with the Russians," Jack said.

Gill frowned, as if he didn't approve of the glib turn of phrase.

"It looks that way," he said.

"And you think the fire could be connected. Started deliberately?" Jack said.

"We can't discount it. Too much of a coincidence. But of the three of them, Connor was the least likely suspect. He's junior. No access to confidential papers, launch plans, or missile codes. And we've gone through his records. Can't see any time during his career, or before, when he would have been approached, or even any motivation. We're drawing a blank. What's your take on the guy?"

"It would have helped if you'd told me this before," Jack said, not bothering to hide his irritation. "Connor's a mess—psychologically, physically. He's going to have a hell of a lot to deal with. The burns on his hands are going to make life much harder for a long time. As for his face . . . like I said, it'll be hard."

"Do you think he's lying about not remembering?" Gill said.

"I do. He's defensive. But that doesn't necessarily mean he's your spy. Could be he thinks we won't believe whatever he says, so it's safest saying nothing. Could be he doesn't want to say something that gets Henry in trouble. He liked Henry, but he told me Henry and Stiglitz didn't get on. Says Stiglitz was sarcastic and arrogant. They had some kind of falling out earlier this year. It festered. I need to know if it's true. Then I can work out how much I trust what he says." He took his report out of his briefcase and placed it on the desk. Gill ignored it.

"And how do you do that?" he said.

"I'd like to talk to other people who were stationed there. People who knew the three of them. Get another perspective."

Gill shook his head.

"No deal. We don't have support from the military. If we start asking questions it'll get back to them."

"What about someone who's no longer serving?" Jack had taken the files out of his briefcase, running his finger down the list of names.

"There was one, the chaplain. Left the army in summer. File says he has a parish over in Forestville now."

Gill and Coty were silent. Arms folded, Coty said, "You really need this?"

"I do," Jack said. "Otherwise we've only got Connor's viewpoint. I need background, some more context. The chaplain would be a good person to talk to. Part of his job was listening to people."

"Try and get a sense of his loyalties first. We don't want to stir things up. Not yet anyway," Coty said.

Gill still didn't look happy.

"I get it," Jack said. "Softly, softly." Like a cat in goddamn cashmere pajamas, he thought.

6

Washington, DC
December 27, 5:00 P.M.

Jack sat in the passenger seat of a brown Ford Fairlane as it rumbled through the Washington suburbs smoking one cigarette after another, his arm hanging out the window. Head woolly with lack of sleep and the pileup of information from Coty and Gill. Light was leaking out of the gray December sky and the snow that had fallen was icy and brittle. He liked the stillness; air cold, snow dampening the sounds.

He didn't like the fact that Coty hadn't given him the full picture from the outset. A missile base under the ice, an accident they wanted investigated without the army finding out, and now the revelation that either Connor, Stiglitz, or Henry kept heading out into the snow to send coded signals to the Russians. As if one secret wasn't enough.

Coty hadn't always been like that. It was as if the Agency had seeped into him over the years, building up habits of secrecy. Walls around walls. Rooms within rooms. Conversations that could only be opened with a key. When Jack had first started working for him things had been simpler. He'd interview a potential senior appointment. Review an agent's suitability for a particular mission. Now Jack was always looking for the question behind the question. He went along with Coty's game, not sure if it was habit or because he enjoyed the insight into a clandestine world, peaking through the gap in the curtain to see how Langley worked, to see how certain kinds of men wielded power. It was more than he got from the patients who came to his clinic. Although at times there was little difference between the behavior of the referrals from the state hospital and the senior Agency staff. A few years back Coty had tried to get him to work for the Agency full time. Jack turned him down. Small doses. Ring-fenced projects. That was enough for him. Except that this time there was more to it. He'd never been introduced to Gill before. This was bigger. He was intrigued and annoyed in equal measure. No, that wasn't true. The intrigue was winning.

"Must be near," Jack said to the driver, checking the address he'd noted in his pad.

The driver grunted and turned off Marlboro Pike onto Ritchie Road.

"It's up here," he said. He was lean and capable-looking. Jack wasn't sure if he was watching him or watching out for him. Whatever the case, he didn't say much.

They pulled into the parking lot by the Epiphany Episcopal Church. Jack got out. The driver looked around then switched off the engine. The streetlights flickered, unsure whether it was time to light up in the early dusk.

The church sat square on the snow, red brick at ground level and then white wooden cladding all the way up to the bell tower. The large sign welcomed all brothers and sisters in Christ in serious-looking black letters and announced the reverend's name, *William Peterson*, with an italic flourish directly below. The paint still fresh and crisp. The main doors were open, ready for Evensong. He entered and took a seat near the back. No one else was there yet.

Reverend Peterson walked quickly from the vestry to the altar, humming without any discernible tune and trailing a cloud of smoke from a thin cigar. A tall figure with a slight stoop. He checked something on the shelf beneath the altar. Didn't look up. Then hurried back to the vestry.

A few moments later he appeared again, draped in his black cassock, clutching a series of cards in one hand and swinging incense with the other. Jack wasn't sure if it was to cover up the cigar smoke or part of some old Anglican ritual. He placed the cards carefully on the pulpit alongside the Bible. Checked the order. Mouthed a few words.

He looked up. Saw Jack for the first time. Jack gave him a mini salute.

"Good evening, sir," Jack said.

"Welcome, welcome," the reverend replied, almost falling over his feet in his rush to greet him. "I do apologize. Caught up in my own world here."

Jack stood and took the hand he offered.

"It's always a pleasure to have visitors. Especially at this time of year," the reverend continued. "What brings you to our little church?"

Jack smiled. Other people were starting to arrive and the reverend was nodding and waving hellos at them.

"Just visiting. Don't let me distract you from your congregation. Perhaps we can talk after the service?" Jack said.

"Of course," the reverend said cheerfully, then turned away and began to greet the steady stream of hats and coats that came through the main doors.

Jack mumbled the songs and listened to the sermon, which was more fervent than he was expecting. The central heating gurgled and cranked as if it was possessed, and the twenty or so people that had turned up solemnly swayed up to the altar to take the Eucharist and solemnly swayed back to their pews. They were an old crowd. Jack thought they didn't look like they could do much that needed forgiving. When the reverend had said his goodbyes and waved them off at the door he returned to Jack.

"Well, sir, what can I do for you?" he said.

"Is there somewhere we can talk?" Jack replied. "It's a personal matter."

Jack followed the reverend to a side room. The white washed walls were stained with years of cigarette smoke and strands of cobweb hung from the high ceiling like wisps of fine gray hair. There were three crystal decanters on the desk filled with different shades of gold liquor. A layer of dust covered the top of each one.

The reverend caught Jack's eye.

"A welcome present from my congregation when I arrived in summer. They're very generous. I don't really drink but please help yourself. The pale one in the middle is supposed to be the best."

"Thank you," Jack said, pouring himself a generous measure. He sniffed it and sipped: midrange single malt. Too peaty for his taste.

"I don't use this room much," the reverend continued, filing his cards carefully in one of the drawers. "It could do with freshening up." He sat down opposite Jack. "How may I be of service this winter's evening?"

The reverend lit a thin cigar with a battered Zippo and looked at the crystal decanters as if they were a test of his will power.

"I wanted to talk to you about your time in the army."

The reverend sat up a little straighter.

"You came here to talk about me?" he asked.

"Not about you exactly, about the time you spent in Greenland."

"What did you say your name was?" The reverend's tone was colder.

"I didn't. My apologies. It's Dr. Jack Miller. I'm a psychiatrist. One of my patients was stationed with you. There was an accident at the base in November. He was badly burned. A traumatic experience. He suffered memory loss. We call it *dissociative amnesia*. I'm helping him recover. As part of that process I'd like to understand a little more about who he was. I appreciate it's been several months since you last saw him but I thought it might still be helpful to talk to you. An army chaplain has something of a privileged position in terms of getting to know people."

"Oh, I see," the reverend said, he peered at Jack through the cigar smoke, his eyes half-closed, sitting tall in his chair. "I'm sorry to hear that. Who's your patient?"

"Connor Murphy."

The reverend nodded. "Yes, yes, I knew him. I knew everyone. They were my flock, even if some of them didn't want to be. Connor and I chatted now and then. He talked about his fiancée. He missed her terribly. It was tough out there. Tough on all of them. You say he's lost his memory? And was burned? That sounds terrible. Truly. What an awful thing to happen to a young man. I'd be more than happy to visit if you think it will help."

"Thank you. We're doing what we can for him."

"They were always so careful. Do you mind me asking how the fire started?"

"We don't know exactly," Jack replied. "Refueling accident maybe. An officer called Stiglitz was there too. You know him?"

"Of course. Chief scientific officer. Good man. Exceptional mind."

"You like him?"

The reverend looked like he was about to say something, then changed his mind.

"He was always perfectly pleasant to me," he said.

"Doesn't sound as if you liked him very much."

"I liked him well enough. What's that got to do with anything?"

Jack didn't answer, took a sip of whisky. It tasted better this time.

"I heard he didn't get along with one of the other officers."

The reverend examined the end of his cigar, which had gone out. He applied the flame to it and puffed to get it going.

"I thought you were here to talk about Connor?"

"Stiglitz was caught in the same fire. Only he didn't make it."

"I see. It'd be easier if you just level with me, Dr. Miller. I can't abide dishonesty. Why are you here and what do you want?"

"I am a psychiatrist, like I said. And I am here because I want to help Connor remember. Stiglitz was caught in the same fire, only he didn't survive. So was a man called Henry Carvell."

"Henry too? Goodness. And Connor says he can't remember anything," the reverend said softly.

"You see our predicament," Jack said.

"I do, I think. And when you say *our* predicament who exactly are you referring to?"

"People who need to find out what happened. Connor can't remember the fire or the week leading up to it, but he told me Henry and Stiglitz didn't always get along."

The reverend sighed.

"True. They didn't get along. But they were very different people."

"How so?"

"Henry was headstrong. Born with a, well, not so much a silver spoon as a silver bullet. Military family. Clear pathway through the ranks to the top. He didn't like being stationed in Greenland, no matter what they said about its strategic importance. He wanted something more . . . active. His previous posting was South Vietnam. He distinguished himself there, so I believe. Led a team that cleared out tunnels under the jungle used by the Viet Cong. The men liked him, he was serious when he needed to be but he also liked to fool around. Had the kind of enthusiasm that's hard to resist."

"What about Stiglitz?" Jack said.

"Stiglitz was from a more humble background. He had to work twice as hard as anyone else to get where he was. Didn't mind telling them either. Intellectually brilliant. Intimidatingly so. A touch cold. Arrogant even."

"I heard Stiglitz and Henry had an argument, back in January."

The reverend waved a hand dismissively. "Oh, it was one of those silly things you sometimes get in that type of claustrophobic environment. Things get blown up out of proportion. Henry decided he didn't trust Stiglitz. Was quite open about it. Stiglitz called him out on it. Rightly so. We organized mediation and sorted it out."

"Why didn't he trust him?" Jack said. The reverend sighed. He looked uncomfortable.

"I don't want to go into it. As I say, it was silliness really. Unfortunate. Unpleasant for all concerned."

"I'd appreciate it if you could be a little more specific," Jack said.

The reverend paused and picked a speck of lint off his trouser. "Somehow Henry got it into his head that Stiglitz was, well, he was making people sick."

"I beg your pardon?" Jack asked.

"I know. It sounds ridiculous. It was ridiculous."

"Why would he think that?"

"You have to remember it was a long posting. Henry was exhausted. And he'd been in active combat for several months before he came to the arctic. There was no daylight outside, which upsets the body's natural rhythms. He needed a break, really. Should have had one before he came to the base." He flicked ash onto the floor.

"Why did he think Stiglitz was making people sick?" Jack asked again.

The reverend placed his hands flat on the table.

"Rumors, speculation, and nonsense," he said.

"So give me the rumors," Jack replied.

"I really don't think it's my place," the reverend said.

"I really think it is," Jack said quickly. "I'd like to know what Henry said, even if there's no truth to it."

The reverend looked at him, then said, "Alright. Three people were evacuated from the base. End of December last year. Henry got it into his head that Stiglitz made them sick. That he'd done some sort of experiment on them."

"Why did he think that?"

The reverend cleared his throat and laughed nervously.

"Henry wasn't well. He was very tired. Like I said. He went home for a month or so. Had a break. Came back in the spring. From then on, they seemed to get along ok, or at least they managed to avoid each other."

Jack drank the rest of the whisky.

"People stopped getting sick?" he asked.

The reverend shrugged.

"People will always get ill, but yes, after that no one else was evacuated. It was just those three soldiers."

Jack nodded his head.

"They ever tell you what was wrong with them?"

The reverend frowned.

"Some kind of virus I believe."

"You wouldn't happen to remember the name of the medical officer who signed off the evacuation would you?"

The reverend shook his head.

"I'm not sure I remember, isn't it in your files? There should be a flight log. That'll record the passengers and who signed off their transportation."

"Oh, there's a flight log, it just doesn't record any soldiers being evacuated due to illness."

The reverend was silent.

"Who was the medical officer?" Jack asked again.

The reverend coughed and reached for another of his thin cigars. He put it to his lips but he didn't light it. "There was a team. They changed fairly regularly. Could have been any of them. Might not have even been a doctor. A senior officer could sign off transportation. I don't like to speculate. Now, if you don't mind, I have some notes I need to write up. I have a christening tomorrow morning. Please do let Connor know he's in my prayers. And I am always available to visit."

Jack leaned back in his chair. The reverend was sweating slightly. He looked at the bottles on the table, a longing in his eyes. His lips clamped shut around the cigar.

Jack got up. "I'm staying at the Willard in case you want to talk," he said. He took out his card, scribbled down the name of the hotel. "Leave a message for me if your memory starts to come back."

Jack left the church. He could feel the whisky running warm in his blood and the air cold on his cheeks. It sounded as if Henry had suffered some sort of breakdown, accusing Stiglitz of poisoning his fellow soldiers. As the reverend suggested, possibly the combination of the stress he'd experienced in combat combined with the darkness of the arctic winter had led him to make some paranoid accusations.

Jack wondered if being trapped there in November when everyone else had been able to leave—everyone except for him, Connor, and Stiglitz—had caused these fears to resurface. He wondered if something had happened between Henry and Stiglitz, under the ice in those dark, freezing tunnels; if Henry was once again convinced Stiglitz was somehow experimenting on him and Connor. The human imagination could take on all shapes and sizes in the right circumstances.

Time to go back to the hospital. Connor said he couldn't remember what happened in the week leading up to the fire. He didn't say he couldn't remember what happened between Henry and Stiglitz earlier in the year. All he'd said was they'd had a disagreement. He didn't want to talk about it. Well, it was time he started talking.

He was about to get into the Ford when he noticed a car a couple of blocks away. The only other car on the street. It was parked in the shadows between streetlights.

Jack yanked open the door to the Ford. His driver looked half-frozen. Scarf pulled tightly round his neck. Collar turned up. He looked up sharply and turned off the radio. The engine was on and the heater was blasting out warm air.

"How long has that car been watching you?" Jack asked.

"What are you talking about? What car?" the man replied.

"The one behind us, two blocks away."

The driver looked in the mirror. Annoyed. Stared for a couple of moments. He could just make out the silver fender glinting in the lamp light.

"There's no one inside it," the driver said.

"You can see that from here?"

"No, but . . ."

"Drive," Jack said as he got in. "Let's do an experiment."

The driver put the car in gear and pulled away. Jack kept his eyes on the mirror.

"You see, no one inside. It's not moving," the driver said.

"Keep going. Once we cross the intersection douse the lights and take a left, pull up over there, between those two houses."

The driver did as he was told. The Ford crunched to a halt on the icy snow. Jack looked over his shoulder. Waited. Watched. The driver pursed his lips. His eyes on the mirror. A black Oldsmobile crept past.

"Want to tell me what's going on?" Jack asked the driver. They waited in the alley for a couple of minutes. The driver hunched and cold.

"Probably nothing," he said, blowing into his hands.

"Oh sure," Jack said. "That what they teach you these days in spy school? Ignore anything suspicious?"

"I'll notify Coty," the driver said.

"So will I," Jack said. "Take me back to Walter Reed. And check your goddamn mirrors."

7

Walter Reed Army Medical Center
December 27, 9:00 P.M.

The roads were quiet on the drive back to the hospital. The day's busy schedule of appointments, consultations, and operations had been replaced by a cautious nighttime quiet. In the reception area an elderly lady held an Agatha Christie in her lap without reading it and a young woman was curled up on a chair next to her. The woman's frame was so slight Jack thought she was a child at first. Her body shifted and she turned toward him. Her eyes opened, caught him looking at her. She twisted so her back was to him. He thought he recognized her.

"Can I help you, sir?" The nurse behind the reception desk interrupted his thoughts.

"Yeah, here." Jack showed the CIA badge Coty had given him. "I'm here for Connor Murphy." She looked at it and asked him to sign in.

He found Connor sitting in front of a TV screen in a darkened room. The TV was the only source of light and the sound was so quiet it was barely audible. He was watching a Western. Two men in chaps shooting at a snake, firing from the hip in a way that's guaranteed to make you miss your target. *The High Chaparral* appeared in large letters on the screen before cutting to an ad break for kitchenware.

"Still not sleeping?" Jack asked. "Even with this crap on the TV? It would send me into a coma."

Connor turned awkwardly in his armchair and let out a sigh.

"You again," he said, but his tone wasn't angry.

"What can I say, I missed you. Mind if I join?"

Connor stared at the screen.

"Be my guest. Have you got any of that whisky?"

"I do, but I don't think you should drink it."

"Then just let me sniff it."

Jack took out his hip flask and held it under Connor's nose. Connor drew in a deep breath and coughed a little.

"Where've you been all afternoon? Sightseeing?" he said.

"I went visiting. Someone you know. Do you remember Reverend Peterson? He left the base in summer. Tall fella. Kind of serious."

"Kind of drunk, you mean," Connor replied.

"Was he? Well, he has a parish over in Forestville now."

"Yeah. *Left* the army. There's only so many times you can forget to turn up to chapel because you fell asleep in the middle of the day."

"He seems to have it under control," Jack said.

"Drunks never have it under control. They go sober for a year or two then they hit it harder than ever. What did you talk about with Peterson?"

"He told me about Henry and Stiglitz, about what happened between them in December last year." Jack paused, waiting to see if Connor would talk. He didn't. "He said Henry thought Stiglitz was making people sick. He said that was why they fell out. Did you know about this?"

Connor shrugged.

"Why didn't you tell me?" Jack said.

"Because that was over. It was months ago. And if I told you you'd think Henry was the problem. And he wasn't. Henry was ok," Connor said. "He just lost it for a bit back then. It was a long winter. He took time out and he came back and he was his old self. Henry was a good guy. It was all over months before we were stuck together in the goddamn storm. It was Stiglitz who was . . ." He stopped.

"Who was what?"

"Difficult," Connor said.

"How so?"

"Arrogant. Like you said."

"The reverend said the people who got sick were evacuated. What happened to them?"

Connor frowned.

"How should I know?" he said.

"Did they come back?"

"Yeah. Maybe. Some of them. Or maybe they went somewhere else. The team changed all the time."

Jack got up, switched off the TV, and turned on the light.

Connor blinked and lifted a bandaged hand to his eyes.

"So you don't know if they came back?" Jack asked.

"Check the logs. I wouldn't know if some of the missile crew weren't there. There were over a hundred people on the base at any one time, they worked shifts so you didn't always see everyone. People get sick, so what? No big deal. Why are you interested in them anyway? I thought you wanted to work out how the fire started."

"Just curious," Jack said. "Given what happened to Henry and Stiglitz, I wanted to find out why Henry was so suspicious. It's a pretty wild accusation."

"Well, like I said, Henry wasn't doing too good. It was a long winter. But he went home. Got it sorted."

"Yeah, you said that," Jack said. It was clear whose side Connor was on. He wasn't going to say anything negative about Henry. Jack opened his briefcase and took out the photograph of the fire site, holding it face down so Connor couldn't see it.

"I want to show you something. It might help you remember, but it's not a nice thing to see. You ok for me to show you a picture of what the fire did?"

Connor shrugged. "I guess."

"What it did to your two colleagues?" Jack watched him closely as he said this. Looking for fear in his eyes, a tightening in the muscles around his jaw, a tension in his body. Anything that indicated the image could cause him psychological shock. He remembered the police officers who'd turned up next to his hospital bed, all those years ago, wanting to ask him about the crash that killed his wife. The photo they'd shown him of the two cars, his Buick crumpled, blackened by fire, the Chevy truck that had hit them on its side further down the road. There were no bodies in that picture and still he'd found he could barely look at it. He'd tried to pull her out, held on to her as the fire ate up his arm.

Connor didn't flinch. All Jack saw was a cold curiosity.

"If you think it'll help then go ahead and show me," he said.

Jack passed the photograph of the burnt-out cabin with the two bodies to Connor, who held it in his bandaged hands.

"*Fuck,*" Connor whispered, then, "I was lucky. I guess." He shook his head. "That fire got everything. Poor bastards." He looked at it for a moment longer. "What the hell." He passed the photo back.

"Does it help you remember? You were found just outside this room. Door was open, what was left of it. Any idea what happened?"

Connor closed his eyes and raised his hands to his head. His breathing was sharper, more restricted.

"I, I don't know. It was fast. It all happened so fast," he said.

"You remember?" Jack said.

Connor didn't reply. He shut his eyes. His breathing was heavy and restricted. Jack waited.

"I remember hearing something," Connor said. "The sounds were echoey in the tunnels. Like someone was banging a pipe. Far away. That's what I thought at first. Just a faraway sound. Henry or Stiglitz trying to fix something. I was somewhere else. Sorting stuff. The noise went on. I just listened. That's all I did." He stopped, sniffed. His body tensed and he was staring straight ahead, his gaze not fixed on anything in the room, instead focused on some indistinct point in the past.

"And I remember it got louder. Faster. Like they were really going at the pipes. I was wondering what the hell they were doing. Dumb Henry. Probably breaking something because he couldn't fix it. Too much force. That was his usual style. The noise didn't stop. I went to find them. Guess I was annoyed. Sounded like it was one of the maintenance tunnels. It was dark and my flashlight was dim. And it was cold, you know? I mean, you don't want to do anything unless you have to. Even leaving the cabin meant I had to get all suited up. Gloves, furs. Everything." He paused. "I went down Park Avenue. That's what we called the main tunnel, it led from the rec rooms to the workstations, the loading bays, the labs."

"You can remember?" Jack asked. "It's coming back to you?"

Connor nodded slowly. "I tried the service tunnels. Doubled back on myself a few times. The banging was still going but, now that I was closer, I could hear something else. Shouting. I didn't know what they were doing. I guess I panicked a bit. I started to run. The ice was slippery. In some places there weren't even duckboards. I think I fell. Knocked my head. I could hear my name. Shrill, a scream. Someone calling me." Connor looked down. His hands were shaking.

"I turned a corner and the cabin was glowing. Whole thing was like a giant furnace. All fired up. I ran to it, pulled at the door. Tried to get it open."

Connor's legs were shaking now too. He looked like he was about to have some sort of fit.

"Take it easy," Jack said. "Have some water."

Connor didn't seem to hear him, he was back to staring into a place Jack couldn't see. "I could hear their voices," he said. "I could hear their screams." His hands were gripping the arms of the chair. "I got the door open somehow, the ice pick, I guess. I couldn't feel my hands. They were on the door. Felt like they were part of the door. The heat swallowed up my face. Came in a rush. Like someone stripping your skin, one sudden yank, a tear. I've never felt anything like it." He stopped talking. His body still shaking.

"They were inside," he said softly. "On the floor. Two figures. They were moving. I swear they were moving. They were black, charred. Like pieces of charcoal. I couldn't get near. But the heat, the smell. The smell of burnt skin and hair and fuel . . ." His eyes closed and his head fell forward. His body was shaking.

"Connor? Connor, can you hear me?" Jack said.

Connor didn't reply.

"Connor, come on. Focus. Can you hear me?"

Nothing.

"*Shit*," Jack muttered under his breath. "Nurse, nurse!" he yelled.

Connor's body twisted in his chair, his head jolting from one side to the other, as if electricity was running through him. The bandages loosening.

"Nurse!" Jack yelled, getting up. *Goddamn it.* "Nurse! I need help."

Connor's head was hitting the sides of the armchair, and each time it did the bandages loosened further. They started to come off. His skin underneath stuck to the leather, making a sucking sound. The layers of new skin tore, blood seeped through the grafted flesh. It stained the headrest. Bandages hung from Connor, the dressings leaking and torn.

Jack stared at the face underneath. The structure was gone. The nose just two rough holes, as if someone had pressed a screwdriver into raw flesh and twisted it. The left cheek was concave, stripped away. Holding the patchwork of grafts in place were thick black stitches. Stitches that Connor was pulling at with his bandaged hands as he rocked back and forth.

"Nurse! Where are you?" Jack shouted, trying to control Connor, taking hold of his arms, holding them down.

At last hurried footsteps entered the room.

"You need something to sedate him," he said.

"What's he had already?" she asked, scanning his chart.

"I don't know. Painkillers. Morphine maybe."

She jammed a needle into his arm. The shuddering of his body lessened, the breathing relaxed. His eyes closed.

8

Walter Reed Army Medical Center
December 27, 10:30 P.M.

Jack stood outside the hospital. Deep breaths. The air was cold but he didn't feel it. A car rolled past, its wheels crunching on the ice. He didn't see it. He could only see Connor. The wounds opening up, bandages torn, blood seeping through.

Connor remembered. And the trauma of remembering was too much.

Jack had expected the photograph to create a psychological jolt, but he hadn't expected such an extreme physical manifestation of the trauma he had suffered. Not given their conversations so far. He hadn't seen anything like that in a patient before, not if they hadn't previously exhibited symptoms. And he'd wanted to look at the photograph. He'd appeared calm. He'd asked to see it.

It was the memory coming back that brought on the fit, not the photograph. He should have prepared better—had someone on hand to sedate him. Shit. Jack shook his head. Took a sip of whisky from the flask. You bring these things out slowly, at the right time, with the right support. He knew this from his treatment of veterans after the war. He knew this from his own experience in combat. The difficulty he'd had processing what he'd seen, and what he'd done. It was the reason he'd become a psychiatrist in the first place. If not to beat it, then to learn to live alongside it. And help others do the same.

Connor had survived something that had killed the people he worked with. One of whom was his friend. Jack knew what that felt like. He reminded himself to go easy, no matter how soon Coty and Gill wanted answers. He got into his car and told the driver to take him to his hotel.

The Willard was a half-hour drive downtown, close to the Capitol. It was old-fashioned and expensive. The lobby ornate and gilded with dark wood furniture and chandeliers hanging from the high ceiling. It felt surreal after the sparse interior of the hospital. Jack could make out a piano playing in a bar somewhere and the distant buzz of conversation.

He checked in and collected his key, then went up to his room. His suitcases were already there. Coty had sent them on. He stared at them, but the effort of unpacking was too much. He hadn't slept in over twenty-four hours.

He sat on the bed instead, took the files out of his briefcase and flicked through the papers. Found the photograph of the burnt-out cabin. He stared at the photo, wondering what had happened between Henry and Stiglitz. Was what he was looking at the aftermath of some awful paranoid attack by Henry? A fight, fuel spilt. A dropped cigarette or lighter and the whole room ignites. The door jams. A hot, fast fire sucks the air out of the room.

What was it Connor had said?

He'd managed to get the door open, seen the two bodies on the floor. They looked as if they were moving but they were black and charred.

Jack stared at the photograph. Stiglitz's body was still recognizably human in shape. Henry's body wasn't, there was barely any body at all. Just a pile of ash and loose fragments of bone and teeth. The more he stared at it, the stranger it seemed. Stiglitz was closest to the heat source, the generator, and that had buckled due to the extreme temperature. So why was he still in one piece? Why was Henry more burned? He was further away. Why was there hardly anything left of him?

Jack looked through the notes to see if there was any commentary in the accident report to explain the different state of the bodies, but there was no mention of it.

He sat back on the bed, his eyes growing heavy. Maybe it didn't need explaining. Maybe Henry was holding a can of fuel when the fire started. Maybe that was why he'd burned quicker. And kept burning till there was almost nothing left. And in the split second between opening the door and turning away Connor had seen burning human shapes. He wouldn't have taken in the extent to which they were burned. He would have turned away immediately from the heat, fallen back on the icy floor of the tunnel.

But there was no can in the photo, no discarded container that could have had fuel in it. There should be something, if Henry was holding a can of diesel it should be somewhere close to him.

Jack's brain was running in circles, chasing its tail. He shut his eyes.

Why weren't the two bodies in the same state? He couldn't let go of the thought, despite the deadweight of tiredness that hung around his neck. It needled him. The fire had burned itself out. The bodies had been exposed to it for the same amount of time. Why was one more burned than the other?

Still no answer. Did it need an answer?

He put the photograph and the files away. He didn't have an answer. He needed to talk to someone who knew about fires. It was probably nothing. Probably something an expert could easily explain. But he needed to show the photograph to an expert to be sure. He'd ask Coty. Coty would pull a face. So what? He wanted an answer.

He laid down on the bed, thinking he would rest for a couple of minutes before unpacking, but he found he couldn't move. Couldn't keep his eyes open. Sleep came over him like a slow, awful drunkenness. He sank through the bed into the floor. High walls, growing taller still, all around him. A tunnel under the ice. Then Connor's face. Misshapen, broken, telling him he didn't do it. He remembered that he didn't do it, whatever it was. So why did he keep asking him questions? The head disappeared into a dark tunnel. Two lights appeared, blinking, like animal eyes in the distance. They grew larger. Headlights.

He'd had this dream before.

Even in his unconscious state he recognized it. It was always the same. The lights came toward him, bearing down on his car, veering to his side of the road. His wife beside him telling him to stop, to pull over. He didn't because they would move. They had to move. No one could be that stupid. Realizing too late they wouldn't. Turning the steering wheel but the car didn't change direction. Hands gripping it. Knuckles white. Spinning it.

In the dream he tried to make things right, to steer out of the way, but it never worked. The wheel spun in his hands, the car stayed straight.

9

The Willard
December 28, 6:30 A.M.

Jack could hear a noise. Beside his head. A ringing. He checked his watch. The room was pitch black save for a yellow line of light under the door. He reached across and picked up the receiver.

"Yes?" he mumbled into it.

"It's Coty."

"Ok," Jack said.

"I'd like a briefing this morning. The doc says you put Connor out of action. He's under heavy sedation. Won't let us near him. Won't let us wake him up. What did you do?"

Jack frowned. Rubbed his eyes.

"I went to see him."

"Last night?"

"There were some questions I wanted to ask."

"Likewise. I'm coming to your hotel. See you at seven." Coty hung up.

"Wonderful," Jack replied, and put the receiver back in its cradle.

His legs felt strange and heavy. He looked down. He was still in his clothes, his shoes, too, lying on top of the bed. He got up, his body stiff and reluctant. Struggled with his laces. Used his good hand to untie them then kicked them off. He undressed, turned the shower as hot as it would go to get some life into his muscles then switched to cold to wake him up, ran a razor over his face, cut the mole on his neck and got a spot of blood on the collar of his clean shirt. Happened at least three times a week. He massaged his knuckles and placed his arthritic hand on the radiator while he took turns smoking a cigarette and coughing. When he was done he went down to the dining room.

Coty had chosen a table at the back. He'd wasted no time ordering breakfast. A pot of coffee and a rack of toast was laid out in front of him.

"What the hell, Jack?" he said as Jack approached. His voice a high-pitched whisper.

"Good morning to you too," Jack replied.

"I get a call at half one in the morning from the medical supervisor saying Connor had some kind of fit and he'd managed to tear off half the skin they were grafting on. What did you do?"

"Went to see him. Asked him some questions. Showed him a photo of the burnt-out room with the two bodies."

"And what? He started pulling off his face?"

"No. He started remembering. He started talking."

"Ok. That's something at least." Coty relaxed a little in his chair. "What did he say?"

"He said he heard some shouts, went to investigate, opened the door to the cabin with the generator, saw the two bodies, and got burned in the process."

Coty leaned back, shaking his head.

"No shit. I think we worked that out already. Did he talk about what happened before the accident?"

"If you're asking whether he said that Henry or Stiglitz kept going outside to radio the Russians then no, he didn't."

"You think he'll give us more once they've fixed him up?" Coty asked. He picked up his knife and dipped it in the butter. He pushed the butter right to the corners of his toast and then scraped the knife clean on the edge of the butter dish, leaving a gritty deposit of crumb and fat. Jack found it intensely irritating.

"I don't know, maybe," Jack replied.

Coty finished his scraping, then said, "What about Reverend Peterson? Did you learn anything from him?"

Jack took a sip of coffee.

"I did," he said. "He confirmed what Connor had told me about Henry and Stiglitz. They didn't get on. But he told me something else too. He told me," Jack paused as Coty took a bite of toast, "he told me Henry had made some wild accusations against Stiglitz earlier in the year."

"What kind of accusations?" Coty asked, mouth full.

Jack frowned. "Henry accused Stiglitz of poisoning soldiers. This was back in December, almost a year before they were trapped together."

Coty put down the toast.

"Poisoning soldiers? That's what the reverend said? Henry accused the chief scientific officer at a military base of poisoning his fellow soldiers?"

"That's what the reverend said. And Connor confirmed it last night."

"It's not in any damned army report."

"Henry took some time out. Went home for a while. Sounded like he was either suffering from a breakdown or on the verge. He'd gone straight from active service to an underground base just before the arctic winter. I'm guessing it was too much for him.

He went home for a month or so. Got better. My theory is he had another paranoid episode when the three of them were trapped there in November. Except this time he couldn't get away. Maybe Stiglitz and Henry were caught up in some kind of argument, there was an accident. The fire started."

Coty shook his head.

"*Poisoning* people. Why would Henry think that?"

"They evacuated three soldiers. Stiglitz was chief scientific officer. I suppose Henry decided he must also be experimenting on people. Do you know what Stiglitz was working on?"

"Ice-core samples," Coty replied. "He had a team of geologists looking at ice and rocks. That was the cover for the base. They did research. They published reports. Meanwhile, the army maintained missiles for short- and long-range ballistic deployment."

Coty drew a deep breath. He lit a cigarette, eyes on the far side of the room. "I guess Henry lost it. It's not unheard of. The isolation. Lack of daylight."

Jack nodded. "The human brain can really go to work on itself in that kind of environment." He stirred his coffee. "But I still think we should check up on the three soldiers they evacuated. Reverend Peterson said he didn't know what had happened to them. I don't believe him. And he wouldn't tell me who signed off on their transportation back home."

Coty leaned back in his chair.

"Shit," he muttered, his eyes scanning the room. "I'll see what I can find out. I'll also find out where Henry went for his period of rest. If it was a medical institution I'll get the notes."

He looked at the cigarette and stubbed it out, then raised his hand to his face and rubbed his temples with his thumb and forefinger. He said, "Connor will be in surgery today. They need to reattach the grafts. He's torn some of the stitching. They had more grafts to do anyway, it's a slow process. Tomorrow he'll be resting. I'll call you. You can go back to New York for now."

"Thank you, I might just do that. There's one more thing," Jack said.

"Oh yeah?" Coty looked up, eyes weary.

"The two bodies in the photograph, anything strike you as odd about them?"

"Not that I can remember, why?"

"Only one of them is still what you'd call a body. The other is mainly ash. Human debris. There's nothing in the report to explain it."

Coty shrugged. "Maybe it doesn't need explaining. Maybe it's just, I don't know, the way fire works. The type of clothing he was wearing burned faster. Or he was closer to the heat source. Or something blew up next to him."

"Maybe. But I don't like making assumptions. We've got some time. I'd like to talk to someone about it."

"Who?"

"Someone who knows about fires."

"What are you going to do, call up the goddamn New York fire department?" Coty shook his head impatiently. "I know someone who might be able to help. Guy called Nathaniel Bramwell. He's deputy fire chief for Brooklyn. We've used him before. I'll set something up. See if he can meet you for lunch somewhere near the fire station. Just don't tell him who the people are, where it happened, or why you're asking the question."

"Can I show the photo?"

"Guess you'll have to." Coty looked from his empty plate to his empty cup of coffee. Nothing left to eat or drink. He drummed his fingers on the table. "But don't tell Gill we've gone outside or he'll bust a blood vessel. I'll do it later. I don't need more mess."

10

En route to New York City
December 28, 9:00 A.M.

Jack flew back to New York. It was only a couple of hours in the air but he couldn't relax and it was too early for a drink. He chatted to the stewardess about the weather and how long it took to clear the runway of ice as he smoked and sipped a Coke. The stewardess was young and pretty. Talking to her reminded Jack of Connor's fiancée. Connor had looked terrified when he mentioned her. No wonder, given what lay beneath the bandages.

What bothered him was that he was starting to care about the man. It was the sight of the injuries that did it. So much easier when his pain was hidden. His life had changed forever, was over in many ways, and he had to spend his convalescence being questioned by a psychiatrist on behalf of the CIA. He remembered how it'd felt when he was in hospital, the heat in his burnt arm and the pull of the new skin, being questioned by police for what felt like hours when all he'd wanted to do was load up on morphine and float away to a world where his wife had survived.

He had doubted Connor's claims of memory loss, had thought he was trying to protect Henry-Three-Times, and maybe he had been. He took a pencil from his pocket and made a note on his pad—*Henry?*—was all it said. He added *and Stiglitz?* He flicked back to the previous page. All he'd written on that one was *white*. He liked to give his thoughts time to form. He shut his eyes and listened to the sounds in the cabin. The low note of the engines. The rumble through the wings and into the fuselage.

Why would Connor protect Henry? Because he'd done something bad. Because a fire had started and it had all gone to hell. Because, because, because.

The low winter sun streamed through JFK's glass walls like spilt gasoline, making the polished concrete floor glow with head-numbing brightness. Jack had a little time before the meeting Coty had set up with the fire chief so he made his way to the bank of phones next to the departures lounge. He bought a soda to break a twenty and took the stack of coins over to a booth. The booth smelled of stale smoke and disinfectant. So did the receiver. He took a silk handkerchief from his pocket and wiped it, then called his clinic.

He worked from the third floor of a building on West Fourth Street in Manhattan, not far from his apartment. Two other psychiatrists and a secretary shared the office.

"Dr. Miller. Finally. Where are you?" Martina answered. Even though he'd known her for ten years he still couldn't get her to call him Jack.

"I'm still away," he said vaguely.

"When will you be back?"

"I don't know, end of the week maybe. Depends."

"Well, I'll clear out the rest of your appointments. Mrs. Gehry was very disappointed you couldn't see her yesterday. She misses you. And the actor, he was most upset. Used the kind of language that would make a lady blush. Or at least think he was overcompensating for something."

"He's always miserable unless there's a camera and a blonde pointed at him. You should have offered to see him yourself. Sounds like you've got him figured," Jack replied.

"I don't want to have to cancel again next week. You'll have no patients at all. Then what will you do?"

"There'll always be more patients. It's New York. Anything I need to deal with?"

"Nothing urgent. Someone was here yesterday. Asking after you, what you specialized in. I said you were away at the moment. He was disappointed. So, you see, you lose a customer. The other doctors see far more than you."

"I'm sure he'll find someone else," Jack said. He was about to thank her and hang up but something made him stop. "What was he like?"

"A tall man. Softly spoken. Well dressed. I think he might have had short hair. Maybe dark. And he had that look."

"What look?"

"You know, the look people have when they want something but don't want to say what it is. The way patients look."

"What did you tell him about me?"

"I said you'd had to attend an emergency and were away all week. He said he was sorry to hear that." Martina paused. "You're being more inquisitive about this man than you are about any of your actual patients."

"Thank you, Martina. I'll check in again before the end of the week."

Jack replaced the receiver. He was thinking about the car that had followed him last night, watching from the shadows when he went to see Reverend Peterson. He'd forgotten to tell Coty about it; too much on his mind. He hoped his driver had. The man who'd visited his office could be anyone. A potential patient, or someone with a different motive altogether. He'd looked as if he'd wanted something but didn't want to say what it was. Was he with the same people who were following him last night?

That would mean they were in New York and Washington. He cursed inwardly, angry at the not knowing. Angry at Coty. He wasn't a spy. This wasn't his world. He didn't want it spilling over into his life, following him, turning up at his office and asking his secretary about him.

He told himself he was being paranoid. He was simply seeing something normal in a different way. Same as poor Henry, looking at people getting sick and thinking they'd been poisoned.

Jack put the thought out of his mind, drank the soda, and flipped the empty bottle into a trash can.

The traffic flowed smoothly from the expressway onto Woodhaven Boulevard. Once they got to Forest Park it snarled up and became irritable and congested. Same as ever, Jack thought. He lit a cigarette and opened the window, savoring the cold after the stuffiness of the cab. He could see Manhattan in the distance, the sight of it making him less worried.

Coty had organized a meeting at a deli on Cadman Plaza in Brooklyn, close to the fire station. The cab pulled up outside an apartment block on the east side of the park. Jack stepped out into the deep shadow it cast, paying the driver and collecting a receipt.

People pushed past him, as if he'd arrived there for the specific purpose of getting in their way. Jack didn't mind. He was back in the bright cold of New York and starting to feel less like he'd been handed a part he didn't want to play. Less worried about people turning up at his office, asking to see him. More at home, on his own patch. He crossed the street to the deli.

The lunchtime crowd was impatient and loud, the tables crammed together. A tinny radio played over the background hubbub, adding another layer of indistinct noise. A mix of workmen, firemen, and businessmen jostled for service.

Coty had told him Nate was five foot five and *all of it angry*. Red hair, ruddy complexion, barrel-shaped. He scanned the back of the restaurant for him, then pushed his way through the closely packed diners.

"Nate Bramwell? I'm Jack, Jack Miller."

Nate stood to shake his hand, bumping the marble tabletop with his belly and spilling a little cola as he did. He didn't smile.

"You're five minutes late," he said.

Nate signaled to the one of the men behind the counter.

"Traffic by Forest Park. Sorry. You get table service? In this place?" Jack asked.

"I'm the deputy fire chief," he muttered in reply.

"I'll have whatever he just ordered," Jack called out. The man behind the counter nodded, scribbled something on a piece of paper, and pinned it to the counter.

"Thank you for seeing me and sorry to crash your lunch," Jack said.

"Coty said it was urgent. I've only got twenty minutes." He flicked his watch out from under his sleeve and glanced at it. "More like fifteen now."

"It's appreciated. Ok. Background," Jack said. "I don't know how much Coty told you but I'm a psychiatrist. Talking to a burn victim. We need to find out how a fire started. There are two dead bodies. The burn victim says he doesn't remember much but I don't know if he's telling me the truth. Not sure I trust him. I want to. It's terrible. The injuries. But that doesn't mean he's telling the truth."

The waiter elbowed his way through the diners and set two sandwiches down in front of them.

Nate took a bite. "Describe the fire," he said.

"Confined space. Underground, in an insulated cabin. Fuel was stored there. It might be easier if I just show you. If you don't mind looking while you're eating."

"Go ahead," Nate said through a mouthful.

Jack took the photo out of his pocket and placed it on the table. Nate's expression changed, became more interested, as if he'd met someone he actually wanted to talk to. He took a pair of glasses from his inside pocket and put them on. He stared at the photo some more, leaned in closer, nodding his head.

"Must have been a hot fire. Judging by the metal. What kind of burns has your survivor got?"

"Hands and face. They've done some grafts. They'll be doing more. He's got a long way to go."

"So how does he fit into this?" Nate gestured at the photo. "How come he got off so lightly? He can't have been anywhere near."

"He wasn't. He opened the door to it. Burned his hands in the process, face too. The other two were trapped inside."

"But he's talking ok?"

"He is."

"Opening the door on a blaze like this would have sent a blast of burning hot air into his lungs, throat, and mouth. What's he sound like?"

"Croaky, but he talks. They put him in a medically induced coma for three weeks."

Nate frowned and pointed at the photo.

"No way he should be talking now. Not for any length of time. The air would have been too hot. It would have scorched his lungs. Can you tell me where this was?" he said.

"It was in a very cold place. Subzero. Would that make any difference?"

"Maybe. What are we talking about here, a fire in an icebox?" Nate said, his face incredulous.

"Something like that. Let's say he's lying on ice. So was the room that caught fire."

Nate stared back at him, waiting for him to say more.

"I can't give you anything else," Jack said.

"So the blast of hot air cools fast," he said. "And I'm guessing it couldn't spread once he opened the door."

"That's right. It's an isolated room. Cold environment. There was nowhere for the fire to go. The location was built with this kind of scenario in mind. It's the sort of place where you couldn't let fire spread."

"Is that your way of telling me this was a missile base?" Nate asked.

Jack frowned.

"I couldn't say. Anything else not look right?" he asked.

"Yeah."

"Yeah?"

"This body here. It's almost gone. Burned to ash. The other isn't."

Jack sat back in his chair and nodded. "That was bothering me too."

"See this misshapen hunk of metal?" Nate said, pointing at the generator. "You need over a thousand degrees to make steel buckle like that. If that's the temperature in the room then these two bodies should be nothing more than ash and bone. This one has burned away to nothing. The other is still recognizably human in shape. Now, if two people are in the same room for the same amount of time, next to the same fire, then it doesn't make sense for one of them to be more burned than the other."

"Any reason you can think of for why they might have burned at different rates?" Jack said.

Nate shrugged. "I can think of one reason. But you won't want to hear it. What ideas have you and Coty been throwing around?"

"Different clothing? One of them is wrapped up in something fire resistant? The other isn't?"

"Not likely to help if the fire is this hot."

"One of them was holding a can of gas? Or spilt some on himself?"

"Is there a can of gas amongst all that human debris?" Nate said, looking at the photo. "I can't see one, and I'm guessing no one moved it out of shot. But even if one of them burned faster the other should have caught up. Looks like the fire burned itself out, judging by the mess. Your boy in the hospital can't have opened the door on the room and found them both inside. If that was the case both of the bodies would be ash," he said.

"So what happened?" Jack asked.

Nate shrugged. "Only one explanation," he said.

"What's that?"

"They weren't burned in the same fire."

Jack had his sandwich halfway to his mouth. He put it back down on the plate.

"They weren't burned in the same fire?"

Nate nodded. "This room and that sorry pile of ash makes sense to me. This other body doesn't fit. Your boy's lying," Nate said. "But I think you knew that anyway, otherwise you wouldn't be here."

"I was kind of hoping what he said would check out," Jack said. "Hoping there might be some kind of explanation that made this easier."

"No, not from where I'm sitting." He stared at the photo a moment longer.

Nate checked his watch, took his glasses off, and slipped them into his pocket.

"Gotta go. I'll check through the fire reports at the station. See if I can find anything similar. Different burn rates but both bodies in close proximity to the same fire. You never know." He stood to go.

Jack nodded. "Thank you. Here," he said, handing him his card. "Call me if you find anything."

He put the photo into his pocket as Nate made his way through the crowd and out of the deli.

The two bodies weren't burned in the same fire.

Things had just got a lot more complicated.

11

Manhattan
December 28, 2:00 P.M.

Jack decided to go back to his apartment and write up his notes. Try and make sense of what Connor had told him and what Nate had said about the fire. He caught a taxi back to Manhattan. The cables of the Brooklyn Bridge diced the low sun so it fell in quick slices and the skyscrapers shimmered in the distance. They looked as if they might dive into the Hudson and swim away. Jack rubbed his eyes. He felt as if everything Connor had told him had done the same: dived into the water, swam away. Two fires. He didn't open the door and see the two of them. Couldn't have. Henry and Stiglitz didn't burn in the same fire.

Connor was lying. Why? What had he seen? What the hell had gone on between the three of them? He'd had to hold Connor's arms down just to stop him tearing off his own skin when he'd questioned him last night.

Jack's apartment was in a back house in Greenwich Village, just off Waverly Place. You had to go through another building to get to it and it didn't get much light, but it was spacious by New York standards and strangely quiet without the noise of the street. There were only two stories. The woman on the first floor looked about 150 and had lived there forever. Pretty much since it was built. She filled the courtyard with plants he couldn't name and wrapped the pots in blankets to keep out the frost. He looked in on her a couple of times a week, mainly as an excuse to take out her trash. They'd had roaches two summers before and it had been hell to get rid of them.

He walked quickly to the front door, as was his habit. If she saw him she'd come out and give him a list of chores.

If his head hadn't been so full of fires and questions he might have paid more attention to the lock, which bore fresh scratches on the brass plate. And if he'd seen that maybe he would have walked more quietly up the stairs, listened for other sounds. He might even have walked away, taken up position somewhere discreet on the street and simply watched and waited.

But he didn't. Because he wasn't a spy and, in all the years he'd worked for him, Coty hadn't given Jack any training. And he was in a hurry to get home, write up his notes, make some calls, and then get himself on the next flight to Washington. So he opened the front door, thinking he was lucky to get in without being cornered by his neighbor, climbed the stairs without listening for any noises coming from his apartment, and when he got to his door he took out his key, went to open it, and paused. It took him a surprising amount of time to realize that the door was ajar, with no need to put his key in the lock at all. He looked dumbly at the sliver of light that spilled out into the hallway by his black shoes.

That wasn't right. He knew that now, key in hand, door already open. He probably should have walked away at this point and called the police, but instead he stood and waited and listened, and since there was no noise coming from inside he pushed open the door.

It was an old, heavy door and it swung inward slowly, creaking loudly. Jack stayed where he was, outside, on the threshold. There was his hallway. Same as it always was. Same as when he left it. Occasional table. Mirror. Telephone. Faded red rug. Window at the end and dust motes wriggling in a warm slice of winter sun.

He shifted to one side. Looked in the mirror. Caught the reflection of the kitchen. Stayed very still. He could feel his heart beating. He listened, but all he could hear was the sound of his own breathing. He waited. It wasn't that he was playing a game, trying to catch them out. He simply couldn't move.

Nothing.

Ok. The door wouldn't be open if they were still there. If they were inside it would be closed. You wouldn't leave a door open while you were inside burgling a place. You'd close it. They must have gone and left it open. It was simple.

He stepped inside.

The movement was so fast he barely saw it. Just a blur in the corner of his eye. A hand, and in it something, something sweeping toward him. He ducked to one side and it caught his shoulder.

The trepidation he'd felt was replaced with a rush of anger. He swung the palm of his right hand upward, felt it connect, felt teeth crunch together and heard a dull groan. Then a fist hit his cheek in a reply that jolted his skull sideways. He stamped his left foot forward into the man's kneecap but missed and scraped his shin. Jack hit out with a jab that half connected with the man's neck. The man gasped but didn't go down. He was big, bigger than Jack, and there was no room to fight in the hallway. Jack couldn't get an angle, could barely see him. Just a blur of movement. Close-cropped hair. Sandy colored. Blood from the lip Jack had split ran down his chin.

The man's arms tangled around Jack, tried to fling him onto the floor. He was behind Jack now. Twisting him, trying to get him in some kind of choke hold. He had ideas, this one. He was well practiced. Jack wasn't. He'd had his fair share of army brawls but that was twenty years ago. The muscle memory was long forgotten. The desire to hit back wasn't.

The man managed to twist Jack's arms behind his back. Jack could smell cigar smoke on his short, sharp breath. Stale and bitter. He jabbed his elbow into the man's stomach, heard him gasp. The hold loosened. Jack tried to get away, fell forward, and, as he fell, he saw another figure. This one swinging something black and heavy toward him. His telephone? Was that his damn telephone in the man's hand? He couldn't get out the way. Nowhere to go. It hit him on the side of his head and the room span away from him, once more, a second hit and it blurred and dissolved.

The last thing he saw was the red rug rising up to meet him.

12

Manhattan
December 28, 3:00 P.M.

His world was confused. There were sounds in the distance. Voices he didn't recognize. Footsteps on the floor that he could feel through the side of his head. He opened his eyes. Tried to. One was stuck shut with something. Dried blood. The world was lying on its side. He wasn't where he should be. He stayed still.

"I think that fucker broke my jaw." The voice was high-pitched. The accent Southern. The tone resentful. Jack felt a twinge of satisfaction.

"It ain't broke. If it was you wouldn't be talking. You're just sore you got beat by an old man." The second voice was lower and more measured. Sounded like a mix of Lower East Side and Eastern European.

"Did you see the size of him? You had to hit him twice with the damn telephone. I thought you said he wasn't going to be here."

"That's what his secretary said. He's meant to be out of town."

Jack could see two sets of shoes moving. A pair of brown brogues, polished and expensive, and a pair of leather boots that tapered at the toe.

"You find anything in the study?"

He heard the sound of furniture scraping along the floor.

"Nah, just books. Endless fuckin' books. And photos of him with some Jap broad. He's young. In a marine outfit. A Jap broad after the war. Jeez. Some people."

"Let me see," the other voice said. He looked at the photograph. Jack had his arm around the woman's shoulders, hair blown across her face and a white-gloved hand pressed against her skirt, holding it down as the wind tried to lift it up. In her other hand a small bouquet of paper flowers. The two of them smiling in front of a burnt-out city. *Miyoko and Jack Miller, Tokyo, March 2, 1946* written in careful black ink on the back. A starting point. The beginning of a journey. The man dropped it casually on the floor and the glass cracked.

"You think we should wake him? Ask him questions?"

"No. He wasn't meant to be here. What's in his briefcase?"

Jack felt a foot brush his back as the man stepped over him and picked up his briefcase.

"It's locked."

"So break it open."

He heard the tear of metal splitting fabric. Fought the urge to check the photograph in his pocket.

"What've you got?"

"Nothing much, just a notebook. There's a few lines of shorthand and then these three words. *White*, *Henry*, and *Stiglitz*. What is that, some kind of code?"

"Who knows. Make a note then put it back. We're not supposed to take anything."

"Can I cut him?"

"Cut him? No! What's wrong with you?"

"My lip. It's still bleeding. Eye for an eye is what I say."

"He didn't blind you."

Footsteps toward him. He felt a rough hand take ahold of his hair and lift his head, felt the same stale cigar breath he'd felt on his neck earlier. Did his best to play dead.

"Just a nick, here," the voice said.

Jack felt something cold pressed against his cheek.

"Leave him alone. He wasn't meant to be here. Let's go."

The hand let go of his head and it dropped to the floor. Pain shot through the inside of his skull. It was the same side of his face they'd introduced to the telephone. He clenched his teeth so he didn't yell. The door to the apartment closed softly with a click. He remained still. His heart beating hard. A mixture of anger and relief and helplessness flowed through him. His breathing was tight. He drew deep breaths, pulled his knees up close to his chest and rolled back so he was resting against the wall, felt for the photograph in his jacket pocket. Still there. Slowly he got up.

They had made a mess. The table in the hallway was on its side, the plaster wall had a gash in it, the mirror hung at an angle. Books were strewn all over the floor. He picked up the picture of him and Miyoko and removed the broken glass carefully out of the frame. He placed it back on the shelf. It was their wedding day, shortly before they returned to the US. They had paper flowers because he couldn't get real ones. The dumplings they'd had for lunch were real though.

He reached for one of the books they'd thrown on the floor. Her copy of *Tender Is the Night*. Some of the pages had been torn out. She was in this book, her neat handwriting in pencil throughout the margins. The questions she'd asked about what certain words meant, her notes in kanji. She'd been studying English before she started working for the US army as an interpreter. He remembered her delight when he explained new words and expressions, as if she'd been given a present. A new word could hold a whole new world, she'd told him. He collected the pages, then searched through a cupboard for a roll of tape and some scissors. He cut thin strips of tape, carefully setting the pages back in the right place, putting her back together, and placed the book on the shelf next to the photograph.

Dumplings and flowers. Feed the soul as much as the body. After the war he'd needed that. He'd needed her. Her curiosity, her appetite for new things. Her hope. He still did. Fifteen years since she died, but she was still with him.

He felt a surge of anger at the two men, wished he'd hit them harder, then he straightened the mirror. A cut on his hand left a swipe of blood on the wall, which he didn't notice. Into the bathroom. He turned on the hot tap and started to fill the sink. As the water ran he went into the study. On the mantelpiece was a brass tobacco caddy and in that was the key to the desk. He took out the key and unlocked the bottom drawer. A Colt .45 lay on its side. He took it out, checked the action, and took it with him into the bathroom. He placed it on the washstand and proceeded to wash the blood off his face.

The mirror steamed up. He wiped it and decided he didn't look too bad, considering. The blow had been to the side of his head. There'd be a bump but it would be covered by hair. His chin was tender but he'd always had a strong jaw. He unbuttoned his shirt and stripped down to his vest. His shoulder was stiff. He'd hardly felt the blow but the skin was hot and red. He went to the icebox in the kitchen, crushed some ice, and wrapped it in two towels, holding one against his shoulder.

He returned to the living room, poured himself a whisky, and sat on the sofa with ice on his shoulder and ice held against his head. It hurt but he'd known worse, he thought, looking down at the skin graft on his left arm.

He placed the whisky glass on the table beside him. His heart rate was coming down. His breathing was more even. The rational part of his brain was regaining control.

They weren't expecting him to be there. That was clear. They'd been asked to find out about him. They'd gone to his clinic and then to his apartment. Nothing more. It was his bad luck he'd disturbed them.

Who were they working for? Was it the same people who'd followed him when he went to see Reverend Peterson? Somehow he doubted it. They'd sat discreetly in a car. Lights off. Waiting. These two seemed more like low-rent private eyes. Jack dragged himself off the sofa and put on a fresh shirt. He stowed the Colt in the bottom drawer of his desk and locked it. He took out his notebook and flicked to the end and wrote down everything he could remember about the two men who'd been in his apartment. Shoe size. Voices. He thought about calling the police but decided he should run it by Coty first. He lifted his hand. It was shaking.

He'd never experienced anything like this before. Not in all the years of working for Coty.

Jack dropped an ice cube into his whisky and winced as pain shot through his shoulder. In spite of all of it, he wanted to get to the truth. He liked Connor. Even felt bad for him. But Connor was lying. The two men didn't burn in the same fire. The whole thing was a mess, as Coty said. There were unanswered questions lying on the floor like broken books. He picked up the telephone. It still worked, despite its recent encounter with the side of his head. He called Coty. Told him what had happened. Then he checked the flight times to Washington, finished his whisky, and tried standing up. It was a lot harder than he remembered.

13

En route to Dulles Airport
December 28, 7:30 P.M.

The flight back was unpleasant. The pressure in the cabin increased the ache on the side of his head and he couldn't get comfortable with his shoulder. A mother and her two boys were in the seats behind him. The boys were fighting. Fighting over a toy car. He could feel sporadic kicks in his back. The mother was drinking a Bloody Mary and doing her best to ignore them. Jack decided to do the same.

Coty sent a driver to meet him at the airport. It took Jack a while to work out that it wasn't the same driver he'd had before. He wore the same dark gray suit and had the same neat haircut. The difference was that this one seemed to be looking for a fight, instead of pretending one was never going to happen.

"We've got two sets of eyes, so you see anything you tell me straightaway," the man said, shaking Jack's hand and scanning the other passengers. "Coty said you're not field."

"I'm not what?"

"Armed. Trained."

"No. Well, I was trained twenty years ago, but that suitcase isn't a flamethrower and I don't have a machine gun in my jacket."

"If I need to draw I'll shout *down*. Don't get up unless I tell you to."

"Does anyone get up before you tell them to?"

"You'd be surprised. First instinct is to run. Don't run. Not unless I say so. Name's Frank by the way. The car's outside. Wait here." Frank went outside, looked quickly up and down the taxi rank, then unlocked the doors of a brown Ford Fairlane. He went back into the airport and cast another quick look around.

"In," he said, nodding toward the car. Jack got in. Frank checked the rearview mirror and pulled away. He drove fast but without impatience, weaving through the airport traffic and taking corners at the limit of what the heavy car could handle.

"I'm taking you to see Coty and Gill. Not to the hotel." A lit cigarette appeared between Frank's lips as he was saying this. Jack wasn't sure how he did it, it was a magic trick, but he found it strangely reassuring.

"They want to talk," he continued.

"That's good because so do I," Jack replied.

At Langley, Frank stayed with him all the way to Gill's office on the eighth floor. Jack felt like a teenage girl being chaperoned by an overprotective aunt.

"Come in, Jack," Gill said. "How's the head? I see where they hit you. You want us to get a medic to check you over?"

"I'm ok, just a little bruised," Jack replied.

"You sure?" Gill asked. "Your call, guess you're a medical man yourself." Gill seemed half-embarrassed, half-indifferent. "Sit," he said, pointing at a chair. He turned to Coty. "Fix us some drinks, won't you?"

Jack sat in the chair, sitting at an angle so it didn't push on his shoulder. Coty filled three tumblers with whisky.

"I'm sorry, Jack," Coty said. "This came out of the blue. You sure you're ok?"

Jack took a sip of whisky. It caught in his throat and he coughed. He put it down.

"I'm a little sore. Side of my head and chin took the worst of it. Shoulder's stiffening up too."

"Get a look at them?" Gill asked.

"Not much. Apart from the shoes. Who did it? Same people that were following me yesterday when I went to see Reverend Peterson?"

Gill and Coty exchanged a look.

"Those guys held back. Out of sight. Your driver told me he didn't think there was anyone there at all. Not anyone suspicious. He thought you were seeing things in the shadows," Coty said.

"Is that why I have a new driver?" Jack asked.

"It is. And Frank's more than a driver," Coty replied. "But I can't square what those thugs did to you today—breaking into the apartment, throwing things around, beating you—with what happened yesterday. Completely different style. Those men today were unprofessional. Stupid, even. The people yesterday were ghosts."

"Are you saying there are two sets of people on my tail?" Jack asked. "Because if that's the case this is getting a little rich for me."

"It's possible," Coty said. "We don't know who was following you yesterday. We think maybe it was the military trying to find out why we're talking to Connor. Spying on the spies. That seems most likely. This town is paranoid."

"So what about today?"

"Best guess is Henry's father, General Arthur Carvell," Coty said.

"Henry's father?" Jack said, trying to take it in.

"He's been making a lot of noise. Not getting any answers. Wants to know exactly how his son came to die in a locked room in an abandoned military base in Greenland. Understandable. The military uses the word *accident* to cover up a multitude of sins."

"And this shit stinks," Gill added. "He can smell it all the way from West Point."

Jack frowned.

"Why get them to beat me?" he asked.

"I don't think he did. I think that was on them. God knows how he found those two. Maybe he asked someone to look into it and they hired a couple of goons. I've met the General. This isn't his style. He wouldn't have wanted them to beat you. No point. I think it's all on them. But he must be desperate to find out why his son was brought back to him in a box. And he obviously doesn't believe whatever reason he's being given by his friends in the army," Gill said.

"He's in town later this week," Coty added. "I'll arrange a meeting. Ask him about it. Try and give him some answers. A little quid pro quo. He's not getting them anywhere else."

Jack shook his head. "So I've got an unidentified tail in Washington and hired thugs trashing my apartment—and me—in New York. Anyone else about to join the party?"

Gill poured himself another drink. Smaller this time. Coty was already on his second.

"If you want to walk you can," Gill said. "You're not trained for this. If we'd known where it was headed we'd never have asked you to talk to Connor."

Jack nodded, but he didn't entirely believe him. They knew where most things were headed. They knew there was a spy at the base and they hadn't bothered to tell him until after he'd spoken to Connor.

"Appreciated," he said. "But I don't want to walk away. Not now. Anyway, I've got Frank to look after me."

He got up to pour himself a drink but Coty intervened and got one for him.

"How did it go with Nate?" he asked.

Jack stared at the whisky, swirled it round in the glass, then took a sip.

"You're not going to like this," he said, looking up at the two of them. "I showed him the photo. Gave him a little background."

"And?" Coty said.

"He said it looked like a hot fire, given the way the metal had buckled."

"That was in the report already." Coty frowned.

"He looked at the state of the two bodies. Tried to work out if there was anything to explain why one was more burned than the other."

"Like an accelerant," Coty said. "Fuel spilt on one of them."

Jack nodded. "But he said that even if one body was covered in gasoline it shouldn't make that much difference, given the fire had burned itself out."

Gill and Coty stared back at him.

"So what was his conclusion?" Gill said.

"His conclusion was that they weren't burned in the same fire."

"He said what?" Gill replied.

"Not the same fire," Jack said, and swallowed the rest of his whisky.

Gill looked like he was going to crush the crystal glass in his hand. He set it down heavily on his desk instead.

"If Stiglitz wasn't burned in the same fire it means what little Connor's told us about the accident is bullshit. Running to find them, trying to open the door of the cabin to save them, seeing the two bodies in there," he said.

"How long before I can talk to him again?" Jack asked.

"Tomorrow morning," Coty replied. "Before he goes into surgery. We should be able to get thirty minutes or so before they prep him."

"Two damn fires," Gill said grimly. He drained his glass then reached behind him and took three files off the desk. "Here, take these. We pulled together detailed personnel files on Henry, Stiglitz, and Connor: education, time in the army, interviews, assessments, whatever we could find. We were looking for evidence of communist sympathies, vulnerability to blackmail. Anything that might indicate they were a target for Russian intelligence. Read up, maybe you'll spot something we missed there too."

"And this," Coty said. "Medical file for Henry. Came in this morning. From his time at the Alexander Institute back in February. His little period of rest and relaxation. Courtesy of one of the most discreet and expensive asylums in the country."

14

The Willard
December 28, 10:00 P.M.

Frank drove Jack to his hotel. The sky was dark and a light snow was falling. The delicate flakes danced sideways in the wind while the radio played Christmas songs. Frank didn't seem to mind. Jack did. He switched it off. His jaw hurt, and the side of his head. The music made it worse.

The two of them entered the hotel and stopped by reception to check for messages.

"Here." The man behind the desk reached for an envelope and passed it to Jack. "Someone called for you earlier. A Mr. Peterson."

"He did? What time?"

"Couple of hours ago, I believe."

Jack looked at the envelope a little suspiciously, then turned away and opened it.

I have looked further into the matter we talked about. If you'd like to discuss I'll be at the Old Ebbitt Grill this evening. Yours, Rev. Peterson

He read the note again then folded it and placed it in his pocket. The reverend had seemed unwilling to talk much about the men they evacuated from the base yesterday. He was evasive, almost defensive. Something must have changed his mind.

"What is it?" Frank said.

"I'm going to meet someone," Jack said.

"Now? Where?" Frank replied.

"Follow me and you'll find out. But try and stay out of sight. I don't want to scare him off."

Jack locked the files in the safe in his room then left the hotel and walked around the corner to 1427 F Street. The Old Ebbitt Grill had a wood-paneled facade and was hung with three ship's lanterns that looked ready to topple on the first unsuspecting drunk of the night. He went inside and let his eyes get used to the smoke-filled gloom. Someone had evidently decided the room would look better if stuffed animal heads and dead fish took up all the available wall space.

Reverend Peterson was by the bar. His tall figure was too long for the stool so his body made a loose letter "z" from floor to elbows. He shifted awkwardly when Jack got there, sliding off the stool then gripping the brass rail that ran around the bar to steady himself.

He held out his hand.

"You made it, Dr. Miller," he said. "I was about to head home."

"You look like you've been here a while."

"Hour or two at the most." The reverend smiled nervously and looked over Jack's shoulder.

"What's your poison?" he asked.

Jack shrugged. "Whatever you're drinking."

"I'm not much of a drinker," the reverend said. He turned to the barman. "Two old-fashioneds, and bring them to the table in the corner."

Jack followed him. The reverend moved easily through the semi-darkness, despite the booze in his blood. Jack sensed he'd made the journey many times. They sat opposite each other and the reverend looked at him a moment, trying to work something out.

"Something's different about you," he said, looking a little puzzled. Jack touched his jaw and felt the slight swelling under the skin. The reverend was perceptive, even in this state.

"Took a knock on the chin," he said. "Nothing serious. Wasn't looking where I was going."

The barman placed two drinks on the table.

"That why you've got that fella following you? The one who looks like he got lost on the way to a funeral? To make sure you don't walk into anything?"

Jack smiled.

"I don't think he could stop me walking into something. I'm pretty clumsy. He just wants me to remember to duck if the bullets start flying."

"Well, I am unarmed," the reverend said, holding open his jacket theatrically. He took a small sip of the old-fashioned and placed the glass gently down on the table.

Jack leaned back, waiting. The reverend ran a finger round the top of his glass and it squeaked on the crystal. His eyes drifted to the bartender, who was making light dance through tumblers and pouring golden liquor in a series of smooth, well-practiced movements. The reverend smiled appreciatively. "I do like the way a good bartender makes fixing a drink into a performance. A ritual. Even if he's only got an audience of one."

"I suppose it's not a million miles from your job," Jack said.

The reverend made a little snorting sound. "Guess not," he replied. "And sometimes I don't have many more customers." He took a small sip and licked his lips. "Our little chat yesterday got me thinking," he said. "About the people who got sick at the base. I guess because there were so many people there, and because all the crews worked different shifts, I never really thought about what happened to them. I thought I might look one of them up. You know, seeing as you mentioned them. I was curious. In some ways I miss the army; not Greenland, that was not a good place for someone like me." He looked uneasily at the old-fashioned. "But it was good to be around young folk. Not like my current congregation."

"I thought you couldn't remember who was evacuated?"

"No, well. You turn up at my church asking questions, you can understand why I might not want to talk too much. And I'm still not sure I should be talking to you now either. But you're not army."

"Is that good?"

"Given what I found out yesterday, I'd say so. What are you? FBI? Agency?"

"I do some vetting and psychological assessments for the Agency. But I don't work for them. I have a clinic in New York."

The reverend nodded. "I checked you out." He twisted the glass, watching as it caught the light. "I called up my old unit yesterday, spoke to the sergeant. I said I was going through my things and I'd found a Bible belonging to a guy called Cooper, that was the name of one of the boys who'd been evacuated, said I wanted to post it back to him." The reverend held up his hand. "A little white lie, before you ask. I had no Bible. The sergeant went all quiet, then said he was sorry to tell me that Cooper had died in February. I was surprised. I asked what from, that would have only been a month or so after he'd got back from Greenland. He said he'd taken his own life."

"I'm sorry," Jack said.

"So was I, and I was angry that no one had told me or anyone else about it at the time. No memorial service or anything. I asked about the other two who were evacuated with him. The sergeant went all quiet on me. Said he didn't think he should be talking about it. I could sense that he wanted to. You get to know when someone is carrying a burden in my job. I told him if he wanted to talk I was always here. Still a man of the cloth. In confidence. He thanked me, I left it at that. He called me back this afternoon."

"And?" Jack said.

"He said the three of them were shipped out from Thule under sedation. By the time they got back to the US they were all wide awake. The sergeant said he'd never seen anything like it. They were terrified. He said it was like they were under some sort of spell. They were seeing things."

"What kind of things?"

"Apparently they thought a dark figure was watching them. They'd point at him. They couldn't describe it very well though. It was just there, somehow. And he said they would see bugs, on the floor and on the ceiling. Crawling all over the place. Crawling out of cracks or under doors."

"So they weren't ill with a virus or anything like that? They were suffering from hallucinations?"

"That's what he said. Said he'd never seen men look so scared."

"And they all suffered similar symptoms, they all described the same thing?"

"Sounded like it. He didn't have much time with them before they were sent to an institution in Kentucky. But they were all in the same state, all terrified." The reverend lifted his glass, went to drink, then realized it was empty. He started to lift a weary arm to signal the bartender to bring over another two.

"I'm fine," Jack said, interrupting his request. "Been a long day. If I have anything else you'll have to scrape me off the floor."

The reverend ignored him.

"When you've heard what I have to say next you'll thank me." The bartender went through his ritual one more time, then brought the drinks on a tray. He took away the empty glasses and slipped back into the shadows. The reverend sipped his old-fashioned carefully and licked his lips.

"It wasn't just Cooper who took his own life. One of the others did too."

"Two of them? At the same clinic?"

"That's what the sergeant told me."

Jack frowned. "Shouldn't have happened. They should have been under observation after the first one died. What happened to the other guy, you said there were three of them?"

"He went AWOL. Tried to escape from the institution by swimming across an ice-cold lake. They think he drowned. They dredged it but couldn't find him."

"Fuck," Jack said softly, then, "Sorry."

"If I thought God was offended by cussing I wouldn't have joined the army," the reverend replied.

"Do you have his name?"

"Here." He took a piece of paper from his pocket and passed it to Jack. *Archibald Bell* was written on it. Jack read it, then held the piece of paper over a candle and watched as the flame ate it up.

"Thank you," he said.

The reverend nodded. Jack picked up the old-fashioned and swallowed it whole.

"Do you think there was any truth to what Henry said? That Stiglitz had poisoned these three people?"

The reverend looked uncomfortable. "At the time Henry just sounded paranoid. We were all worried for him. He was a nice guy and he was obviously going through something. But accusing Stiglitz, it was ridiculous. It sounded ridiculous. And it wasn't the only thing he accused him of." He looked up, embarrassed.

"What else did he say?" Jack asked.

"They had a dog at the base. Against all the rules, I know, but it was a gift from the Inuits who helped them sight and build the place. A husky. Henry found the dog all mangled and beaten in one of the tunnels. He said Stiglitz did that too."

Jack stared. "Why did he say that?"

"I've no idea. And Stiglitz just looked at Henry like he'd lost his mind. We all did. You can't accuse the chief scientific officer of mutilating a damn dog. The base commander made an arrangement with Henry's father, General Carvell. Get him home, treat him privately before he says or does something that might end his career. They wanted to keep it quiet."

Jack nodded. No wonder Henry's father wasn't willing to accept that Henry had simply died in an accident.

"And nine months later Henry and Stiglitz find themselves trapped together under the ice in the middle of an arctic storm," Jack said.

The reverend picked up his drink. The glass was empty. He seemed to have once again forgotten. He put it down. "With only Connor between them," he said. "I guess the chance of it ending well was always pretty slim."

15

The Willard
December 29, 12:30 A.M.

J ack sat on the edge of the bed. Felt his chin, which had a numbness to it. He wasn't sure if all the whisky had helped or made it worse. Three people suffering similar forms of psychosis at the same time under the ice at the northernmost tip of the world. Four if you included Henry. It didn't stack up. Symptoms of psychological distress did not manifest themselves in the same way in different people at the same time. And as for Henry, he hadn't just accused Stiglitz of making them sick, he'd accused him of killing a dog. No wonder he was taken away as discreetly as possible.

Jack opened the curtains and switched off the lights. The windows looked out onto Pennsylvania Avenue and the park beyond. Tall trees lined the street and their branches tangled themselves in shadows on the wall behind his bed. The city was silent and fresh with powdered snow. He took out the three files Gill had given him from his briefcase, sat on the bed, and switched on the lamp. Stiglitz first.

Was there anything here that suggested he was capable of the kind of behavior Henry had accused him of? He opened the file. Objective reading. Noting his actions, the outcomes he achieved, patterns of behavior, his motivation.

Jack mapped out a timeline. Stiglitz took his first degree in the late fifties, then completed his PhD. After that he joined the army's Engineering Corps as a noncommissioned officer.

He'd written papers on warfare in subzero temperatures, the effect of the cold on fuel efficiency, ballistic deployment, and time to launch. Optimal additives for cold weather. Frequency and volumes. Power-to-weight ratios in mid-axle engines. Lubricants. Everything to keep the army moving through the cold. And moving faster than whoever they were moving toward.

Jack could feel his eyes starting to close. Stiglitz's work was not interesting. Not unless you had a fleet of trucks and several hundred missiles you needed to move about in the arctic. Which, he supposed, was exactly what the Russians had. He flicked through the pages of diagrams and formulae he didn't understand, looking for something he did. The personnel files were collated at the back.

Works with dedication, applies scientific rigor and imagination, enabling him to incorporate and build on the theories of others. More time in the lab will help refine his theoretical work. I have no hesitation recommending him for and supporting his postdoctoral research in fuel-cell containment and subzero dispersion.

Another one, this time from the army promotions board:

His work has proved vital in allowing the military to expand its strategic defense objectives. He is to be highly commended.
He has succeeded where others failed. His brilliance is matched only by his dedication.

There were more, all singing Stiglitz's praises. An exceptional intellect. A dedicated and imaginative scientist. A generalist, in the best sense of the word. Able to turn his mind to any problem and find a practical solution.

Work. It was always about his work. There were no references to how he got along with others. How well he managed them, whether he inspired them, whether he annoyed them. On his personal qualities they were silent.

The file was arranged chronologically. Jack went as far back as he could, to his time at college. He found a review from the *Cornell University Chronicle*. Stiglitz had appeared in a production of *The Merchant of Venice*. It was one of those undergraduate pieces where the writer is more intent on crafting their own witty one-liners than telling you anything much about the play, but there were a couple of lines about Stiglitz:

> *The most surprising thing about the show wasn't when part of the set fell onto Shylock's head, nor was it Peter Mendelson's ability to continue to perform whilst in the grips of one of the most violent coughing fits the stage has ever witnessed, it was Owen Stiglitz's Antonio, likeable, forgivable, and able to recall all his lines without sounding like a drunk Larry Olivier. Which was more than could be said for the other players. Most of whom probably were drunk, but were definitely not Larry Olivier.*

Stiglitz could act, apparently. Or at least he could act better than the other people in the play. His only other activity outside of academic work was athletics, where he'd run middle distance but never distinguished himself.

At the end of the file he came to a handwritten note from a Dr. Rauschenberg. It was the last page of a complaint file, dated June 1958, Cornell University.

It is unfortunate that mediation hasn't worked, and the relationship has deteriorated to the point where the two parties will no longer communicate. As explained at the hearing, we found no evidence that Owen Stiglitz tampered with the work of Peter Mendelson, nor have we found evidence that Mendelson plagiarized Stiglitz's work on ice-core formation in his own thesis. Since mediation has failed and neither side is prepared to resolve the situation Mendelson has been assigned to another supervisor and will move to lab block C.

Something interesting. A hint of discord, Jack thought. He took out his notebook, opened it on a clean page and wrote *Peter Mendelson, Cornell* on it. He looked back over the review of the play, Mendelson was mentioned here too. Someone it might be worth talking to in order to understand more about what kind of person Stiglitz was. He appeared to be the only person who'd ever made a formal complaint about the way Stiglitz behaved. The only person other than Henry. He'd ask Coty to set it up.

He opened Connor's file. It was a whole lot slimmer. He wanted to read it but his eyes disagreed and closed on him. His hand held onto the papers, his arthritic fingers gripping tightly, till the pages slipped from them and onto the bed.

16

The Willard
December 29, 7:00 A.M.

He was woken by a banging on the door. Frank calling his name. He was still in his clothes. Second time he'd fallen asleep without undressing. He got up, his body stiff and aching in more places than he remembered being hit, as if fresh bruises had bloomed overnight. His chin was still sore, the side of his head hurt. He fumbled for a cigarette on the bedside table but there were none. The pages he'd let go of covered the bed and slipped onto the floor as he moved. He collected them.

"Time to get up," the muffled voice called through the wall.

"Ok, ok," Jack called back. He got undressed and turned on the shower, waited until the bathroom was filled with steam, then let the hot water loosen his muscles. He wiped the steam off the mirror but it clouded again. As far as he could tell it was still his face, just a little misshapen.

"We haven't got long," Frank called. Jack ignored him and put on a fresh shirt. It was starched as stiff as cardboard. Trousers slowly pulled on as if he was putting on a suit of armor. Socks next. Goddamn socks.

He could do this. He shook his head, almost laughing at himself as his arthritic fingers hooked the sock and yanked it over his ankle.

"Come on," Frank called out again. Jack put on his shoes, tied the laces, then got up and opened the door. Frank looked immaculate, not a crease in his charcoal gray suit. His face smoothly shaven. Eyes clear and bright.

"Don't tell me you've been standing there all night," Jack said.

"I got a room across the corridor," he replied. "You can see Connor, Coty wants me to take you there now. We've only got an hour before he goes into surgery."

It was a cold, bright day and the sky was a pale ocean blue, crisscrossed with vapor trails. The sun was low and it bounced in a thousand silver balls off fenders and mirrors and shop windows. Frank drove in his usual style. Finding a way through the early morning traffic when it didn't look like there was a way. Jack was keen to see Connor and get some answers, but wary of how he'd react given what he'd done to himself when he saw the photograph.

In the end it didn't matter. When they got to the hospital the chief medical officer wouldn't let them through.

"Coty said we could have an hour before you started prepping him for surgery, what's changed?" Jack said, not bothering to conceal his annoyance.

"Well, you can't." The chief medical officer stood with his arms folded. "I had to bump him forward. We've got a boy fresh from Saigon who's scheduled for ten A.M. and it's going to take the whole team. Seventy percent burns. They flew him back on ice. We patched up Connor's cheek first thing this morning. He's in recovery now and won't be awake for a couple of hours. Then he'll be drowsy the rest of the day. What happened to your face?"

"Nothing. I took a knock. Couldn't you have told me or Coty earlier?"

The doctor raised his eyebrows.

"Guess I was too busy working out the practicalities of how to save someone's life," he said.

"When can I see him?"

"This evening. Maybe. Depends on his recovery. Now if you'll excuse me, we need to prep. Don't go walking into anything else." The doctor disappeared through a pair of swinging doors looking very pleased with himself. Jack wasn't sure if this was because he was about to work on a patient who had seventy percent burns or because he had managed in his small way to inconvenience him. He suspected the latter.

He turned to Frank. "You got a smoke?" he asked. Frank performed another of his magic tricks, making a cigarette appear between his fingertips. Jack took it.

A steady flow of visitors and patients moved through reception. Jack looked around, curious as to what kind of injuries the soldiers would be bringing back from Vietnam. If it was anything like the Pacific, the challenge would be taking care of jungle wounds before they got infected. Sepsis was at least as dangerous as the enemy. That and snake bites. He shuddered at the thought. He'd been brave once, now he struggled to tie his damn shoelace.

"Is there anywhere I can take you?" Frank asked.

"Back to Langley. I've got papers to read through," Jack replied. He was about to leave when he caught sight of a woman sitting on one of the chairs. She looked as if she'd just woken up. She sat up straight and brushed her hair out of her eyes with her fingers. She realized Jack was looking at her and stared back at him defensively. She got up and slung the overnight bag she'd stashed under the chair over her shoulder, it was heavy and weighed her down on one side. He stared at her a moment longer. It was the same woman he'd seen the night before last.

He turned to Frank.

"You go wait in the car, I'll be out in a minute," he said.

Jack followed the young woman along the corridor. She disappeared into a restroom. He took a sip from a water fountain and waited. It was twenty minutes before she came out with fresh makeup and her hair brushed. He turned his back so she didn't see him. He knew where he'd seen her now. It wasn't just the other night in the hospital. She looked like the girl from the photo in Connor's file. Hair a little longer, different style too. She didn't have bangs in the photo.

The young woman was talking to the lady behind the desk in hushed tones. The woman was shaking her head, checking through papers. The girl looked desperate but her voice stayed quiet. Then the woman behind the desk passed her something, a bar of chocolate. The girl slipped it into her bag. She did the same furtive movement he'd seen earlier, brushing her hair away from her eyes.

"Excuse me, ma'am," Jack said. The woman turned toward him, her manner challenging. Now that he was close he could see she was a little older than he'd first thought, maybe twenty-five. Which in Wyoming probably meant she was an ageing spinster. "I was wondering if perhaps we're here to see the same person, a Mr. Connor Murphy. My name's Dr. Jack Miller. I'm helping him with his recovery," he said.

The woman took a step back. Her expression fierce.

"Then maybe you can tell them to let me see him. They keep saying no visitors. He's in surgery. He needs rest. He doesn't want to see me yet. I don't believe it."

Jack rubbed his chin. "It's complicated. Maybe you would be so good as to join me for breakfast or coffee? He's in surgery this morning. I'm going to see him later today, if I can. I'll tell him you're here. I could pass on any messages."

The woman's eyes welled up but she didn't let the tears fall. She stared back at him.

"I'm not leaving here till I see him."

"How long have you been here?"

"I don't think that's any of your business." She clutched her bag. It looked as if it contained at least half her worldly possessions.

"Join me for some food and I'll tell you how he's doing. I've visited him a couple of times."

The woman looked like she was making up her mind about something. Jack wondered when she'd last eaten. And how long she'd been camping in the hospital, sleeping on chairs and using the restrooms to freshen up.

"I'm Chrissie, Chrissie Johnson," she said.

"Well, Miss Johnson, there's a diner across the street. I want some pancakes and bacon. And coffee. Join me."

17

Shane's Diner
December 29, 9:00 A.M.

They sat at a corner table. Chrissie shunted her bag onto the bench. It took up half the seat. The diner was busy and bright and full of other people's business. It was noisy, too, but in a good way. Cutlery moving hurriedly over china, the sizzle of eggs on the hot plate behind the counter, orders shouted and chased.

"Looks good," Jack said as the waitress slid a plate of bacon and eggs in front of him. It almost felt normal. Breakfast in a diner on a bright winter morning. Then he saw that Frank had followed them and was sitting at the counter.

Chrissie glanced around, not paying much attention to the place. Or her food.

"So you're a doctor at Walter Reed, are you?" she said.

"I'm a psychiatrist," Jack said. "Not at the military hospital. I have a practice in New York, they brought me in to help with Connor's recovery."

Chrissie frowned.

"Why does he need to see a psychiatrist? I thought he was burned."

"The injuries are . . ." He paused. "They really haven't told you what condition he's in?"

"Wouldn't even tell me which hospital he was in, I had to drag it out of his sergeant. You should have heard him, like he was so important and I didn't deserve to know anything because I wasn't kin. I said I was his fiancée and we were as good as kin and he said that wasn't enough."

"But he told you, in the end."

"Yeah, he told me in the end, guess he got tired of me hollerin'." She smiled guiltily, then her face reset and her eyes filled with worry. "Tell me about Connor," she whispered.

Jack nodded.

"It's going to be difficult for him," he said. "He won't be the same. I mean, inside he'll be the same, but what's inside is going to have to adapt to what's on the outside. To how people see him. He won't look the same."

Chrissie's lips tightened.

"His head and hands are eighty percent third-degree burns. Which means they have to go to work replacing the skin. And the tissue underneath was damaged too. They graft on sections from other parts of the body. Here, let me show you something." Jack took off his jacket. "Would you mind undoing the link on the cuff? My fingers are pretty useless for this kind of thing."

Chrissie put down her knife and fork and looked at his misshapen fingers. "Looks like my grandma's hand," she said as she adjusted the cuff link and slid it through the eyelet. She placed it gently on the table. A neat gold square with "M H" etched discreetly in the corner.

"Thank you," Jack said, rolling up his sleeve. "You see this?" He held out his arm. The skin was stretched and smooth from the wrist to the elbow, slightly indented, paler in color, and hairless.

"I got a nasty burn in '52. Car accident. They used skin from my thigh to fix my arm. Stitches hold the skin in place till it takes. Hurts for a while then it settles down. Looks a bit different though."

Chrissie looked at it with interest.

"Like putting a patch on old clothes," she said. "Can I touch it?"

Jack nodded. She felt the skin with her fingertips.

"Do you have feeling?"

"Mostly, not all over."

Chrissie sat back in her chair and stared out the window.

"You said he had burns over his head, on his face, I guess you're saying . . ."

"He won't look the same. It'll still be him. But they have to try and put him back together. It'll need more than just grafts. He'll need reconstructive surgery too." Jack thought about the face he'd seen under the bandages, the two holes where his nose should have been, the sunken cheek.

Chrissie looked away. Pushed her bangs out of her eyes. Then her fist balled and she brought it down hard on the table, making the plates jump.

"You know why he took that posting?" she said. "Because it was extra pay. He wanted to do things right. To marry me and give me a home. Not some army digs. We were saving. I was waiting." Her fist opened slowly. She picked up her napkin and dabbed her eye. "I'm already twenty-six. My sister has three kids and she's only twenty-four."

"I'm sorry," Jack said. "It's an awful thing to happen. Just awful."

"They said he didn't want to see me," Chrissie said.

"I know. It'll be hard for him. He'll have to deal with the way people respond to him, with how they react. He won't look like everyone else."

"He never did," Chrissie said. "He didn't look like anyone. He was the prettiest boy I ever saw."

"He won't look like that anymore," Jack said gently.

Chrissie screwed up the napkin and dropped it on the tablecloth.

"Well, I'm not going. I'm not leaving. And I don't care what he looks like."

Jack had rolled his sleeve back down and was struggling with the cuff link. She pushed it through for him, somewhat impatiently.

"If he's said he doesn't want to see you, it'll be because he wants to protect you, he doesn't want you to feel you have to stay with him," Jack said.

She shook her head. "That's not Connor. Connor wouldn't be like that. He knows I wouldn't just leave him. And he wouldn't ask me to neither."

Jack leaned back on the bench and took a sip of coffee, then said, "He's been through something awful. It can change a person. Did he tell you what it was like living out there at the base, under the ice? I guess it would've been strange. Especially for someone used to being outdoors."

"Connor didn't mind. He was doing it for me. For us. He said some of them thought the roof of the tunnels would collapse. He didn't. The weight of the snow held it in place. He told me why it all made sense. How the weight of the snow and ice on the arched roofs made them stronger. He said they lived in these little cabins inside ice tunnels. They put them on rails so the heat from the cabin wouldn't melt the snow underneath. He's so smart. Goddamn army thought he was some dumb mechanic. He was smarter than all of them. He could fix anything. He could pretty much make anything. He was going to build our house."

Chrissie looked down at her plate of food. She'd hardly touched it.

"He must have been proud to serve his country. Not everyone would have what it takes," Jack said.

Chrissie stared at him as if the thought had never occurred to her.

"I guess," she said.

Jack didn't say anything. He let the silence lengthen. Chrissie picked at her food. Then she opened her purse and took out a photograph. It was a color print. Chrissie in a red-spotted dress and sunglasses and Connor in plaid shirt and slacks, one arm around her shoulder. She leaned into him. The two of them were standing in front of a brand-new Oldsmobile sedan. He was struck again by Connor's appearance. He was one of those people the camera brought to life. Put a lens in front of them and click and they get a charisma overload.

Jack stared at it for a moment longer. Couldn't help himself. A beautiful young couple, the future in front of them. A picture of hope. Hell, if you were selling automobiles, you couldn't have framed a better shot.

"Nice photo," he said.

"My sister takes them. She has a good eye. Wanted to be a painter before her husband and children came along. This was out at her place. She married into a big farming family. That's her husband Hal's car. He's not much to look at but he's pretty decent—apart from when he's drinking. Connor wanted a picture with the car. He said he'd get me an even bigger one. I said I didn't care. What am I supposed to do with a great big car? Men get stupid ideas sometimes. You married?"

"No, not anymore. I was. She passed. Car accident."

"I'm sorry. Is that where you got the burn?"

Jack nodded.

"Long time ago." She was the same age as you when it happened, he thought. Didn't say it. It was already pretty clear that her and Connor's life was not headed toward a hand-built house with a picket fence. Chrissie put the photo carefully back into her purse.

"I still don't understand why he doesn't want me to see him. Tell him not to be so darned silly."

"I will. But you need to give him time," Jack said. "His brain will take a long time to process the trauma. And they only brought him round from a medically induced coma a few days ago." Jack stood. "I'm gonna get some smokes, you want a packet?"

"No, thanks."

He bought a packet of Lucky Strikes from the vending machine by the counter. Offered one to Chrissie. She shook her head and watched as the waitress poured more coffee. She added cream and three spoonfuls of sugar. Jack liked her. There was a brightness in her eyes, an energy, a toughness.

She drank the coffee, then said, "Thank you for breakfast, Dr. Miller, but I really must be getting back." She stood, smoothing out the creases in her dress.

Jack got up as she did, wondering where she was getting back to.

"Where can I reach you?" he asked. "In case Connor says he's ready to see you when I talk to him later."

"I'll be at the hospital."

"Don't you have somewhere to stay?"

"Of course I do," she said. "I just prefer to wait at the hospital. Good day, sir."

Jack watched her leave then sat back down. Frank was still at the counter, reading the *Washington Reporter*.

He stared at the uneaten food on Chrissie's plate. The eggs had congealed and the cold yellow yoke was stuck fast like spilt paint. She was holding it together but he could see she was going out of her mind with worry. And fear. The army hadn't told her a damn thing. And he was sure Connor would have written to her about everything that happened at the base, including what went on between Henry and Stiglitz. He wasn't sure what she knew but he was sure she was smart enough not to tell him about it. Not until she trusted him. He'd have to work on that. Maybe he'd tell her more about his past. That might help her open up. He'd been close to telling her more about the accident, how he burned his arm. Letting her know that he lost his wife in the fire that consumed the car. Lost their future.

The accident.

That's what he called it. It wasn't an accident. But to explain more meant he'd have to explain the whole thing. Tell the whole story. Not just the fact that a dumb kid had run them off the road in his truck, or that he hadn't steered out of the way in time. He'd have to tell her about the argument in the bar earlier. The names Miyoko had been called. The fight that followed. His inability to walk away and the kid he'd left with a broken nose and wounded pride. The same kid who'd gotten in his car, blood dripping down his face, raced past them before disappearing into the darkness and circling back around to face them. The same kid who'd driven straight at them, headlights charging toward his Buick.

It wasn't the first time someone had started in on Miyoko and usually Jack let it pass, but that time he hadn't because he'd had a couple of drinks himself. And even though he knew it was all on the other guy, he couldn't take himself out of the story. So he stopped telling it, that part anyway. It was now just "the accident."

"Mr. Miller?"

Jack looked up. Two men were standing over him. One in a police uniform the other in a suit.

"That's right."

"You mind coming with us?" The man in the uniform was doing the talking. The man in the suit stood back and looked Jack over. He wasn't unfriendly and he wasn't friendly. He just looked like he was used to looking people over.

"Come with you where?" Jack said.

"The station. We'd like to ask you a few questions," he said. Jack tried not to look at Frank, who was still sitting at the counter, his eyes intently focused on the *Reporter*.

"What about?" Jack replied.

The man in the uniform placed his hand on the table. He was starting to get impatient and he wanted Jack to know.

"It's about Reverend Peterson," he said softly. His teeth were small and yellow and folds of neck hung over the white of his collar like undercooked pastry.

"What about him?"

"The detective would like to ask you a few questions. And he doesn't want to do it here, so be a good sport, get off your ass, and come with us."

Jack smiled. Small man syndrome. Funny how you could get it in regular-sized guys too. He didn't like to label people within a few seconds of meeting them but it was practically tattooed across the man's angry little hands.

Jack got up and tried not to make the man feel any smaller.

"It's your town," he said. He took out his wallet, paid for breakfast, and left the waitress a large tip. He realized everyone in there had stopped eating and drinking and was either staring at him openly or trying not to be too obvious about staring at him. He also saw that Frank had left. He assumed he'd follow and let Coty know about whatever the hell was happening.

18

Georgia Avenue, Washington, DC
December 29, 10:00 A.M.

The policeman led him two blocks down the street to an unmarked Plymouth Fury. In Jack's head a dark cloud was forming. He couldn't think of any nice reason why they'd want to talk to him about Reverend Peterson. The detective followed several steps behind. Jack could feel his eyes on him.

He got into the back of the car. The detective slid in next to him. He didn't say anything. Page one of the detective's manual on how to unsettle someone. Don't give anything away. Observe their reaction. Innocent people started asking questions and showed shock and fear, whilst the guilty were prone to silence. The theory was they knew why they'd been taken so were less likely to start challenging. Sometimes the manuals had it the other way around. The innocent went silent out of shock and the guilty started asking questions to show they were innocent.

It wasn't exactly a science and the theories were generally bullshit as far as Jack was concerned, dangerous, too, because they gave the detective a justification for whatever subjective feelings they had about the person they'd picked up.

"You going to tell me what this is about?" Jack said.

"At the station," the detective muttered, giving him a sideways glance. He was more interested in trimming his thumbnail with his teeth. Close up Jack caught the scent of his cologne. He'd never met a policeman who wore cologne before. No reason why they shouldn't, he thought. Except that you hoped the first thing on their mind when they woke up was making the city a safer place, not how sweet they smelled. He glanced down at the man's shoes. They shone in the gloom of the foot well. Good quality leather. A fashionable shape. This was a man who paid attention to detail. At least when it came to his appearance. He was maybe ten or so years younger than Jack. Which meant he'd missed the war. Some younger guys could be funny about that. Especially ones who felt like they had something to prove.

They drove to the police station on Indiana Avenue. It took twenty minutes and each of those minutes was silent, heavier, and longer than the last. Jack smoked two cigarettes and thought about what kind of trouble the reverend might have got into, and what it had to do with him.

The cop pulled over. In front of them a tow truck with "Abernathy Automobiles" emblazoned on the side waited, its engine ticking over. The cop sounded the horn and the truck moved forward, it didn't seem in any hurry to get out of the way. They pulled into the space. The sweet-smelling detective got out. Jack followed. The detective was already halfway up the steps of the police station. He turned, waiting for Jack to catch up, and gave him that half-interested stare he'd shown in the diner: I see you but I don't see a person. Just a set of possibilities.

He waved, not at Jack. Jack turned, thinking he was waving at the cop, but he'd already driven away. It looked like he was waving at the driver of the tow truck.

"This way," the detective said, leading him through the main doors and into the lobby. "You need to check-in your briefcase."

Jack did as he was told. The detective led him down a nondescript corridor, past a series of unmarked doors and rows of filing cabinets. It was the kind of place where case files went to die. They went down more steps, along another corridor, this one decorated with framed prints of police officers who either held their hat or wore their hat. As far as Jack could tell the choice depended on the amount of hair they had left.

At last the detective decided they'd done enough walking and stopped by a door. He fished about in his pocket for a set of keys, flicked through them, and unlocked it.

"In," he said, gesturing to a windowless room that smelled of cigarettes and stale coffee. Maybe that was why the detective was wearing cologne, Jack thought. He walked into the room. The detective didn't follow. Instead he shut the door on him.

Jack sighed. Page two of the detective's guide on how to unsettle a suspect—leave them alone in a room so they can stew on how guilty they are and how much trouble they're in. Jack sat in an uncomfortable chair with his back to the door. There was another one opposite. He decided most people would choose the one facing the door, waiting to see what was going to happen. Jack didn't. He knew what was going to happen. They were going to ask him some questions, they may or may not believe what he said, then Coty would arrive and get this all straightened out.

After fifteen minutes the detective reappeared. He'd brought a friend with him. A red-faced man with an angry gray-black buzz cut who looked like he could split wood with his teeth. The detective took a seat opposite Jack. The man with the red face stood behind the detective. He breathed loudly. The long walk to the interview room had taken its toll on his lungs.

"I'm Detective Hayes," the sweet-smelling detective said. His voice was soft, with the tiniest trace of a lisp. He didn't introduce the bulldog.

"Could you confirm your name?"

"Jack Miller."

"Occupation?"

"Psychiatrist."

"And the purpose of your visit to Washington, DC."

"Business," Jack said.

Detective Hayes made notes on a yellow pad, his writing precise and tidy.

"How do you know Reverend Peterson?"

"I don't exactly know him. I've met him twice." Jack paused, wondering how much he could say. He decided as little as possible.

"So why did you meet him?" the detective said slowly, as if he was talking to an idiot.

Again, Jack paused, editing his thoughts.

"He was helping me with a patient," he said at last.

"Who was the patient?"

"You'd need a subpoena before I could tell you that."

"Is that a fact? Thanks for the advice. Maybe we'll get one. When did you last see Peterson?"

Jack suspected they already knew the answer to that one.

"Last night," he said.

"Where did you see him?"

"At the Ebbitt bar." Another one they already knew the answer to. Jack had a bad feeling about where this was going. The reverend was either missing, or something worse had happened to him. If he was missing, Jack didn't think they'd have brought him in for questioning, they could have just taken notes somewhere less intimidating than a Washington police station.

"What's happened to Reverend Peterson?" Jack asked.

The detective looked over his shoulder at the heavy-breathing bulldog behind him. The man shook his head.

"You often meet people in bars to talk about patients? Sounds to me like that would be a breach of confidentiality."

Jack lit a cigarette.

"Sounds to me like you don't know what you're talking about," he said. "Are you going to tell me what happened to Reverend Peterson or are you going to continue playing amateur detective games?"

"You said you met him twice."

"I'll take that as a *yes*."

"When was the other time?"

"Should I have a lawyer present? I'm not clear what the status of our conversation is."

"You think you need a lawyer?"

"Everyone needs a lawyer. You'll need a lawyer if you don't tell me what you want," Jack said. There was a limit to his patience and he didn't respond well to power plays by men who thought they were smarter than him.

The bulldog twitched. He unfolded his arms then folded them again, looking even more tightly coiled than before.

"This is just a conversation, Mr. Miller," Detective Hayes replied. "A friendly chat. You're helping us work out what happened to one of our city's residents, a pillar of his local community, no doubt. Now why do you think, out of all the people in Washington, we've decided to ask you to help us, Mr. Miller?" His voice was slow.

"I really don't know," Jack replied.

"Well, let me elucidate. Reverend Peterson was pulled out of the Potomac this morning. You arrived in town yesterday afternoon. Met him in the evening. Far as we can tell you were the last person to speak to him."

Jack took a deep drag on the cigarette. Letting the man's words sink in.

"I'm sorry to hear that," he said.

"So, you see, the fact that you turn up here, night he dies, saying you're a psychiatrist who meets people in bars to talk about other people's business. It doesn't look so good." He looked at his pad. "You said you met him a couple of times. When was the first time?"

"Tuesday."

"The day before yesterday?"

Jack stared back at the detective, fighting the urge to explain that Tuesday was indeed the day before yesterday.

"That's right."

"But then you flew back to New York on Wednesday morning. Then came back Wednesday evening."

"That's right. I had some business back home."

The detective made a note of this on his pad.

"These are very unusual movements, Mr. Miller. If you don't mind me saying. Of course, I appreciate you're a medical man. So maybe you have a different way of working, flying all over the place at a moment's notice to see people. To talk to them about your patients." His voice was heavy with sarcasm. Jack was beginning to resent the man. He caught the thought. Don't let him get under your skin.

"It happens," he said. "You put the client first. I don't mind traveling." He raised a hand to his face and was about to rub his jaw. It was still sore. The detective caught the movement and stared at him.

"Side of your face looks a bit swollen there, Jack. Is that some bruising I can see under the skin? And on your head, too, near your temple?" He turned to the man behind him. "What do you think, Bob?"

Bob leaned closer, breathing his heavy breaths, slurping up the air. He placed a hand on the table and used the other to clamp the side of Jack's face. He twisted it so it caught the sheen of the lightbulb. Jack flinched and tried his hardest not to push the man away.

"I'd say this man's been in a fight. Recent one too. Those bruises are pretty fresh. Still got some color to come into them." He let go of Jack's head. Jack could feel his hands shaking. He drew a breath to control it. Anger wasn't going to help him.

"My friend here is an expert in bruises. You been in any fights, Jack?" Detective Hayes said, his dead fish eyes wide open with mock surprise. "Anything you remember? Maybe a fight last night after you left the bar, down by the water? Something you and the reverend disagreed on?"

Jack rubbed his jaw and stared back at them. He could feel his stomach turning into a tight knot.

"Why don't you show me those hands too? The right knuckles look grazed. It doesn't look good," the detective continued. "Maybe we should move into one of the other rooms. I can see why you wanted to talk to a lawyer. I think I would if I was in your position. What do you think, Bob, think you'd want to call a lawyer if you were in Mr. Miller's position?"

Bob nodded, a slow, thoughtful nod.

The detective continued. "What happened after you left the bar, Mr. Miller? Did you go for a walk with the reverend? Get into an argument near the water, maybe he tried to hit you first? The barman told us he was pretty lit. Maybe you were defending yourself from some drunken punches and he slipped. How does that sound?"

"Sounds like you should be a crime writer. You seem to like making stuff up. What injuries did the reverend have?" Jack asked.

Detective Hayes ignored him.

"You know what I think we should do?" he said. "I think we should leave Mr. Miller here a little while, allow him some time to gather his thoughts, then get him to write out a statement taking us through yesterday evening."

There was a knock at the door.

"Yeah?" Detective Hayes shouted. The door opened, a gray man in a gray suit walked in. He had the look of a man who spent most of each day bending paper clips. Then bending them back.

"Chief wants to talk to you," he said.

"Now?"

The man looked at Jack.

"Now."

Detective Hayes got up and left the room. Jack and the bulldog stared at each other, then the bulldog made a humphing sort of sound. He left the room, closing the door. Jack wondered if it was locked. He got up and tried it. It wasn't. He fought the urge to run, closed it again, and sat down. The walls felt as if they were getting closer.

After ten minutes the door opened and the detective reappeared.

"Out," he said, standing on the threshold, not bothering to enter. Jack got up. The detective walked back along the corridors. His feet tapping out an impatient rhythm. "This way," he said, leading him to the lobby. Jack followed. He was starting to feel light-headed. The detective seemed even more angry than before. And it smelled as if he'd ladled on another dose of cologne.

They reached the lobby. He turned to Jack, he looked like it was all he could do not to spit in his face.

"You're free to fuck off," he said, then turned and disappeared down another corridor. A few gray heads looked up from their desks. Jack stood motionless in the center of the room. Then collected his briefcase.

Coty was sitting on a bench near the entrance. He got up when he saw Jack.

"Want to tell me how you managed to get yourself arrested?" he said.

19

Indiana Avenue, Washington, DC
December 29, 12:30 P.M.

Frank was waiting outside in the car. He started the engine. Coty got in the front, Jack sat in the back feeling like a naughty kid.

"They rough you up at all?" Frank asked.

"Nah, although if it had gone on much longer they might have."

He nodded.

"Some of those guys have tempers," he said. "The one who picked you up. I know him. He's been investigated twice for aggravated assault. Fully exonerated both times."

"No surprises there," Coty said. "Didn't he break up a used-car racket a few years back? Washington PD made a big play about it in the press. That detective got his face all over the papers."

"That's him," Frank said. "They called him *the dashing detective*." He started the engine and pulled away from the curb. The tow truck was still there, but now it had a police car loaded onto the back.

Jack fumbled in his jacket pocket for his cigarettes, took one out and lit it. His hand was shaking. He opened the window and breathed in a lungful of cold air.

"What did you say to make them let me go?" Jack asked as they turned onto Sixth Street. Whatever thoughts Coty was furiously chewing over they weren't making it out of his mouth.

"I just said you were Agency," he replied tersely.

"That's it?"

Coty drummed his fingernails on the windowpane.

"I might have said it was a matter of National Security so they should hurry up and let you the fuck out of there before I have the commissioner demote them to traffic police."

Coty twisted awkwardly in his seat and directed his stare at Jack.

"Want to tell me how you ended up in there?"

"Sure," Jack said. "Frank tell you I went out last night?"

"He did."

"He tell you who I met?"

"Reverend Peterson."

"That's right. He'd traced the soldiers who were evacuated from the base. Wanted to talk about it. He was pretty high. Drinking like it was all he had left. Anyway, turns out I was one of the last people the reverend spoke to. They pulled him out of the river this morning. I don't know if it was suicide or murder. They wouldn't say. I got the impression they thought it was murder and because I'd spoken to him last night I was suspect number one."

Coty twisted back around in his seat.

"*Shit*," he muttered under his breath. "And they were straight onto you this morning? An outsider with no known address or priors. And not only that, they know exactly where to pick you up?" He turned to Frank. "I take it you didn't tell the police you saw Jack hit Peterson over the head and dump him in the river?"

Frank laughed, unsure whether Coty was joking.

"Because right now I don't see any other way they could have known Jack talked to Reverend Peterson last night. And I don't see how they could have tracked Jack down to the diner this morning. Unless you called it in yourself, Jack. You didn't pick up the phone to the police this morning, did you?"

Jack didn't answer. He stared out the window as they sped past the stone-faced facades of government buildings.

"Normally it would take them at least two weeks to get to this point. Someone told them everything. Which means someone was watching Jack last night when he was drinking with the reverend and you missed it, Frank. Someone was watching him this morning, too, and guess what?"

"I missed it."

"Damn right."

"They must be good."

"Yeah, but no one's that good. Not the army. Not the police. No one I've seen before anyway."

Coty was silent. So were Jack and Frank, thinking over the implications of what Coty had just said.

"What did Peterson tell you about the soldiers evacuated from the base?" Coty said at last, his hand raised to his forehead, thumb and forefinger massaging his temples.

"They were sent to an institution in Kentucky. Suffering hallucinations. Two killed themselves. One tried to escape. They think he drowned."

Coty shook his head. "The shit we're wading through just keeps getting deeper. And these are the boys Henry accused Stiglitz of poisoning?"

"That's right."

"Did you get any names? What about the one who tried to escape?"

"Archie Bell."

"We need to find out if he made it," Coty said. "I'll get someone on it. We should talk to him."

"When can I talk to Connor?" Jack said. "There's the small matter of Stiglitz and Henry not being burned in the same fire and I'd kind of like to get his thoughts on it."

Coty sighed, looked out the window.

"Connor's back in surgery," he said. "There were complications after this morning's procedure."

"So we have to wait?"

Coty nodded. He stared at the gridlock of cars in front of them. "Why aren't we moving, Frank? Can we take another route?" he said.

Above the car horns they heard the sound of chanting, a wash of voices, indistinct, gaining in volume. A drum being hit, the bass note bouncing off buildings to add another layer of messy noise.

"Protest march," Jack said.

"On Constitution Avenue? The police said they wouldn't let it happen," Coty replied.

"Well, it's happening," Frank said. "Maybe they were too busy questioning Jack to stop the antiwar brigade."

Coty snorted. "You joke," he said. "But knowing those guys . . ." He wound down the window and angled his head out, straining his neck to see further up the road.

"I can see a lot of peace signs," he said eventually. "And people wearing coats made of dog hair." He pulled himself back inside and closed the window. Frank twisted to look behind him, past Jack, through the rear window. They were blocked in. Cars on all sides. Jack noticed a change in Frank. He was no longer slouched. His back was straight and his eyes kept flitting to the side- and rearview mirrors.

Jack had never felt a greater desire to get out of an automobile. The cigarette was done. He flicked the butt out the window. It bounced off the car next to them and hit the ground. He felt tired and sick to his stomach. He reached for another cigarette, but he didn't light it, he just flipped it over and over between his finger and thumb.

"What's the matter Jack? You're not afraid of the hippies are you?" Coty said.

Outside the chanting grew louder. They could hear whistles too. The protestors were walking amongst the cars, tapping on the windows and handing out leaflets. Their breath formed clouds in the cold air. It was like coming across a herd of animals on their way to some new destination, a watering hole or food source. The people flowed around them. Jack noticed Frank's hand was inside his jacket.

They marched by, calling for an end to the bombing. Calling for prosecutions. The war was better served by the press than the one he'd fought in. You could even watch it on TV. The public had never had such an opportunity to witness what happened when you set machines and fire against fields full of people.

Jack watched a young woman as she approached the car. Her gaze fierce, her fist clenched. He found himself thinking about Chrissie, her determination to find out what had happened to Connor, sleeping at the hospital till he said he'd see her.

We were saving. He was going to build our house.

Jack wanted it to be true. He wanted Connor to be a pure-hearted hero. Like he wanted to believe Chrissie would stay with him even though his face would be changed beyond all recognition. But Connor was lying about the fire. And he was the only one left alive. And whatever had happened between Henry and Stiglitz when they were trapped under the ice went back further, much further. It went back all the way to the three boys who were evacuated in December. It went back to Henry's paranoia, his accusations that Stiglitz was poisoning them. Hell, it probably went back to the damn dog he said Stiglitz had killed.

20

Langley, Block B basement
December 29, 2:00 P.M.

Jack switched on the desk lamp in his makeshift office. Connor was out for the rest of the day, which meant he had time to look through the personnel files Gill had given him, and the medical notes for Henry. He read through Stiglitz's file again, checking he hadn't missed anything. Wrote a quick memo to Coty to track down Mendelson, the man who'd made a complaint about him at university. Then he took Henry's file out and placed it on the desk.

He read through three successful applications for promotion and a series of glowing recommendations from senior officers. Henry was described as a man who could inspire loyalty and obedience in equal measure. Never afraid to place himself at the center of the action and lead by example.

Everything looked spotless until he took the posting in Greenland. It was a further promotion, a reward for the diligence and bravery he'd shown working with the South Vietnamese army. It was noted that he'd requested a different posting. He wanted to continue to be able to contribute "actively and in combat," especially once America committed to deploying troops.

The request was denied. The Greenland posting was where the army wanted him. Henry had reluctantly accepted. His time in Greenland had started well enough. He organized morale-boosting activities outside. Games of football, snowball fights, a makeshift obstacle course.

Once winter set in it was a different story. The report noted that a dog, a husky, had been found mutilated in one of the tunnels. Henry accused Chief Scientific Officer Owen Stiglitz of butchering it. Stiglitz refuted the accusation in the strongest possible terms. The report found no evidence to support Henry's assertion. Shortly afterward Henry left the base for a period of "rest and respite."

No information was given about what had led up to the incident. There was no mention of Henry accusing Stiglitz of poisoning people. No suggestion anything might be awry with his mental health.

Whatever else Henry had accused Stiglitz of, the army hadn't reported it. Just like they hadn't recorded the evacuation of the three soldiers to a mental asylum in Kentucky. Or made anyone at the base aware that two of them had taken their own lives.

He checked the rest of the papers. Educational history. Henry's time at military school. Then he opened the medical file Gill had given him. It contained the notes from the private clinic Henry had been admitted to.

The first page was a summary document of the kind Jack had written many times himself. A patient assessment and treatment plan.

Henry Carvell was admitted at two P.M. on Wednesday, January 14, 1967. His father described him as suffering from insomnia and exhibiting unusual behavioral patterns and irrational thoughts.

Following initial interviews, I formed the hypothesis that Henry's recent posting in Vietnam, which he described in some detail and was clearly harrowing, coupled with the darkness of the arctic winter, induced an almost dreamlike state that left him unable to distinguish reality from his imagination. It was my view that his mind did not have sufficient time to process the trauma before he entered the darkness of winter.

Henry was generally calm, engaging, and often charming during his stay. Over the next four weeks, through a process of analysis and the administration of mild sedatives, we were able to establish that these irrational thoughts were merely the projection of his subconscious.

He showed a significant degree of mental resilience and a keenness to work to understand his condition and overcome it. Following a period of rest and therapy, I am satisfied that he is now fully fit and capable of returning to active service.

The transcripts of the interviews with Henry were clipped to the summary sheet. Jack stared at them for a moment. Here was Henry's voice, transcribed verbatim. He felt a strange mixture of curiosity and sadness as he read it. And a useless impulse to interrupt and warn him not to go back.

Thursday, January 15, 9:30 A.M.
Henry Carvell, Dr. Milton Brown

Dr. B: Did you sleep well?

HC: Yes, thank you.

Dr. B: And the room's to your liking?

HC: It's perfectly pleasant.

Dr. B: That's good. Surroundings are so important, I find. You're on the east side. A view over the gardens. They're the best rooms. The sun streams in first thing, quite a wake-up call in summer. I'm glad you were able to rest.

HC: The pills helped.

Dr. B: So they should. Think of them as a cast, something that allows a broken bone to heal. Only the cast is supporting your mind, slowing things down, helping it recover. Have you had a recurrence of the visions or voices you experienced in Greenland since you arrived here?

HC: You make it sound like I'm crazy.

Dr. B: We don't use that word. No one's crazy. The mind finds ways to cope with the things we've seen and experienced. Sometimes it doesn't function as it should and sends the wrong messages. My job is to help it reset, get things back on the right pathway.

HC: Well, I haven't seen anyone or anything following me around. And for the record, I knew it wasn't real when I did see it.

Dr. B: That's good. I understand you were pretty anxious about it. Your father said you fired a gun into a bedroom wall when you got home.

HC: That was stupid. I was angry. I was angry because I knew it wasn't real. I guess I thought letting off a couple of rounds would shake things up a bit.

Dr. B: It certainly would. If that happened in my house I think everyone would have been a bit shaken up.

HC: Well, like I said, I fired because it wasn't real. I knew it wasn't real, but I could see it.

Dr. B: I'm glad you're able to say it wasn't real. I'm glad you understand that. It's a good first step. I'm going to ask you questions about what happened in Greenland now, do you feel able to talk about it?

HC: It's what I'm here for.

Dr. B: Excellent. I want to understand when you first started seeing and hearing this presence. Understanding what led to its appearance can help you process why you started to see it. Once we know that, then if it appears again we've got more weapons we can use against it. More things we can point and fire at it. A bit like your gun, but hopefully more effective. Can you let me know when you first became aware of it?

HC: Early December, I think.

Dr. B: Do you remember where you were?

HC: In one of the tunnels, on my way to the rec rooms. I felt as if someone was beside me. Heard a voice. I turned. No one there. I turned again. A figure was walking away from me. I called after him. It was hard to see him clearly. In the tunnels you had deep shadow, then around the lights you got this bright glare from all the ice crystals. I called out. No one answered. Then I felt him brush past me again.

Dr. B: Did you see him this time?

HC: No, there was no one there.

Dr. B: Had you ever experienced anything like this before? When you were younger, at school or college?

HC: Hell no. First time. I was sure it was real.

Dr. B: Did you tell anyone about it?

HC: One person.

Dr. B: Who was that?

HC: One of the mechanics. Connor Murphy. I trusted him.

Dr. B: What did he say?

HC: He said it sounded like someone was playing tricks on me. Next time I should chase them down.

Dr. B: And what happened next time you saw it?

HC: Next time I was sitting with Connor in the rec room playing cards. I got up to put some music on and I thought it was just the two of us, but then I realized this figure was sitting in the corner of the room.

Dr. B: That must have been most unsettling. Was it someone you recognized?

HC: No, it's hard to describe. And it was turned away. Like it didn't want to look at me.

Dr. B: What did you do?

HC: I tried to ignore it. It was silent. It wasn't bothering me. But then it started talking, talking softly to itself. I couldn't hear it. Not clearly. Now I knew it wasn't real, that was obvious, but seeing something you know isn't real as if it is real is . . .

Dr. B: Very frightening.

HC: Yeah, but it made me angry too. Anyway, I must have gone off-color because Connor asked if I was ok and I said I wasn't exactly feeling well, and I think maybe he guessed I was seeing the same thing I'd told him about because I was shaking.

Dr. B: What happened next?

HC: Someone else came into the room. Chief scientific officer. Owen Stiglitz. He sat at a table in the corner and he pretended to read a magazine but really, he was watching me.

Dr. B: What makes you think he was watching you?

HC: I know it. I could feel it.

Dr. B: You can't know it, Henry. He might have just turned up in the recreation room by chance.

HC: He didn't. First he was in the tunnel and now he was in there, watching me.

Dr. B: What do you mean he was in the tunnel?

HC: First time I had the vision, Stiglitz was there too. Almost ran into him.

Dr. B: I see. You know, Henry, the mind is a curious thing. It will interpret the world one way based on our previous experiences. It's a kind of inbuilt bias we all have. You saw him the first time you suffered from this delusion, and you saw him the second time, so you drew the conclusion that he was in some way connected to what was happening. He was watching you.

HC: You don't get it. You don't know the guy. If you knew the guy you'd be more than suspicious.

Dr. B: So you'd had a few run-ins with him before?

HC: We had a couple of minor disagreements. He always spoke to me like I was an idiot. He spoke to pretty much everyone that way.

Dr. B: I see. This is all useful background, Henry. It's really good. I think we're going to make excellent progress.

HC: You don't believe me, do you?

Dr. B: I believe what you were feeling was real to you. And in some ways, I think it's a perfectly reasonable response to a difficult situation.

HC: But you don't believe Stiglitz was behind it, you don't believe he was responsible for what I was seeing? What about if I said there were three other people suffering the same as me?

Dr. B: I would say that the human brain has a need to rationalize and make sense of things that can't be easily
understood. To make connections, to find coinci-
dences. It's a natural impulse. I think you fixated on
Stiglitz as a target to try and find a basis in reality
for what is, and should be, a temporary disorder of
the mind. An illness you can recover from.

HC: Then how come Connor thought the same thing?
How come Connor agreed with me about Stiglitz?
Connor is smart as a whip. He said he didn't trust
Stiglitz either. He said he'd had to fix the pipes in one
of the labs and it didn't look like they were working
on ice-core samples and whatever else they were supposed to be doing. Not as far as he could tell.

Dr. B: I mean no disrespect to your friend, and it's helpful
that you had someone you could trust and confide in.
But you can't really expect a mechanic to understand
what work the chief scientific officer was carrying out
on ice-core samples. I think we should leave it there
for now. We've made good progress this morning.
Let's take a break. Have you walked round the
grounds yet? There are some beautiful trees over by
the lake, they'll be sparkling with the morning frost.
Or you could try the indoor pool. I know you'll be
wanting to stay fit while you're here.

Jack realized he was holding tightly to the papers as he read. He placed
them down gently on the table and rubbed his hand, it had stiffened up
again. He held it close to the lightbulb and let it absorb the warmth.

The transcript of the interview echoed in his head. He felt as if he'd
been in the room. He could hear Henry's voice. His confusion. His

reasonableness and frustration. His need to make sense of something that couldn't be explained in any rational way. Jack thought he seemed pretty stable, all things considered. He'd had to deal with a series of visions and voices that would have created a more extreme reaction in many people a lot sooner. Perhaps the reason he'd held it together for so long was because he believed there was a rational basis for what he was experiencing. He believed Stiglitz was somehow responsible for it. Connor seemed to think the same, which must have been some comfort.

He took out the photograph of Henry. He still looked like the picture of entitled youth, but then that's what he was, and the photograph was taken before he was sent to work with the South Vietnamese army. The experience would have changed him.

He put down the photo and read through the next set of interview notes.

21

Langley, Block B basement
December 29, 3:00 P.M.

Friday, January 16, 2:00 P.M.
Henry Carvell, Dr. Milton Brown

Dr. B: What I'd like to cover in this session is what I see as the root of your problem, this belief that one person, Owen Stiglitz, was responsible for the delusions you've been suffering from. I'd like you to tell me more about him, how he made you feel, what type of interactions you had with him.

HC: You mean like conversations and stuff?

Dr. B: Exactly.

HC: I didn't talk to him much. He was distant. He ran the research project. Acted as if he owned the place, as if the whole setup was there for him.

Dr. B: It wasn't?

HC: Hell no, that was just . . . look, I can't talk about this. But trust me, the purpose of a military base in Greenland is never going to be scientific research.

Dr. B: I see what you mean. So you didn't like him?

HC: Nobody liked him. I doubt even his own mother liked him. He was arrogant in that sneaky way, the way that puts people down with little comments.

Dr. B: For example?

HC: I don't know. Maybe he'd tell the chef the food was good considering he didn't have all the right equipment, knowing we had the best kitchens the army could get. Or he'd keep offering the chaplain another drink. *You look like you need a drink, Reverend Peterson. Put a little color back in those cheeks,* he'd say. The last thing the chaplain needed was another drink. And he'd come into the rec room when we were messing around and put on opera. The boys don't want to listen to that on their downtime, but they couldn't tell him not to do it because even though he was an NCO he was still their superior, and you know what? He enjoyed it. You could see it on his face. He liked the fact that they had to all sit there listening to whatever he put on and couldn't tell him to shut the goddamn thing off.

Dr. B: Are you sure he didn't just want to share his love of music?

HC: Oh, I'm sure. Same as he didn't organize chess tournaments in order to share his love of chess. He only did it because he knew he'd win and he wanted others to feel small. He always did win, too, and in the end the only people who'd play him were Connor and the chaplain. They both lost all the time, until one day Connor beat him. Connor was like that, he'd take things apart, see how they worked. He did it with machines and he'd done the same thing with Stiglitz. Stiglitz knew it, too. He knew he'd been beat good and proper but he couldn't accept it so they played again and he lost again. Then they played again. And again. He made Connor sit there half the night; they must have played another three, four games and Connor won every single one of them. After that Stiglitz never organized another chess tournament, so go figure.

Dr. B: I see. But surely everyone disagreed with each other at some point? Each person must have acted in a way that annoyed others on occasion?

HC: Of course we did, but you're not listening, you're not getting it. Stiglitz wasn't like everyone else. There was something about him. He was . . . I don't know. Closed off.

Dr. B: Interesting. From your perspective you've described a man who was capable of acting out a terrible punishment on the people around him, someone who would deliberately alter their perception of the world to psychologically and physically endanger them. But to me, so far all you've described is a disagreeable character, who may well be a bully, may even have certain narcissistic tendencies, but you haven't described a sociopath, which is what he'd need to be if he was intent on somehow poisoning people so they see strange visions.

HC: What about the fact that he was there the first two times I saw this thing?

Dr. B: Pure coincidence. The human brain likes to insinuate causality.

HC: And the fact that Connor saw he wasn't working on ice or whatever he was supposed to be studying?

Dr. B: I mean no disrespect to Connor, he's obviously a friend of yours, and clearly a very capable chess player. But can you say with all certainty that he would understand the scientific parameters of whatever geological studies Stiglitz was running?

HC: Ok, well, you tell me this, you've got drugs here, all kinds of drugs. Drugs to slow people down, speed them up, stop them seeing things. Make them sleep. Make them wake up. Are you telling me it would be impossible for you to dose me up so I start seeing things again, if you so wanted?

Dr. B: There are psychoactive compounds, things that disrupt the senses, and if applied in the right amount they could certainly alter your perception of reality, but just because something is possible doesn't mean it happened. Are you suggesting an officer in the US military went out of his way to endanger the lives and well-being of his fellow soldiers? Not only that, he had the knowledge to execute the specific doses required?

HC: Stiglitz could. He had about three degrees and a PhD. He studied everything. He could work it out.

Dr. B: Again, what you're describing is reasons why *you* believe he was responsible for your delusions. What you're describing to me is an intellectual with poor social skills.

HC: You never met him, sir. You didn't know him. It's different from what you're saying. It's . . .

Dr. B: Would you like to take a short break? I can see this is becoming emotional for you. We can pick up again later. I know it's difficult to hear a point of view that contradicts your own but it's important. It's important you consider an outside perspective and allow it to sink in. I think you're in a place where you can do that. This is good, some patients take months to get to this point. Some never get to it. But you're listening and responding. And that's good.

Henry was agitated, but I was reluctant to let the session end. I considered his emotional response a positive indicator of understanding, of engagement. He didn't like what I was saying, but he responded to it and sought to argue against it, which meant he grasped the possibility that I could be correct and he could be wrong. This is a critical stage in terms of the patient's ability to move on from an irrational, subjective view to an objective one. However difficult for him, I was keen that we continue to explore those possibilities.

Dr. B: Are you happy to continue? I'll order some water or a juice if you prefer.

HC: Orange juice. Thanks.

Dr. B: Great. Now, as I was saying, you've told me how you felt about this man, Stiglitz, and you've told me about the negative character traits he showed in some of his interactions. Can you describe a specific event that made you believe he was responsible for poisoning you?

HC: Ok, well, Connor said there was another cabin at the back of the labs. A secret space. He'd seen it on the plans. He knew because the pipe work led to it. He wasn't allowed in it though. No one was.

Dr. B: Did Connor say he thought Stiglitz was carrying out experiments in there?

HC: No. He hadn't been inside.

Dr. B: Henry, that could have been a storeroom, it could have been anything. Just because there's some kind of cupboard doesn't mean Stiglitz was poisoning you. I'd like to return to one of the points you made yesterday, where you said you thought he was responsible for poisoning the three men who were evacuated from the base too. The question you haven't answered is "*why*." Why do you think he poisoned you? Why do you think he poisoned them?

HC: I don't know why he did it. You could work that out. You're the head doctor.

Dr. B: Did you tell anyone other than Connor you were seeing things?

HC: Hell no. I'd have been out of the army. End of my career. And with my father . . . I couldn't let him down. I didn't tell anyone. I just told a few people I thought Stiglitz had made the others sick.

Dr. B: That wasn't the only thing you accused him of, was it? There was an incident with a dog too. Would you mind telling me some more about that? I understand this was the trigger for you agreeing to take some time off. You accused Stiglitz of hurting this animal, didn't you? What happened exactly?

HC: Alright. If you want. We had a husky that ran about the place. He was there long before I arrived. Mukluk, he was called. I like dogs, we've always had lurchers. They're great, but this husky, he was a real character. I kind of adopted him. He joined me for runs in the tunnels. I went to fetch him one morning, and he was all curled up. I thought he was sick. Normally he would jump up and run to me, you couldn't keep him back. But he just laid there. I got close and saw his fur was all matted. I touched it. He was bloody. He wasn't moving, barely even breathing. Now I was close I could see his front legs were all twisted and mangled. I was upset. I was angry too. Looked like someone had hit him and broken his legs. Or run over him driving a snowplow through the tunnel. Then I hear a voice over my shoulder. *Oh dear, did he have some kind of accident?* I get up and he's standing right there, Stiglitz. And I don't know how long he'd been behind me but he was staring at me, watching me. Not just looking at me, but staring. Same way he was watching me in the rec room. And the way he said it. He did it. I just knew.

Dr. B: I see. This seems like a very stressful event, very sad too. An animal can be a great comfort, a great companion, especially somewhere like that. But you must be able to see how strange it would look for you to say that Stiglitz had somehow deliberately mutilated a dog. The chief scientific officer mutilates a dog. No reason. You can hear how strange it is when I say it, can't you?

HC: Yeah, it does sound strange. Imagine how sick you'd have to be to do it.

Dr. B: That's one way of looking at it, that's your way of looking at it. I want you to try and see it the way everyone else would look at it. Simply an accident, with what must have appeared to be a strange reaction from you. Can you see that?

HC: Why are you on his side? Jeez, if you'd met the man you'd get it. You'd know what he was capable of.

Dr. B: And I need you to understand that the conclusions you've reached are based on your perception—and that perception was driven by visions that would be deeply disturbing for anyone to have to go through. Your mind was trying to find a way to rationalize them, to understand them. You blamed Stiglitz for the visions. You blamed him for what happened to the dog. I think the key to those visions lies in the experiences you had in combat. I know this is hard, and I'm sorry you have to revisit painful places, but it really is worth it. I'm pleased you haven't seen this character, this dark figure again. I think the further we get from that the more likely you are to see that the visions you suffered from, and the belief that Stiglitz was the cause of your problems, were generated by external events—by your mind trying to find a way to cope with trauma. You hadn't had time to process what happened to you in combat before you entered the arctic night. In time you'll come to see that this was all your own invention. A perfectly natural way for the mind to cope, to dream, to process information, to expunge it. It's just that normally we do all that dreaming while we're asleep. This was more of a waking dream. There were tunnels under the jungle in Vietnam, too, weren't there? In your file it says you helped clear them and were commended for bravery. I'd like to talk about that next time.

HC: That wasn't bravery.

Dr. B: Come, now, don't be modest, Henry. It's important that you can rationally appraise your achievements as well as your fears. Don't belittle them.

HC: It wasn't bravery. Clearing the tunnels was tough, but there's only one place the enemy can be and that's in front of you. Not coming at you from all sides. How's that for rational? I chose the tunnels over the jungle because it was less dangerous, not because I was braver than anyone else.

Dr. B: But it was still extremely dangerous work. Stressful. Difficult for people like me to even imagine.

HC: I had a gun and I had men and when I hit someone they bled. There weren't shadows chasing me. Watching me. You see a shadow in those tunnels you better fire quick or you'll feel a knife across your throat. This thing at the base, the way it watched me, but didn't fight me, sitting there invisible to everyone else . . . try and imagine that. Imagine seeing something real no one else can see. It's like someone's turned your brain inside out. I preferred the jungle. Maybe that does make me crazy. But it's not crazy like you're saying.

Dr. B: I'm not saying you're crazy, Henry. I think you were brave, and I think what you're saying now is brave. It takes a lot of courage to talk about these things. What you need to understand is that we're only just beginning to recognize the long-term impact of the type of trauma you've been through, how the memories can stay with you, come back at you when you least expect it. I know I can't understand what's in your head completely, but looking from the outside I see a bigger picture. That's why you're here. And we're making excellent progress.

22

Langley, Block B basement
December 29, 3:30 P.M.

Jack skimmed the remaining pages. He thought the psychiatrist treating Henry had taken the right approach. At least, he took a rational, helpful approach. The only problem was that the psychiatrist had to start from the basis that Henry was wrong. There was no way Stiglitz was the cause of his delusions. There was no way Stiglitz would have killed a dog. There was no way he would be watching Henry. Jack had another perspective. He had to consider the possibility that Henry was right. There was a spy at the base, after all.

And the more he read about Stiglitz and Henry's relationship, the more convinced he became that something had happened between them when they were trapped together during the storm. Something Connor didn't want to tell him about. Henry had confided in Connor. He had trusted him. Connor didn't want to say anything that would get his friend in trouble after his death, or might tarnish his reputation. Or maybe he thought they wouldn't believe him. Was that why Connor was lying about seeing them both burning in the fire, not wanting to say that there were actually two fires?

He looked up, the door handle was rattling. It turned. Coty appeared, belly first, a triumphant grin on his face.

"I got him," he said. "Archie Bell. I know where he is."

"Really? Ok," Jack replied, eyes still skimming through the details in Henry's file.

"You don't sound very interested."

"I am, I'm just distracted. I've spent the last couple of hours listening to Henry Carvell talk about what it was like to lose his mind in the middle of the arctic."

"That's pretty impressive considering he's dead. What did you do, hold a séance? It's not something the Agency's ever tried but if it works . . ."

Jack held up the file and waved it at Coty. "The notes from Henry's stay at the Alexander Institute. Transcriptions of the interviews. He was suffering from similar mental disturbances to the boys they evacuated. But he was convinced it was all down to Stiglitz. Comes across as well-balanced and rational, even in the grip of these delusions."

"You think there might be some truth to what he's saying? Stiglitz was behind it?"

"We can't discount it. So where's Archie Bell?"

"William Grade's Automobile Repairs in Holden. Which is little more than a strip of houses and trailer park developments on the edge of Bangor in Maine."

"How did you find him?"

"Phone log from the Institute in Kentucky. We got the outgoing calls from January and February from the exchange. Cross-referenced them with Archie's friends and family, where they live, where they work. The number he called belongs to a payphone at the garage. Garage is owned by a Mr. William Grade. William Grade is married to Patricia Bell, Archie's aunt. We called to book a job, asked how many people they had working there. They said three. Only two employees listed on their tax returns."

"You're sure it's him?"

"It fits. The last call was made two days before he ran away from the asylum. I figure someone drove down to meet him on the other side of the lake. Saved him from freezing to death."

"Are you going to bring him in?"

"I thought it might be better if you go and talk to him."

"What about Connor?"

"Connor's still out, there were complications. He needed a transfusion, and somehow they got the wrong blood type. Sent his body into shock. They had to put him back into an induced coma. He'll be out for at least another twenty-four hours. I won't send you on your own. Frank will accompany you. Come on, admit it, you're curious to find out about whatever strange mental affliction came over these three soldiers, and Henry, all at the same time. If not for your country then at least for the greater scientific good."

Jack shrugged.

"I'm curious to find out how my actual patients are doing in New York. But I guess you've already booked the flights."

"I did take that precautionary step. Didn't want to find there were no seats available, it being the end of the holiday season and all."

"When are we going?"

"Tonight."

"For God's sake, Coty. Maybe I wanted to get some sleep?"

"Sleep on the plane. You'll be back tomorrow. Look, I know you'd rather be playing records and smoking cigarettes and having difficult conversations with ageing actors about why no one loves them anymore, but if anyone can get this guy to talk it'll be you. Frank can't do it on his own. He'll scare him off. And if I try it'll feel like an interrogation. You've got a way with people."

"Stop flattering me."

"I mean it. In a professional sense, they open up to you. You have an instinct."

Jack leaned back in the chair. He felt bone-tired. His eyes stung from reading in low light.

"Fine," he said.

"I've given Frank a file on Archie Bell. There are a couple of photographs from when he joined the army."

"And you really think he'll be there?" Jack said. "He could be anywhere."

Coty shook his head. "He's there. It's a small town. Barely even that. Just one main road. Technically he's AWOL. He needs people around him he can trust. And if you were going to choose somewhere to live a quiet, secret life then Holden is perfect. I can't think of many quieter places."

23

Washington, DC
December 29, 6:00 P.M.

Coty drove Frank and Jack to the airport. He took a circuitous
route, stopping twice on side streets, waiting till the stoplights
were about to turn then powering through. He toured the whole
of the outer Washington suburbs like a lost taxi driver. In the dark
Jack wasn't sure how he could tell whether or not the same set of
headlights were following them or whether they were different ones,
but eventually he pulled onto the freeway and drove at a breakneck
speed to Dulles Airport.

The car was warm and Jack was tired. He'd drunk coffee before they
left, but it had no effect anymore, and he could feel himself drifting
in and out of sleep, his head tilting forward as the world frayed at
the edges and soaked up darkness. He saw the policeman from that
morning staring a dead-fish stare at him through the car window, his
finger tapping on the glass but making no sound. He saw Chrissie
sleeping on a hospital bench while Connor pulled at his bandages and
screamed a silent scream in the next room. He saw Henry walking
around the gardens of the asylum on a beautiful winter's morning,

dressed in white with charred black hands and a charred black face, but mostly he saw darkness intercut with dashes on the road that sped toward him like bright white darts.

Eventually they arrived at the airport, and he was awake again, but the images he'd seen in his broken sleep still swam in and out of his vision.

"We're here," Coty said, jerking the car to a stop outside the entrance. "You've got thirty minutes before takeoff."

Dulles Airport shone bright against the night sky, the roof a vast concrete butter curl over glass and steel walls. Jack felt no desire to move, but he pushed open the door. A blast of cold air hit him. He felt the side of his chin, the cold made it ache. He touched the swelling gently, at least it wasn't getting any bigger. Frank took their overnight bags out of the trunk. He slammed it shut. Coty gunned the engine and skidded away.

"Come on," Frank said. "We don't have much time."

The journey passed in a blur. He drank whisky from his hip flask, but the sleep that had sunk him under its warm waves in the back of the car had gone into hiding. The plane's engines were noisy, the seat was uncomfortable.

They took a taxi from the rank outside the airport, its engine ticking over and vibrating the hood so it looked like it was shivering. The driver tried some small talk, but Frank's curt responses made it clear he wasn't interested.

The overhead cables on Bangor Main Street were hung with icicles, and a row of parked cars were gradually being turned from sleek metal and chrome into white, fluffy toys. No one was out. The windows of the department store glowed hopefully at the restaurants opposite. Only one responded. An Italian place, holding onto the last customer of the night.

They pulled onto a side street and the driver stopped. Jack peered through the window at a small townhouse set up as a little hotel. He could see pale pink nets hanging over the windows and drapes so dusty they looked as if they'd been coated in a fine spray of concrete.

"Looks delightful," Jack said as he made his way up the steps.

"Don't blame me," Frank said. "I didn't book it." He rang the bell and waited. The owner was an elderly lady. They could hear her shuffle toward the door. She let them in and opened a ledger, writing their details in a careful, slow hand.

"Breakfast is at seven," she said. "Hot water comes on at six A.M. and goes off at eight A.M. In the evening it's available between eight and ten P.M. You've missed it, but there might still be a little something left in the tank. Is it just the one night?"

"I hope so," Jack said.

"Yes, thank you, ma'am," Frank replied.

"Check out is at eleven A.M. If you're still here after that we'll charge you for another night whether or not you stay. That all clear? Here." She handed them two room keys. Jack's came with a large blue silk pom-pom attached to it via a tassel. Frank's was pink. Jack was too tired to make a joke.

"You're both on the first floor. Will you be wanting a cooked breakfast?"

"No, thank you," Frank said.

"French toast for me," Jack replied.

"That's not on the menu."

"Normal toast then."

"That's in the noncooked menu. You can have it with the cooked menu, too, but it's not part of that menu. Doesn't come with jam if you have it with the cooked menu."

Jack stared at the woman a moment, his brain too tired follow the logic of the tiny rules.

"I'll just have bread," he said eventually.

His room smelled of lavender and cats. Jack didn't care. There was a sink in the corner. He turned on the faucet and heard what sounded like a submarine emptying its ballast tanks in the basement of the building. He turned it off and splashed his face with cold water. He loosened his tie and laid down on the bed. He would have preferred it if a picture of the crucified Christ hadn't been staring down at him from the opposite wall and the mattress had been stuffed with springs instead of mashed potatoes, but his body ached for sleep, and sleep it did.

24

Bangor, Maine
December 30, 7:00 A.M.

Jack took breakfast in the floral dining room on the first floor. Outside it was still dark, the fresh snow marked with a single set of footprints. Frank had already gone to pick up the rental car and check out the garage where Archie was working.

The owner brought him bread, cold toast, hard butter, blueberry jam, and coffee. He put the butter dish on the radiator and tasted the coffee, then wished he hadn't. He missed New York—he almost missed Washington. A radiogram played in the corner of the room. A local station. Weather broadcast. A snowstorm was coming and *boy was it a biggie.*

Eventually another guest joined him, a young man in a smart suit who wished him a cheerful good morning and smiled a salesman's smile.

"Might be a cold one but at least we've got a great breakfast," he said, tucking into bacon, eggs, beans, and hash browns. The man could barely suppress his smile as he ate.

"Yeah," Jack mumbled, wondering whether to ask if he could change his breakfast order.

"Lot of folks don't like this weather," the man continued, barely pausing between mouthfuls. "But for me it's like Christmas."

"You like to have snow at Christmas?"

"Oh no, I didn't mean that. I'm in insulation. Reduce heat loss and cut your heating bills by up to forty percent, and that's guaranteed. Got some samples with me if you're interested."

"No, thank you."

"Well, here's my card anyways. Charlton Skinner. Home Proud Insulation. Pleased to meet you."

Jack slipped the card into his pocket. He looked the man over as he ate, then read yesterday's paper. After a while the other guest bid him a cheerful goodbye and set off in his coat and hat to make as many houses as he could up to forty percent cheaper to heat.

Jack stared out the window. The darkness outside was gradually giving way to a gray dawn. The snowstorm hadn't gotten up to strength yet, it was still dancing through the air, blowing this way and that, teasing the city.

He went to the front desk. There was no one there. He took the man's card out of his pocket, picked up the telephone, and dialed the number.

A distant voice answered. "Good morning. Home Proud Insulation. How may I help?"

Jack put the phone down; being around Coty and Frank was making him doubt everyone.

A car pulled up, snow chains crunching. Frank got out, hunched over, rubbing his gloved hands together. He looked cold as hell as he jumped up the steps to the front door.

"Well?" Jack said.

"They opened the garage at seven. He's there. Two other men with him. One arrived while I was watching. Neither looked like a threat. I mean, far as I could tell." He looked over his shoulder, then continued softly, "One was elderly, wiry-looking. The other maybe in his thirties but out of shape. Course, you never can tell until you're close up if they're the kind of person who'll pull a gun. Maybe up here they are. It's tough country. But those two didn't look like the firing type."

"The firing type?"

"Some people pull a gun, you know they're never going to fire it. Others, you know they will, they almost have to stop themselves pulling the trigger."

"That so?" Jack said. "You could try psychology if you ever get bored of this gig. What about me? Would I fire?"

"You wouldn't pull a gun. You'd talk. But if you ever did," he glanced Jack over, "sure. Body shot. Head if you were in a bad mood."

Jack almost smiled. "I was given a flamethrower in the war. You had to get close before you could light it up. Worst job in the whole damn army. You carry a bomb on your back till you're in spitting distance of the enemy and hope to God you don't get hit. I didn't try talking to them first. How did Mr. Archibald Bell look?"

"He was wrapped up, and I only caught a glimpse of him as he switched on the lights on the parking lot. He's staying in a trailer parked round the back."

"You're sure it was him?"

"Looked the right size and height."

"We better go. Once the storm gets in we might not be able to go anywhere. Want some stale coffee to warm you up?"

"Please," Frank muttered.

They drove along Main Street and crossed the Penobscot River, granite gray and flowing slowly as molten rock. Holden was a couple of miles south of Bangor. They joined a convoy of slow-moving trucks carrying timber to the harbor. The snow was coming down more thickly and Frank kept sniffing.

"You think you can get him to talk?" Frank said.

"No idea. It comes down to whether he trusts us. Whether he thinks we're the good guys."

"Well, we are, aren't we?"

Jack stared out the window, white as far as the eye could see. Gray sky above. At least they had daylight. He couldn't imagine only seeing a night sky over snow for the whole winter.

"We're on his side," he said eventually. "I'll make sure he understands that."

Holden was no more than a few houses and businesses strung out along the main road. There were two billboards promoting new park homes, retirement estates for the elderly on one side and holiday homes on the other. They looked like they were under construction but no one was working today.

"S'over there," Frank said, pointing at the gas station. He pulled across the road into the garage parking lot. A large red clapboard garage sat behind the pumps. White letters painted over the door set out the name.

Frank parked next to a pickup truck and switched off the engine. A row of rusting cars and tractor parts were piled up on the far side of the parking lot, with a layer of white frost covering them. The door to the garage was closed but yellow light pooled underneath it and they could hear a radio playing inside. The radio was interrupted by occasional hammer bangs and the whir of an electric drill. Frank knocked. No one answered. He knocked again. The banging stopped. Footsteps moved toward the door. It was opened by a large man in his thirties, who must have been at least six five and carried a gut in front of him that could hold about a gallon of beer. He wiped his hands on a rag.

"Ye-ah?" he said, peering at them.

Frank smiled. It was a good effort, warm, friendly, reassuring.

"My name's Frank O'Neil, this here's my colleague Jack Miller. We've come up from Washington. We'd like to talk to Mr. Bell."

The man shifted so he blocked the doorway.

"Mr. who?"

"Mr. Bell, I understand he's staying with you at the moment."

"No one here by that name."

"Come on. We know he's here."

"You army?"

"Do we look like army?"

"Nah. You look like realtors."

"We're from the government. We've come a long way. We need his help," Jack said.

"Supposing he doesn't want to talk to you?"

"Supposing you go ask him?" Jack replied. "We're here to talk. We're not about to arrest him."

The man disappeared inside. Jack wasn't sure whether he'd emerge with Archie Bell or a shotgun.

He opened the door a few moments later and said, "Bring your car round the side. There's a barn. You can park inside. Wait there."

Frank and Jack got back in the car and eased it over the freshly fallen snow into the barn.

"You know this is exactly what they'd do if they wanted to make us disappear?" Jack said. "First get the car out of sight. Then take us out. Dump our bodies somewhere in the snow."

"I know," Frank said. The idea didn't seem to perturb him. Jack sensed the same keen air of anticipation he'd felt coming off him when they had first met at the airport.

"I get the feeling you like your job. In your assessment of who pulls a gun, where do these guys fit?"

"That big guy would fire, no question. But he hasn't pulled a gun. We're on their side." Frank switched off the engine. "Where's he gone anyway?" He twisted in his seat and looked out the rear window. Beyond the entrance to the barn he could see trucks rumbling along the highway, the lights glowing yellow against the gray sky. The man hadn't followed them into the barn. They waited some more.

Jack wanted a cigarette, but it was cold and he couldn't decide if he wanted one more or less than he wanted to take off his gloves. Less, he decided, pushing his hands deeper into his coat pockets. He stared at the gray-black shapes stacked on the back wall. The bones of a hundred dead cars. Jack kept looking. There was a man standing amongst them. At least he thought there was. He was standing so still Jack wasn't sure if it was a person or a coat on a hook.

"You see a thin fellow over there in the shadows?" Jack said. Frank leaned forward to get a better look.

"I believe I do."

"You think he's the firing type?"

"Let's find out," he said. "If he is just remember to duck, like I told you last time." They got out of the car.

The coat struck a match against the wall, lit a cigarette, and breathed out a cloud of smoke.

"That's close enough, thank you," he said.

Jack and Frank looked at one another. Frank leaned against the side of the car.

"I'd give you about two hours in the open in those clothes," the man said. His voice was soft, with a rising intonation. "First things to go are the extremities. Tips of your fingers, your toes, end of your nose, too, if it ain't covered. You ever seen someone with frostbite of the nose?"

"Can't say I have," Frank replied, squinting into the darkness.

"It goes black. The flesh dies. That's what happens when the cold gets inside you, it switches off all your little veins."

The man still hadn't moved. As Jack's eyes got used to the gloom he realized he was holding a hunting rifle. Frank had realized it too. It wasn't exactly pointing at them, but it wasn't exactly pointing away either. The man took a step forward.

"How d'you find me?" he said.

"Called the asylum. Got the number of this place. Wasn't hard," Jack said.

"Too hard for the army."

"Yeah, well, we're not military."

"Now you've found me what do you want?"

"We need your help," Jack said. "We need you to tell us what happened at the base in Greenland when you got sick. And what happened after."

Frank reached into his pocket, slowly. He took out an envelope.

"There's five hundred dollars in here." He threw it on the ground. "In case that helps you make up your mind."

Archie reached down and picked up the envelope, the gun balanced across his forearm. He flicked through the bills.

"You sure ain't army," he said. "Follow me."

The snow was deep enough to reach Jack's ankles, and the wind was getting up, whipping freezing flakes across the flat, white fields.

"Looks pretty bleak, don't it?" Archie said, leading the way to a small trailer. It had been white once but now looked dirty gray against the pristine snow. He dropped his spent cigarette. "You got the Penobscot River about two miles that way. Good fishing once the thaw sets in. In summer you can take a boat out from the harbor."

"You like fishing?" Jack asked.

"No. I don't eat fish. I prefer huntin'," he said. "The woods got elk, deer, and bear, but these days I just track. I don't like the kill." He leaned on the trailer door and gave it a shove with his shoulder. The trailer shuddered. Snow slumped off the small porch. Inside it was as neat as a military barrack, with bench seating and a small table at one end and a stove in the middle. A doorway kept the sleeping quarters private.

"Take a seat," Archie said, pointing at the bench. Jack slid onto it, keeping his coat on. Frank joined him. Archie slung the hunting rifle from his back, opened the chamber, and took out the bullets. He placed them in a box on a shelf and locked the gun in a cupboard. Then he moved to the stove and put a kettle on.

"You want coffee?" he asked. Jack and Frank nodded. Jack was taken with the way Archie moved. He did everything with precision and economy. Not a single wasted gesture. It was only when he brought over the steaming mugs of coffee that Jack noticed the top half of his first and middle fingers were missing.

Archie slid a folding chair out of a cupboard, opened it, and sat down carefully. Outside the wind whistled and rattled the trailer roof.

"Thank you," Jack said.

Archie took a sip of coffee. He stared down at the table. His face was drawn and there were bags under his eyes. In contrast to his slow, considered movements his eyes were restless and quick, unable to focus on any one point for more than a couple of seconds.

"You going to tell me who you're with?" he asked.

"Agency," Frank replied.

"That so," Archie said. "What can I tell you that you couldn't find out for yourselves?"

Jack drank some coffee.

"We can read all the files we want, but they don't describe what happened to you and the other two boys they evacuated."

Archie rubbed his eyes then wrapped his hands tightly around his mug. He shook his head.

"Figured someone would turn up one day asking. You won't believe me. What I'm gonna tell you—you'll think I lost my mind." He frowned and shook his head. "Maybe I did."

25

Holden, Maine
December 30, 9:00 A.M.

Archie took a sip of coffee and extracted a crumpled packet of cigarettes from his jacket pocket. He flicked one out. Jack got out his lighter and held it for him.

"How much you know already?" Archie said.

"Not much," Jack replied. "We know the three of you were evacuated, and we know your two colleagues took their own lives at the institution."

Archie nodded. He took the envelope of cash from his pocket, flicked through the bills again, then placed them in a drawer under the table.

"The three of us were artillery, maintained the missiles and launch equipment at the base. I oversaw the simulations. We ran those most days."

"Simulations?" Jack asked.

"Sure. Main and counterattacks. Like a fire drill. So everyone knows exactly what they're doing if we get the call. So it don't feel like an emergency. Feels like what they're meant to be doing. That's the point of the practice. Take away the twitchiness, get people feeling its normal to be arming a nuke to fire into the big black sky, ready to land on some commie bastard's head.

"I guess we felt like we were doing some good. After Cuba and all that. The Russians weren't going away. They were spreading round the world. The officers reminded us of that. Through all the drills and the endless night. And then the endless day. Main problem was boredom. And they limited the booze. Sensible. But it didn't feel like it. Not when you could see the officers with their own stash, telling us we needed to be strong, think of our country. Meanwhile one of them was pissed as a skunk half the time."

"The chaplain?" Jack guessed.

Archie looked up sharply. "That's right. Nice fella. But it wouldn't have hurt him to share a drink with us once in a while."

"I guess there must have been a few arguments, you guys being all cooped up together. Lot of different personalities," Jack said.

Archie nodded.

"Regular army got on ok. But there were a lot of NCOs working there. The rest of us didn't get told much about what they were doing. Something to do with ice. God knows why you'd need to go to Greenland to study ice. There's enough of it outside the window." He reached across and tapped on the glass.

"Owen Stiglitz was the chief scientific officer, wasn't he? Did you get on with him?" Jack asked.

Archie shrugged. "He was ok, most of the time. But sometimes when we were trying to relax in the rec room he'd come in and start playing opera music. All we wanted to do was play cards, and he puts on a record so loud we can barely hear each other speak. Same thing every time. '*Miserere mei, Deus.*' I don't know any classical music, but I sure as hell know that one. Must've heard it at least five times a week."

"Why didn't you tell Stiglitz to turn it off?" Frank said.

"He was a senior officer. And he, well, he always brought whisky. We put up with the music for the booze. He obviously had his own stash or maybe the rules didn't apply to him or something. And it wasn't like he tried to talk to us or anything. Not much. Whenever he spoke it was kind of awkward. He didn't have much to say to us. Once or twice he tried to discuss a play or some theory. Something about fuel or ice or whatever. Compounds. Technical things. We weren't much in terms of company. Not for him. He didn't like cards, either, would only play chess. The only person who he could talk to about all the technical stuff was a guy called Connor. Connor just got stuff. Like his brain clicked with it. With anything. You tell him something and he remembers it forever. But then Stiglitz stopped speaking to him when Connor beat him at chess," he said, shaking his head. "Like some angry kid. Stupid."

"Can you tell us when you started suffering from the condition that led to you being evacuated?" Jack said.

Archie thought a moment. "Early December," he said. "We were three or four weeks into the darkness. They told us that was a tough time, but I felt fine. The food was good, the guys were friendly, and we were on hardship pay on top of our usual allowance. If you ask me it was better than being bitten by mosquitoes, up to your knees in rice fields in Vietnam while someone you can't even see takes shots at you. But then it started, this feeling." His fingers tapped a rhythm on the side of his mug.

"What kind of feeling?" Jack asked.

"I felt like things weren't in their usual place. Like they were being moved around. Stuff I'd left on my bunk. Personal possessions. And I got this notion . . ." He ran a hand through his hair. "I got this notion that someone was following me." He looked up at Jack and Frank, his quick eyes still for a moment.

"Go on," Jack said.

"Now, I'm not a believer in the supernatural. I don't believe in what's not there. But the thing is, this person *was* there. Following me. It started speaking to me too. I wasn't happy about that. I didn't want to be seeing things. I didn't want to be hearing things. I told myself all I needed was a holiday, some fresh air. Some goddamn daylight."

"What did it look like, this thing?" Jack said.

"Nothing much, it wasn't like it had a face I can recall. It was just there."

"Were you working with munitions at this time? Maybe in one of the rooms where they were stored?" Jack asked. "Could it have been caused by chemicals?"

"No, it came on in the evenings or night, after I'd stopped working."

"Anyone else around when you saw it?" Jack said.

"Not really. Stiglitz once or twice. I remember him asking me if I felt alright. I must have looked pretty strung out for him to notice."

"Stiglitz, huh?" Jack said.

"Who did you tell about this?" Frank said. "Anyone at the base?"

Archie shrugged.

"It's a difficult thing to talk about, you can't exactly say to people, *Hey, anybody else see a strange-looking figure who keeps appearing and disappearing? Doesn't work here. Whispers in your ear. Makes you think you're going crazy.* It's not exactly the kind of thing you want to broadcast. It made me feel pretty out-there. I spent more and more time in my cabin. Then I saw Cooper had the same thing. Cooper shared the cabin. He had it worse. One time I saw him lying on his bed holding his pillow staring up at the ceiling. He wasn't moving. He said he could see something crawling across the ceiling. *I think I drank too much*, he said. It was like he was having one of those visions drunks wake up with. I asked him what he could see but he could barely talk. All he said was *make it go away*."

"There must have been a doctor at the base, couldn't you talk to him?" Jack said.

"Dr. Parker? Nah, he was an older fellow. Don't get me wrong, he could strap up a broken leg or pick a bullet out of your foot if you were dumb enough to shoot yourself cleaning your gun, but you wouldn't talk to him about something like this. He was more of a put-up-or-shut-up type, guess he'd seen his own share of ugly during the war."

"Did you speak to anyone at all?"

"I told Connor. He said it sounded like I needed to get away, take a break. I didn't. I kept running the drills. Everybody up. To your station. Run through the protocols. Ready to fire. Same thing each day. Same thing each night. That's when it happened."

"What happened?" Jack said.

"One day a rocket goes up. Or maybe it was night. Same thing in winter."

"Wasn't that the purpose of the drills?" Jack asked.

Archie paused and shook his head, as if he still couldn't believe it.

"Not this one. This one just sort of went up. On my watch."

Jack and Frank stared back at him.

"Holy shit," Frank said.

"It wasn't armed, but it would've still made a pretty big hole in the ground if it hadn't gone into the sea. Damn thing is I couldn't tell you how it happened. I couldn't tell them why it happened." He raised a hand to his forehand and pushed a lock of dark greasy hair away from his eyes. "They found me outside, didn't have my gloves or my coat on. I swore the sun was shining even though it was pitch black. Said I'd blown a hole clean through the night sky to let the daylight in."

Jack and Frank were silent.

"Did you have that on file already, or was that something new?" Archie asked, as if he'd just told them what he'd eaten for breakfast.

"We didn't have that," Frank said.

"No, well, I guess they kept that away from any file you guys could get your hands on. They told me there was no hole in the sky. I remember arguing with them. The man who'd been following me, he told me to do it. It all made perfect sense at the time. I agreed with him. They said I needed to come inside. I didn't want to. I ran. Don't know how long I was out there, not long. But I lost two damn fingers. Could have been worse. Could have lost my toes too. Or my nose. I ain't exactly pretty but I look a whole lot better with my face in one piece." He smiled quickly, his teeth small and sharp. For a brief moment he looked for all the world like a normal young man making a dumb joke. Then the shadows returned.

"I was feverish and shaking and they must have pumped me full of something pretty strong because when I came to I was at the base in Kansas. First few days back I don't think I made much sense. The other two were with me. Cooper and another guy."

Jack lifted his cup.

"Mind if I get some more coffee?" he said.

Archie reached for the pot on the stove and poured the black liquid into Jack's cup.

"Thank you. May I say you've been incredibly frank and open with us, and we appreciate it. It can be an extremely hard thing to talk about this kind of thing. Can I ask what you think was going on? Why you and the others started seeing things, why you stopped being able to distinguish reality from your imagination?"

Archie frowned.

"At the asylum they kept telling us it was being stuck underground in the darkness. They wanted us to take a whole load of pills. I wouldn't do it. I wouldn't do it because I know I felt just fine up there in winter. It was dark. It was boring. People got grouchy. That's it. More you tell 'em you're fine, more they think there's an issue. More pills they want you to take. The other two kept taking the pills, and look what happened to them."

"Did your visions stop?" Jack asked.

"They did. But it kind of opens something in your soul. Hard to describe. I get flashbacks sometimes. Like I had a bad trip."

"What do you think caused you to see things?" Jack asked.

Archie shrugged.

"Gas leak maybe. Or some other chemical exposure. Something in the building. In our rooms. Wasn't the munitions. That would have affected the whole crew. Same exposure for all of us, and there were about seventy, all told. So just us three. I don't know why. You find out then you tell me."

"After the three of you had gone one of the men there, Henry Carvell, he started accusing an officer of poisoning people."

Archie looked up.

"Henry said that?"

"He was suffering in the same way as you, seeing things."

"No shit? He hid it well. Why in hell's name did he think an officer was poisoning the troops? I liked Henry. We all did. But he wasn't exactly a genius. Henry-Three-Times we called him. You had to tell him something three times before he understood it." He rubbed his eyes. "Who did he think was doing the poisoning?"

"Stiglitz."

Archie frowned, then said, "That's a hell of a battle he picked right there. I know Stiglitz was a strange one, but still. He was smart. A lot smarter than Henry. Why would he think that?"

"We don't know."

"Well, can't you ask Henry?" His question remained unanswered, and the silence told Archie all he needed to know. "Ah jeez," he said, his head in his hands.

Jack and Frank looked at one another. Jack didn't speak. It was Frank's call how much information they revealed.

Frank said, "Henry died in an accident at the base. A fire, back in November. He was part of the final clean-up crew. He was there with Stiglitz and Connor. The three of them were trapped. Storm came in. They couldn't leave."

"I'm sorry to hear that. I liked him. He was the kind of man who lifted your spirits," Archie said.

"Stiglitz was killed in the same fire. That's what Connor said. He survived. He's in recovery," Jack said.

"Stiglitz and Henry died in the same fire?" Archie said.

"So Connor says," Jack replied.

Archie nodded slowly, his restless eyes settled on Jack. "I can see why you're asking questions," he said. He got up stiffly and reached for the shelf above the sink. Frank's hand moved toward his inside pocket. Archie caught the movement.

"Relax, I ain't going for my gun. It's locked in the cupboard, in case you hadn't noticed."

There was a framed embroidery on the shelf that said "home sweet home." It sat on a neat pile of newspapers and hunting magazines. Archie moved it carefully to one side. He took down a folded copy of the *Washington Evening Star* and opened it on the table.

"Here," he said, leafing through the pages and pointing at a header in the bottom corner of the page. It was no more than three lines, a summary of a police report, the kind journalists pick up from the station on a daily basis: "Reverend Peterson drowned in the Potomac. Former army chaplain. Officers confirmed they are investigating a possible homicide."

"Yesterday's paper. Should I be worried?" Archie asked.

Jack glanced at Frank. "Anyone else turns up saying they want to talk, don't talk to them. Tell your cousin to say you're not here. Better still, use the money we gave you to get away for a while. It wasn't hard to find you."

Frank got up and eased himself out of the cramped space between the table and the bench. Jack followed, he looked at Archie, sitting at the small table in his spotless trailer. He wanted to say something, but he couldn't think of anything, so he followed Frank out into the snow.

26

Bangor, Maine
December 30, 12:00 P.M.

They pulled onto the highway. Frank was hunched over the wheel, gripping tightly. The snow was coming down thickly. There was no traffic, and the road merged with the flat fields on either side, becoming part of the same vast expanse of white.

"He seemed pretty sharp. Eye on the news. He was careful with us," Jack said.

"He'll need to be more than careful. Did anyone talk to you at the hotel?"

"One man. He ate breakfast while I was in the dining room."

"Why didn't you tell me?" Frank said.

"There wasn't anything to tell."

"There's always something to tell. What was he like?"

Jack looked across at Frank. He was squinting into the flurries of snow that were being swept toward the windscreen. He looked tired.

"Midwest accent, late twenties. Clean-shaven with slicked-back hair. Dressed up smart. High-quality wool suit worn smooth on the seat of his pants. Suggesting he does indeed wear a suit every day and spends a significant amount of time sitting on his ass. Ate the cooked breakfast like a man who wants to get every last cent out of his expense account. Oh, and he gave me his card. Here."

Jack passed him the card. Frank held it up and read it.

"*Charlton Skinner.*"

"I called the number. If you want insulation, I'd say he was a good bet. You could save up to forty percent guaranteed."

"Ok," Frank seemed to relax a little. They were crossing the river.

"You're worried about Archie?" Jack asked.

Frank shrugged.

"Someone is tying up loose ends. Trying to stop anyone finding out what went on. Chaplain was first. Archie could be next."

"No, he wasn't," Jack said.

"He wasn't what?"

"The chaplain wasn't first. The two men who died in the asylum were first."

"I thought they were suicides?"

Jack shook his head. "The symptoms of psychosis don't generate the same outcome in two different people at the same time. There are too many variables. The mind is complex. I don't buy it. Maybe if there was more time between them, but not like that, coming so close together. Archie got away. He was smart—or maybe just lucky," Jack said.

The afternoon flight back to Washington was delayed, and it was past midnight by the time Jack got back to the hotel. He sat on the edge of his bed and untied his shoelaces with his good hand, then kicked off his shoes. He poured a large whisky and sipped it slowly.

Archie didn't say he thought Stiglitz had drugged him. He was more circumspect than Henry, but he described a character that was controlling, passive aggressive, and enjoyed manipulating those around him. And it was clear that Stiglitz was watching him and Henry. Jack just wasn't sure whether it was out of curiosity at their strange behavior or because he'd caused that behavior.

Why? It was hard to understand why anyone would do that. But he'd read enough case studies and seen enough patients in his time at New York State Hospital to know that sociopathy took many different forms. As did espionage.

Stiglitz was the key. The catalyst. He took out his notepad and flicked through, looking for the name of the student who'd made a complaint about him at university. Mendelson. That was the man who'd accused him of plagiarizing his work.

He picked up the telephone, called Coty.

"Coty, it's Jack,"

"Do you know what time it is?" Coty's voice slurred.

"No. But I knew you wouldn't be asleep."

"Not anymore."

"You remember I asked you to look into a guy called Mendelson?"

"No. Yes. Maybe." A pause.

"Did you do it?"

"If you asked me to then I'll have sent out the request and we'll have his details on file."

"Good. I want to talk to him."

"Now?"

"No, not now. But I need to know more about Stiglitz. I want to understand him. Talking to Mendelson will help me do that."

"Sure. Whatever. Good night."

Jack put down the phone, shut his eyes, and lay back on the bed, attempted to clear his head. He used a technique Miyoko had taught him, all those years ago as they lay together in her tiny apartment in Tokyo. An attempt to focus on each thought itself, don't be led by it, don't let it pull you in different directions. Hold the image, like looking at a photograph. Then put it to one side. He remembered how he'd laughed. Poured himself a beer. Told her he'd rather look at her. Told her that closing his eyes was a waste when he was with her. Tried to distract her. Succeeded.

He felt his mind slowing. The day sliding away from him. But the last thing he saw wasn't his wife, sitting cross-legged on the wooden floor, trying not to let him distract her. It was an insulation salesman, smiling, wishing him a good day as he stepped out into the snowy streets of Bangor.

27

The Willard
December 31, 6:30 A.M.

He woke early, showered and dressed, then ordered a pot of coffee. While he waited he called Martina. She asked how he was, when he was coming back, she told him his patients were going to leave him. She also told him Nate Bramwell from the Brooklyn Fire Station had called yesterday. Wouldn't leave a message, just told her it was urgent.

Jack thanked her, put the phone down, massaged his stiff fingers, then asked the operator to put him through to the Brooklyn Fire Station. It rang and rang. A man answered. He asked what Jack wanted. Jack told him he was returning Nate Bramwell's call. Jack waited, the coffee he'd ordered came. He poured it. Drank it. Waited some more. Thought it must be a damn big fire station.

"Dr. Miller," Nate said eventually. "Thank you for returning my call. Martina said you were out of town."

"Yeah, I'm all over the place at the moment."

"Same case?"

"Unfortunately. Have you got something for me?"

"I do, a curious thing. An explanation as to how both bodies could be in the same fire but one burn at a much faster rate."

"I thought you said it wasn't possible?"

"It's certainly not probable. But I found something that made me think you shouldn't discount it completely. I went through our fire investigation reports looking for something similar. There was a fire over on Washington Street a few years back. The Meatpacking District. You could smell it for days afterward."

"I remember, Manhattan smelled like a steakhouse all week."

"Yeah, well, the insurers weren't buying the number of carcasses the businesses claimed were lost. Seemed too high to them. There was the usual back and forth. Turned out the carcasses that were charred but more or less complete were in the deep freeze. Anything that wasn't frozen had burned till it was just ash and fragments of bone. The insurers didn't appreciate how much stock had simply burned away. Made me think of your two bodies, unpleasant as it is."

"Hold up," Jack said, trying to take it in. "You're saying that if one of the bodies in my fire was frozen this could explain the different burn rates?"

"It's a possibility. Wouldn't have occurred to me if you hadn't mentioned ice. I know you can't give me details, but if one of the bodies was frozen before the fire started it may have burned more slowly. Frozen food takes longer to cook."

Jack was silent, his hand gripped the receiver. Stiglitz frozen. That meant he would have been dead before the fire started. Same fire. Not two fires. Only one of them was dead before it started.

"Thank you, Nate. That's helpful. I mean, it complicates things, but they were already pretty damn complicated. What caused the fire in the meatpacking plant?" Jack said.

"Faulty wiring. Compressor in one of the refrigerators overheated. Ignited the gases. More common than you'd think. Makes it very difficult to control once they get going. Burns hot, too, the gases act as an accelerant. Not exactly the same as the situation you showed me, but if we're talking about a fast fire, something intense enough to incinerate one body but leave the other intact, then it's worth considering. Was there an autopsy?"

"Not that I've seen. Could you tell if a body had been frozen before it was burned based on what's left of it?"

"Don't ask me. You're the doctor."

"Yeah, and strangely enough I never worked on a dead patient who was frozen then caught fire. Guess we'd be looking at whether there's anything unusual at a cellular level. Freezing might shrink or damage some of the cells. It might show up under an electron-microscope. Although I don't know what state the body's in now," Jack said.

"Check the lungs for smoke damage too. If he was dead before the fire started there won't be smoke particles on the inside. He wouldn't have been breathing. That's if your body's in a fit state for checking."

"I'll do that," Jack said.

He hung up, carefully placing the receiver back in its cradle. Lifted his coffee cup, got it halfway to his mouth before he realized it was empty. Put it down again. The frozen body still holding onto human form, that was Stiglitz. Dead before the fire started. The other body belonged to Henry. He tried to think through what that meant.

Had Henry, going out of his mind with paranoid delusions, locked Stiglitz out of the base, let him freeze to death, then brought him inside to set him on fire and tried to make it look like some kind of accident?

Maybe those delusions weren't paranoid. Maybe he was onto something. Coty had said there was a radio broadcast from outside while they were trapped there. Was that it? Stiglitz outside, away from the others, calling his paymaster? Then Henry shuts him out. And what about Connor? Did he help Henry? Did he refuse to have any part in it? At least until he realized Henry had got trapped in the room where he'd set Stiglitz on fire. It was a theory. A theory he wanted to be true. One that meant Connor was a good guy. Stiglitz the spy. Henry, well, dumb Henry-Three-Times had at least taken out the bad guy, even if he'd got himself burned to death in the process.

There was a knock at the door. He got up stiffly, stretched his shoulders, and massaged his hand.

"It's Frank," a muffled voice said.

Jack opened the door. Frank glanced around the way he always did when he entered a room, as if he was sizing it up for a sale.

"I've got Mendelson's address and number," he said. "Coty said you wanted it. After he completed his studies he was offered a lectureship at Cornell. He moved to Pennsylvania State for a while, then came back a couple of years ago. He's an assistant professor of chemistry now."

"Is he there at the moment? I'm guessing the spring semester hasn't started yet."

"Should be. He lives close to campus. Has a wife and a baby daughter. Did you want to visit or call?"

"Visit. Ideally. Can we get a flight?"

"There are three a week and none of them leave today. Five-hour drive if you want to talk to him face to face," Frank said. Jack slid his feet into his shoes.

"Give me the number," he said. "I'll see if he's available. If he is I'd rather do it face to face." Frank made a strange little sound, a note of displeasure at the thought of driving all day. He reached for the coffee pot and went to pour himself a cup. Two drops spilled into the cup. Frank looked at it violently, then left the room.

"I'll meet you downstairs," he said on his way out.

Jack called Mendelson, told him he was reviewing the suitability of someone Mendelson had known for a senior government role. Mendelson was standoffish and dismissive, then his tone changed when

Jack told him the man's name was Stiglitz. He said he would appreciate the opportunity to discuss him, and would make time that afternoon. Jack couldn't help thinking he was going to talk to someone who had a score to settle.

After he'd called Mendelson he rang Coty and told him Nate's theory that one of the bodies might have been frozen, and that this could explain the different burn rates. He asked him if they could arrange an autopsy.

Coty made a snorting sound. "God knows where Stiglitz is buried. I'll find out. Guess the weather's been cold so there might not be much decomposition. How would they tell if he'd frozen to death before he was set on fire?"

"Extended cellular spaces? Shrunken cells? Let's ask them. They can look through a microscope at a tissue sample. Also, Nate said to check the lungs for smoke particles. If they're clean it means he wasn't breathing when the fire started. So was already dead."

"Ok, makes sense. Good call. And pathologists love a challenge, morbid bastards. I'll get on it. What time will you be back from Ithaca?"

"Some time after nine."

"When you get back come and meet me at The Ascot at 517 Thirteenth. I'm having dinner with someone. You should be there too."

"Who is it?" Jack asked. There was a pause.

"General Arthur Carvell. Henry's father. He's in town. Thought you might like to meet him."

28

Washington, DC
December 31, 10:00 A.M.

Frank circled the Washington suburbs until he was satisfied no one was following them. The drive to Ithaca was long, and not made any shorter by the circuitous route Frank took. The minutes turned into miles. Hour after hour on straight roads, snow banked high on either side. They drove through a few flurries on the way but nothing that slowed them down. Frank wasn't in the mood for talking. Jack flicked the radio on and off and smoked cigarettes. It was three o'clock in the afternoon by the time they got there and the sun was already low in the winter sky.

Mendelson lived in the historic district on the north side of Fall Creek. The road curved up the hill, through woodland, and through the university campus. They passed fraternity houses and smaller properties belonging to the university staff. They had to drive slowly. The road had a layer of packed snow that crunched and slid under the tires.

The clapboard house was tucked behind the tall pine trees and the street was as quiet as is possible for a street to be and still be inhabited by living, breathing humans.

"You wait here," Jack said to Frank. "I don't want him to feel like it's an interrogation."

"How long are you going to be?"

"An hour or so."

Jack walked up the drive. A child's swing hung motionless in the yard, an inch of snow on the seat. There were paw prints around it. The air smelled of woodsmoke and cold. He walked up the steps of the veranda and glanced up at the house. Paint was peeling from the wood and the gutters were filled with leaves. There were stains down the side of building, moss growing on the slate roof tiles. Mendelson didn't appear to be the kind of man who was easily distracted by chores.

Jack stood at the front door and was about to knock when he heard shouting from inside. A woman and a man, their argument in full flow. A door slammed. Footsteps stamped through the house. A baby crying. He stood still for a moment. On the veranda, by his feet, was a collection of cigarette butts. Someone in the house came outside to smoke, either because they weren't allowed to smoke inside or because they needed time on their own.

He pressed the bell but heard nothing, so he knocked on the door and waited. A chair scraped over the floor. Footsteps. The door opened.

"Good afternoon, I'm Dr. Jack Miller," Jack said. "We spoke this morning."

"Peter Mendelson, pleased to meet you."

Jack shook the man's hand. Mendelson was tall with black hair that curled thickly around his temples but was receding at the front. He was wearing a wool sweater and scarf indoors. A black Labrador sat obediently beside him, looking at Jack speculatively.

"Come in, won't you. Excuse the mess," Mendelson said cheerfully, stepping over alphabet blocks and one and a half pairs of shoes. Upstairs the baby was still crying. "My wife has gone to see if she can settle the baby. Our little bundle of chaos. It's a wonder I get any work done."

He led Jack along the corridor and into a room that looked part study, part playroom, and part dumping ground. The Labrador padded in after him and lay down on the rug next to the fireplace. Papers were piled high on either side of a large desk, books stacked in front of books and on top of books on shelves that bowed with effort. Cardboard boxes sat unopened in the corner of the room.

"We moved in six months ago, just before my daughter was born. Things have run away from us a little since then, as you can you see. Would you like coffee?"

"If it's no trouble," Jack replied, rubbing his hands together to try and get some warmth into them.

"No trouble at all. I'm afraid the heating is a little temperamental. It's unfortunate. University housing you see. I'll get a fire going soon enough." He disappeared into the kitchen. Jack heard him rattling about in cupboards and drawers, as if he was in someone else's house and didn't know where anything was. He emerged a few moments later with a tray and a pot of coffee.

"So, you want to check up on Stiglitz, eh? I don't know how much help I'll be. I haven't seen the man in over a decade. To be honest, I wondered what had happened to him. We all expected him to stay on the faculty, continue his research, find a professorship, and win a Nobel prize before he turned thirty. What's the role he's going for? I'm guessing it's something hush-hush?"

He tapped the side of his nose and smiled. Jack smiled back. The man's voice had a musical quality to it. His eyes a spark of mischief.

"It's standard procedure for us to vet personnel over a certain grade. All government departments do it."

"I don't believe they do, but never mind. Can you tell me what role he's going for?"

"I can't, I'm afraid."

Mendelson added three sugars to his coffee and stirred it carefully, so that the spoon didn't touch the sides of the mug.

"Well, he's a brilliant man. Not just in his field. He was interested in the arts too. Quite the actor when we were at university. But I don't expect you want to hear about the good stuff, do you? Stiglitz is perfectly capable of explaining that himself. And I'm sure he already has, or you wouldn't be considering him for whatever mysterious role it is you've got him lined up for."

Jack took a sip of tea. He tried to put the image of the burned body lying on its back out of his mind.

"Before we go on could I remind you that this is a confidential matter?" Jack said, sensing that Mendelson would be gossiping with his fellow academics at the first opportunity. "I have a paper I can ask you to sign confirming you won't discuss this meeting, but I assume I can rely on your discretion? It's not usually necessary."

"Of course," Mendelson said somberly. "I won't breathe a word."

"Thank you. I might take some notes. Stiglitz will not have access to these notes, or know the identity of any of the people we have spoken to as part of this process. Are you still happy to proceed?"

"Most definitely," Mendelson said.

"Thank you. I was given a whole stack of files on Stiglitz. His work history, time at university, that sort of thing," Jack said. "We're looking at whether there are any, how to put it, vulnerabilities. Character weaknesses. Things that could either make him psychologically unsuitable for the work he is about to do, or put him in a position where he might be blackmailed. For example, if he's a gambler or has some unusual sexual proclivity. We don't judge, it's risk assessment. We need to know what we're getting our hands on. We need to know if there's anything that could be used against him and compromise him." Jack took a sip of coffee, waiting to see if Mendelson would jump in with any stories, try and settle old scores.

He didn't. He sat in his chair and waited for Jack to continue, so he did.

"In the reports I've seen most people describe him in the same terms as you just did," Jack said. "Except for one. Professor Rauschenberg. It was a complaint file from Cornell University. I believe you and Stiglitz had some sort of disagreement. Professor Rauschenberg was the mediator. You accused Stiglitz of plagiarizing your work. It was on ice-core formation."

"Ah. Yes. I accused him of plagiarizing my work because that's exactly what he did," Mendelson said, his tone colder. "He had no compunction about using my results in his studies. He presented them as his own. When I challenged him, he made a counter claim, and accused me of doing the same thing to him. I reported him to the faculty. They investigated. But then they asked me to move to another lab. He was their golden boy. I think they knew he had certain eccentricities and they didn't want to upset him. All the same, they couldn't exonerate him. He was clearly in the wrong."

The floorboards creaked as Mendelson's wife descended the stairs. She appeared briefly in the doorway. The baby was on one arm and there was a slick of burped milk on her blue dress.

"Where's blanny? She can't get to sleep without it. I thought it was in the cot."

"I don't know, somewhere in the kitchen? This is Dr. Miller. Dr. Miller this is my wife, Elisabeth, and my daughter, Una." He turned back to his wife. "Would you mind awfully closing the door, it's government business."

"I could hear you from upstairs," Elisabeth replied. "Hello Dr. Miller. Is this about that man?"

Jack stood to greet her and grasped awkwardly for the hand that was holding the baby.

"Owen Stiglitz," Elisabeth continued. "If you wanted a private conversation you should have closed the door."

"It is about him, yes," Jack replied. "I'm here as part of the standard vetting procedures for government roles, we have to . . ."

"Yes, yes, yes. I heard all that too. The walls in this place are paper thin," she said.

The baby took hold of a lock of her mother's hair, wrapped it between pudgy fingers and pulled. Elisabeth's head bent to one side as she tried to untangle herself from the baby's grasp.

"Elisabeth and I met at Cornell when we were grad students. Elisabeth was studying applied linguistics."

"So you also knew Stiglitz?" Jack asked.

"Hardly. I knew of him. How can you know someone who doesn't bother to speak to anyone he thinks is below him? In fact, I don't recall him speaking to any women at all. I know what he did to Peter, though. The outrageous arrogance of the man. His belief that his work was so much more important. He wouldn't have been able to produce his thesis if he hadn't used your results. He stole your idea. It took you months to get over it. And the way the faculty favored him, it makes my blood boil just to think of it."

"It was only one idea, a long time ago. And, to be fair, he took it further than I'd imagined," Mendelson said, then more quietly, "the man is annoyingly brilliant."

Elisabeth shifted the baby on her arm. She wasn't finished.

"Did you tell him about the dog?" she asked.

Peter looked uncomfortable.

"I hardly think that's relevant to what we're discussing. It was all just hearsay," he said.

"That's not how you felt at the time."

"I know but I don't think it's fair to the man to bring it up now. It was a long time ago," Peter replied.

"What incident with a dog?" Jack asked, his interested piqued.

Peter stayed silent. Elisabeth looked at him.

"Well, if you won't tell it I will. Peter used to feed a stray dog, God knows what it was. Some sort of terrier cross. He ended up adopting it, kept it in his apartment."

"She was a sweet thing," Peter said. "Smart too. Much cleverer than this old bird here." He nudged the Labrador with his toe.

"Well, it wasn't long after he filed his complaint against Stiglitz that the little thing disappeared," Elisabeth said. "She was playing in the yard; there's no way she could have got out. You found her the next day at the side of the road, head was split open. Either a car had run over her or someone had hit her with a shovel."

Peter turned to Jack. "You can see why I didn't bother telling you about this," he said apologetically.

"At the time he was deeply upset," Elisabeth said.

"Of course I was," Peter replied.

Jack frowned. "How does this relate to Stiglitz, other than it happening shortly after you filed your complaint?"

"It doesn't," Peter said. "That's why I didn't bring it up."

"That's not how you felt at the time. You said Stiglitz had made a point of asking you how your dog was shortly after you'd found her dead. You said he'd never shown any interest before, and now he was asking after her straight after she had been killed and you hadn't told anyone she'd been killed because you weren't allowed to keep a dog anyway. You said he had a look in his eye, something strange that made you think he knew what had happened," Elisabeth said.

Peter twisted uncomfortably in his seat. He looked embarrassed.

"I was upset, like you said. It was an emotional time, the stress of the complaint was considerable. It was everything I'd been working for. I felt as if it was being snatched away from me. I'm afraid I'm not one for confrontation, unless absolutely pushed. Then I'm, well, I'm more emotional than I would like."

Jack nodded.

"Thank you. Thank you both," he said, turning to Elisabeth. "All perfectly understandable. This kind of detail is exactly what we're looking for."

"You're not going to record that I accused him of killing a stray dog, are you?" Peter asked, looking horrified.

"No, of course not. But the fact that we're having a conversation about whether or not he could, the fact that it seemed to you to be a possibility, gives an indication of the type of personality we're dealing with. It's clear he can be difficult. He appears to generate and thrive on friction, antipathy even. It's a concern, but not central to the kind of work he will be doing. I'm more concerned with whether he could be compromised. I don't think anything you've said would lead me to that conclusion. I take it he wasn't a gambler? Wasn't someone who would secretly accrue debts?"

"No, nothing like that," Peter said. He looked relieved.

His wife was still standing in the doorway. She shifted the baby to the other arm and said, "Well, I wouldn't want to work with him, for him, or employ him, regardless of his brilliance. It's not hard to be clever if you're born smart. It shouldn't be hard to be a reasonable, considerate human being either."

"Thank you. Is there anything else you'd like to add, Mrs. Mendelson?" Jack asked.

"I think I've made my views clear," she said. The baby had grown tired of pulling at her hair and was fixated on her ear instead, twisting the lobe with one hand and sucking her thumb. "Let me see if I can find the blanket," Elisabeth said, turning to go. "She needs to sleep. Eyes wide open all the time."

Peter poured himself more coffee, then got up and shut the door.

"We're not getting much rest at the moment," he said. "And six months cooped up with Una making goo-gah sounds means Elisabeth is hankering after some adult conversation. As you might have guessed."

"Not at all. And please thank her for being so frank. It's appreciated. One more thing I would like to ask you, if I may. You and he are both scientists. I know that covers a broad range of skills and disciplines, and I know that people choose that type of work for lots of different reasons, but I'd like to know what you think motivates Stiglitz. Did he express any political views? Was he a member of a political party?"

"Are you asking me if he was a communist?" Peter replied with a sly smile.

"Was he?"

"Not to my knowledge. He was interested in it, same way he was interested in everything, he was intellectually curious. But a man like that couldn't countenance the thought of everyone being equal. Which I believe is one of the principals he'd have to adhere to, or at least ensure everyone else adhered to."

"Aside from intellectual curiosity, what else drove him?"

Peter frowned. Jack sensed his reticence.

"Don't worry if it was a long time ago and you think he might have changed. I'm not looking for a definitive answer and nothing you say is going to impact my report in and of itself. To be perfectly frank, Stiglitz is the best candidate for this role by a mile. But it would be helpful to have some color. The lighter and darker tones that make up the overall picture of the man."

"Ok," Peter said. "I'll say one thing for him, which I suppose is why he didn't stick with academia, Stiglitz wanted money. It mattered to him. It matters to everyone, sure, but it didn't seem so important to the rest of us. He didn't talk much about his family, but it was pretty clear they were humble stock. He must have worn the same jacket every day for two years. Didn't own an automobile. Even his bicycle was a rusty old thing. It weighed on him. You could sense it. Made him defensive and arrogant, in spite of his obvious gifts."

"I see. I suppose it would. Thank you. It's been helpful," Jack said, getting up stiffly from the low armchair.

Elisabeth's voice called out from the kitchen, "You're welcome to stay for supper Dr. Miller."

"It's not a social call, dear," Peter shouted back. "Dr. Miller has work to be getting on with."

Elisabeth appeared in the doorway.

"There's no harm in being hospitable, Peter. Can I make you a sandwich or anything before you go? It's a long drive back to Washington."

"No, thank you. I've taken up too much of your time already." Jack put on his coat. In the hallway he noticed a small silver panel on the sideboard. He hadn't seen it before amongst the clutter of books and baby paraphernalia. He picked it up. It was a piece of foam board coated in silver foil.

"Insulation," Peter said. "Latest heat-saving technology, or so I'm told. I wasn't convinced by the salesman. They send these people out without the slightest grasp of thermodynamics. This man claimed he could save us up to thirty percent on our heating bills. I asked him what percentage of heat loss that entailed. Unsurprisingly he couldn't tell me."

"When did he visit?" Jack asked, feeling a sickness in the pit of his stomach.

"Couple of days ago, I think. We've been talking about getting it done since we got here, but we have to apply through the faculty. They have approved contractors. He just turned up on spec. I suppose it's the best time of year for them. Biggest sales period."

"Must be like Christmas," Jack said, his voice catching in his throat. "Did he leave a card?"

"You know, I'm not sure if he did. He seemed to lose interest when he sensed he wasn't going to make a sale directly. I said we could pass his details on to the faculty."

"Two days ago," Jack repeated softly.

"Are you ok? You look awfully pale," Elisabeth asked.

Jack turned toward her and Peter and smiled a grim smile.

"Yes, I'm fine. Thank you both for your time."

He hurried down the steps, his feet slipping on the ice. Ran through the yard and got into the car. His head was spinning, he could feel blood pounding through the swelling in his cheek. Two days ago? It was the same person he'd spoken to at the hotel yesterday. He knew it. He'd got here before him. He'd already been to see Peter Mendelson. He opened the car door and climbed inside.

"How'd it go?" Frank asked.

"*Fuck,*" Jack replied.

"Fuck?" Frank said, turning toward him.

"The salesman from the hotel. The one I told you about. He's been here too. Couple of days ago."

Frank stared at him.

"The one you said was obviously a salesman. Couldn't be anything else?"

"That's right."

"You're sure. Did they describe him?"

"No. But I know it's him. Has to be."

Frank put the car in gear and skidded away from the curb. A delivery truck was heading up the hill. It honked loudly at them as they slid out toward the middle of the road.

"How would he know to come here?" Frank said.

Jack ran a hand over his face, his breath coming thick and fast.

"I don't know. Mendelson's name was in Stiglitz's files, the ones Coty prepared."

"No one got to see that. Just you."

"My notebook too. I wrote it in there. That's the only other place."

"Ever leave the notebook anywhere?"

"No." Jack thought for a moment.

"What about when they burgled your apartment?"

"His name wasn't in it then. I didn't read Stiglitz's file till I got back from New York. I wrote it down after that. Before I met Chrissie. But at the police station. They took my briefcase. The notebook was in it."

"The police aren't behind this."

"The cop, the one you said was crooked. Maybe someone gives him the lowdown on Reverend Peterson, tells him to pick me up. Goes through my stuff while they're questioning me."

Frank thought for a moment.

"What?" Jack said.

Frank shook his head.

"I don't know. Let's see what Coty says. In the glove box is a Colt .45. You remember how to fire a gun don't you?"

Jack reached forward and opened the glove box. He took out the weapon and held it in his hand. It felt clumsily familiar.

"I have one back home," he said.

"Well, keep this one with you."

Frank accelerated over the bridge, through the old town.

"There's a bar over there. I'll call the garage where Archie works and warn him, then we'll let Coty know what's going on." Frank's voice was calm, but his hands were tight on the steering wheel. He pulled over.

"Archie is smart. And careful," Jack replied.

"These people are smarter," Frank said as he got out of the car.

29

Route NY 13
December 31, 4:00 P.M.

After Frank had made the call they drove back to Washington. He said Archie had listened, then told him if someone was going to come for him they'd better be prepared because he'd be waiting with his rifle.

"He's not going to run?" Jack asked.

"No. Guess he has a score to settle. I called Coty, too, asked him if he could send someone to keep an eye on Archie."

"What did he say?"

"He said he'd look into it."

"What does that mean?"

Frank shrugged. "It means he's working out whether there's someone he can send without drawing too much attention to what we're doing. Archie's still AWOL, after all."

The headlights of the car cut a semicircle of light out of the darkness. Frank drove fast. More so than usual. Jack turned on the radio and skimmed through the stations. He offered to drive, but Frank shook his head and stared ahead, concentrating hard as the blank expanse of gray fields and ink-black sky gradually gave way to the electric lights of the suburbs, to supermarkets, and parking lots. The well-spaced houses served by the capital beltway. Further into the city, the buildings grew taller, the roads got wider, grander. All the way to Thirteenth Street NW. Dinner with Coty and General Carvell.

The Ascot was decorated to look like an English country house. Or at least like an English country house in a low-budget movie. The walls were paneled in dark wood and hung with heavy red velvet drapes. Plaster statues of various Greek and Roman lovelies sat in alcoves, lit up coquettishly. Candles burned in faux antique lamps in the middle of each table.

It was busy too. The crowd formally dressed. Piped music crackled from hidden speakers and mingled with the lull of low voices. Cigarette smoke lingered over the tables, and the lights were dim enough to disguise whatever meat they were serving.

The waiter led them past a plaster statue of Venus and two of her best friends to a table in an alcove. Coty and the general were sitting opposite each other on green leather banquettes. A bronze lamp flickered in the center of the table. Coty's plate was empty, scraped clean. His guest was still eating.

"Dr. Miller, Frank. Glad you could make it. I'd like you to meet General Arthur Henry Carvell," he said.

Arthur Carvell stood up and held out his hand with a rigid formality. Jack took it. The general's grip was firmer than it needed to be. His palm dry and papery. He had neatly cut hair dyed an oily shade of black and eyes that were pale blue and clear as a glass of water. There was a leanness to him, as if he'd recently lost weight, a gap between his neck and the collar of his shirt. But he still looked like he could snap the table in two if it said something he didn't like.

"Good evening, sir, I'm sorry for your loss." As Jack spoke he realized how much he meant it. There was a close resemblance between father and son, so much so that Jack felt as if he was looking at an older version of the young man who stood proud and strong in the photograph. The boy who'd been commended for his service in South Vietnam. Who could keep everyone's spirits up with his games during the endless arctic night. Who needed things explained to him three times. The boy who'd seen ghosts in the tunnels under the ice.

The general nodded quickly.

"Thank you," he said. He was still holding Jack's hand. He pulled it toward him, leaning in and casting about Jack's face with quick, curious eyes. Jack pulled back and the general let go.

"I see what they did. I'm sorry about your face," he said. "I would never have used those men if I'd known what they were capable of."

Jack raised a hand to his chin.

"So that was you?" he asked.

The general sat.

"Not me, but as good as, I suppose."

"Have you eaten?" Coty asked. "Order some food."

Jack sat opposite the general. Frank eyed the seating arrangements.

"I'm going to take a table near the door, keep an eye on who's coming and going," he said, then turned to the general. "An honor to meet you sir." He shook the man's hand and threaded a path back through the restaurant.

Coty had a bottle of Meursault cooling in an ice bucket. He poured a glass for Jack, then topped up his own. The bottle was almost empty. The general's wine glass was still full from whenever Coty had last filled it, beads of condensation on the side. Untouched. Jack decided Coty was at least half a bottle in. He tasted the wine. Cold and dry. Summer and peaches. It didn't taste right on a winter night in a country-house themed restaurant in downtown Washington with a bereft general for company. It was like drinking cola with oysters.

"The general here's had a tough time," Coty said. "We're not the only ones trying to find answers. Turns out no one wants to talk about what was happening in Greenland. Even to him."

"Goddamn ridiculous," the general said. "They send me my son's remains in a box and all they'll say is that he was killed in a fire. Started by accident. It was an insult. I've known their commander for years. We trained together at West Point. He said he couldn't help."

He picked angrily at the meat on his plate. It was unidentifiable in the greasy brown gravy. Jack thought he could smell liver.

"I asked for the accident report. I asked for an investigation into his death. They wouldn't give them to me. I went above their heads. All the way to the chief of staff. In the end they gave me a one pager. Fire in a generator cabin, two deaths, one survivor. That was all it contained. I've no idea who sanctioned this goddamn Greenland farce but they aren't accountable to anyone. Whatever was happening there, whatever it was that caused my son's death, they've destroyed it."

"You think there was more to it than an accident?" Jack asked. He twisted the stem of his wine glass between finger and thumb.

The general stared at him as if he was an idiot, then spoke slowly and deliberately. "You read the private medical files from the clinic Henry stayed at last February, didn't you?" It was part question, part accusation.

Coty spoke before Jack could say anything. "I've been up-front with the general about the Agency's role here. And how you're helping us. I've explained that you're a medical professional. We're on the same side; we're all looking for answers."

"I read the files," Jack replied, thinking it was extremely unlikely Coty had told the general everything.

"Then you'll know very well the chances of this fire being an accident are somewhere between zero and nil."

The general stopped to chew some meat, he swallowed as if he was taking a pill. "You know about the incident last January? The complaint my son made about Owen Stiglitz, a noncommissioned officer?" he asked. "Henry told me all about it. The incident with the dog. I don't understand why no one would listen to him. Henry loved animals. Loved dogs." The general stared straight ahead, looking at some unseen point in the past. A silent movie playing out in front of him.

"Animals know when someone's good," the general said. "They feel it. It's instinct. One time when Henry was a kid the neighbor's bulldog broke into our yard and dug up the roses. Got a thorn in its nose. Right inside, it was all bloody. The dog was whining and scared, you couldn't get near him. Henry walked straight up to him and picked him up. He was strong, even as a kid. And this whining, snapping creature let him pull out the thorn. That was Henry. No hesitation. He was good. He was a good boy. He was a good man." His voice faltered. He waved a hand, as if to push away the past, to push back against the wave of memory. "Like I said, the chances of this being an accident are somewhere between zero and nil."

He cut some more of the liver, tearing through the soft meat with silver-plated cutlery.

"How did you find out I was working on this?" Jack asked.

The general shook his head as if the question wasn't important.

"Private detective. It was his contacts in New York that went to your clinic and your apartment. I didn't know you were working for the Agency and I certainly didn't know they'd beat you. I'm sorry. They shouldn't have done that. I would've never used them if I'd known. I was getting desperate. Hitting a brick wall. Never experienced anything like it. And my son. He was my son. They had a duty to be up-front."

Coty smiled. He could always pull a smile out of the air. It was his party trick, like pulling a penny from a child's ear.

"Jack understands, don't you, Jack? Not your fault."

"Sure," Jack said. He'd mind a lot less if his head didn't still ache when he lay down to sleep. The waiter appeared. Jack hadn't opened the menu yet. There was a smudge of crusted white sauce on the red leather cover. The pages listed meats and sauces and all sorts of heavy dishes he didn't feel like eating. He closed it and handed it back to the waiter, mumbling that he wasn't hungry, then turned to the general.

"Was your detective following me when I went to see Reverend Peterson too?"

"Who?" the general looked blankly back at him. His voice had an impatient tone.

"Former chaplain at the base. Took up a post in a parish on the out-skirts of Washington. He was at the base at the same time as Henry. For a few months at least."

"If he was following you he didn't bill me for it. And these people charge you for everything," he said. "They put five cents in a phone booth, call you to tell you, then expect you to pick up the tab."

"Problem with this town is there are so many shadows." Coty cast a warning glance at Jack not to say anything else. "We might not be able to tell you everything we find out, but we'll give you as much as we can off the record," he continued.

The general nodded and pushed away his plate.

"It's appreciated. And I'm sorry again for what happened in New York. Thank you for being straight with me, Coty."

He lifted a hand to his face and massaged his forehead with his finger and thumb. His eyes appeared to sink a little deeper into their sockets.

"I have to go, excuse me," he said. "Give my regards to Gill. The last couple of months have been very difficult. And I have a busy day tomorrow. This war is . . . different. Hard for the boys to tell who is on their side. It gets to them. Hard for us to know too. We're not exactly winning the public over. Here or in Vietnam."

He got up. Coty and Jack stood.

"Not at all," Coty replied. "Like I said, we're all looking for answers here. And it's been helpful talking to you."

The general nodded curtly, then waved at the waiter and told him to bring his coat. The waiter fetched it and held it out so he could slip his arms in, but the general seemed to find something offensive in this, and took it off him, putting it on himself. He drew the coat close around him. It swallowed him up, a size too big. Jack thought it had probably been the right size last winter. He watched him walk away, shoulders stooped.

"A fine man," Coty said. "Terrible what he had to go through."

"What did you tell him?" Jack said.

"Not much. Just high level. There may have been a security breach at the base in Greenland. We're talking to Connor as part of our investigation. We've seen the files, they don't give us the answers. He's not just angry about being kept in the dark, he feels hurt too. Betrayed even. You can see it. It's breaking him."

Coty pointed at the empty wine bottle and signaled for the waiter to bring another. The waiter arrived and presented the bottle to Coty. He glanced at it, eyes struggling to focus on the label. They watched in silence as the waiter extracted the cork, sniffed it, then poured a splash into Coty's glass. Coty swirled it round the glass and downed it. He nodded to confirm it met his high standards.

"What did you learn from Mendelson?" he said.

"I learned more about Stiglitz. It all points back to him. He gets stranger and stranger. And that thing with the dog with Henry. There's a precedent. Mendelson practically accused him of killing his dog with a shovel back when they were students. He wanted to, but he knew it sounded ridiculous. He was embarrassed when his wife brought it up with me, but you could see it bothered him."

"Two people thought he killed their dog?" Coty said. He stared at his wine glass, he looked as if he was searching for a punchline. "There must be a Chinese proverb in there somewhere. If two people accuse a man of killing their dog . . ."

Jack stared back at him. Coty's eyes were bloodshot, and there was a gravy stain on his tie. His stomach pressed hard against the buttons of his shirt. He raised the glass and drank, looking for inspiration. It evaded him.

"Then you're clearly some kind of fuckup," Coty said eventually.

"When can I talk to Connor?" Jack asked.

"Tomorrow morning. He's resting. They finally got the right blood in him."

Try as he might Jack couldn't sleep—even with the wine swirling through his body. He kept thinking about Henry's father, shrunken with grief. His coat now a size too big. And the reverend, in the river. He thought about whether he'd felt the cold of the water, or if he was already dead before he hit it. And Archie, hiding out in the cold, unaware someone was watching him, a sniper's rifle aimed at him through the trees. A shot. He falls. His body disappears under fresh snow.

He knew why Coty drank. He knew why he stayed out late, either at the office or in some bar. He knew why he worked all hours. The day clung to you, the unanswered questions, the fear, the casual brutality, delivered as easily as a period on typed report. You didn't want to take it home.

Was Stiglitz a spy, carrying out testing on American soldiers for his Russian paymasters? *The Russians.* The words knocked against the inside of his head with a hollow thud. An empty term. He knew what it meant, but he didn't really know what it meant. He imagined a Russian Coty, drinking vodka, staying out late, working himself to death at his desk for the sake of his secrets. Or a radio operator, wrapped up in a coat and scarf in a listening post on the Estonian border, hands curled around a mug of coffee, waiting for a short burst of radio waves from the base in Greenland he could decode and pass on. Thinking about going home.

And the insulation salesman. He'd seen him. Spoken to him. He was American—at least he sounded American. As authentic as anything else in that Bangor guesthouse. But he knew about Mendelson. And he'd visited him. And he could only have read the name in the notebook he'd left in his briefcase when the police brought him in.

Jack felt his skin crawl.

Who were these people? Where were they? Everywhere and nowhere, as far as he could tell.

He rolled off the bed and staggered to the door. He checked it was locked then reached into the pocket of his coat and took out the gun. He placed it on the bedside table and lay back down.

Tomorrow he would talk to Connor. Or rather, tomorrow Connor would talk to him. He would tell him whether or not Henry shut Stiglitz out in the cold, whether he burned the frozen body to try and cover it up. Whether Henry was acting out of paranoia and fear, or whether he was sane and rational and defending them both from a dangerous traitor.

A traitor someone was trying to protect, even after his death.

30

Walter Reed Army Medical Center
January 1, 9:00 A.M.

Frank drove Jack to Walter Reed. It had been three days since he'd spoken to Connor and the last time hadn't exactly been a success. Nor the time before for that matter. His reaction to the photographs had been unexpected, and indicative of a level of psychological trauma Jack hadn't anticipated properly. He had a clearer picture of him now.

He was a man who was used to being underestimated. A man no one had a bad word to say about. Someone who was relied on and trusted by the people he worked with. What was it Henry had said in his interview? *Connor could pretty much run the place.* He said he would take things apart to understand them. He'd done that with Stiglitz when he beat him at chess. And he knew what Henry had gone through. As he entered the hospital Jack looked around the reception area, checking to see if Chrissie was still there.

She wasn't.

He signed in. There were more people in the waiting area than last time. The hospital was filling up: visitors speaking in hushed voices.

A mother trying to contain a toddler with one hand—it was pulling away from her resentfully, stamping its feet—and rocking her baby with another. An elderly Black couple staring straight ahead, not noticing the small child. A young man pacing the floor, impatient, nervous. Jack looked at them all, seeking out the person who didn't fit. Or the person who fit in too well. The perfectly suited salesman. He couldn't spot the odd one out. He glanced at Frank, whose eyes were scanning the room, and spoke in a low voice.

"Who's your money on?" he asked.

Frank shrugged, but he didn't look at Jack.

"All of them," he replied.

The chief medical officer pushed through the swinging doors, trailed by two other doctors.

"Dr. Miller, good morning," he said quickly, handing a form to the nurse at reception, picking up another sheet and scanning it, not casting more than a cursory glance at Jack.

He didn't offer his hand and he sounded as if a good morning was the last thing he wished Jack. Jack stubbed out his cigarette and turned to greet him.

"How's the patient?" he asked.

The CMO didn't reply, he was still scanning the piece of paper he'd picked up. He passed it to the doctor with him, who glanced at it, nodded, and hurried away.

"We brought Connor out of his induced coma yesterday afternoon but kept him sedated," he said. Now going through another form, his little finger poised about halfway through the text. "This morning he had a small amount of solid food and some liquid. He passed fluid and was able to stand. I asked him specifically if he was prepared to see you. He confirmed that he was. If he'd said no I wouldn't let you in, no matter what threats Coty made. This way, please."

Jack followed the doctor along the corridor. He called the elevator.

"Third floor, recovery room C. He's not back on the ward yet. Ask the orderly for help if you can't find him. I'll be up to check that you're gone in half an hour. Don't let him talk any longer than that."

The doctor walked away. Frank watched him.

"Doesn't like you very much," he said.

"No," Jack replied. "It's not personal. If I was him I wouldn't let my patient be interviewed at all yet. Coty is very persuasive."

"Coty can make life difficult for people," Frank said. The elevator came. They rode it to the third floor, then followed the signs to the recovery rooms.

"I'll wait for you outside," Frank said, his eyes scanning the corridor.

Jack pushed open the door.

The curtains were drawn and a thin sliver of pale blue light cut across the parquet floor. Connor was sitting up, a drip attached to his arm. The radiator was on and the room was stuffy and airless. On his side table was a transistor radio, a plastic cup, and a jug filled with orange juice. His hands lay by his side and his head was at an angle, as if he didn't have the energy to hold it straight. Bandages held the dressings in place. They were wound tightly around his head, crossing over the bridge of his nose and his forehead, leaving only slits for the eyes.

Connor moved, almost imperceptibly. His head shifted toward Jack.

"No flowers?" he whispered.

Jack laughed. "Next time. How are you holding up?"

"Mostly I feel pretty numb. I don't know what painkillers they've got me on, but I've spent the morning on the ceiling. When my skin starts to tingle I ask them to up the dose. Pass me a drink, will you?" He gestured toward the side table.

Jack handed him a cup of orange juice with a plastic straw in it. Connor held it awkwardly in his bandaged hands and sipped slowly.

"I don't feel so bad," Connor said. "But maybe that's just the drugs. I'm not gonna die from this." Jack couldn't tell from his tone if he regretted the fact or if it gave him comfort.

"I'm sorry I showed you the photograph," he said. "I should have given you more warning, waited a while."

Connor passed back the drink and made a dismissive gesture with his hand.

"You weren't to know," he said. "Neither was I. Guess I've been trying to avoid thinking about certain things. It was tough, seeing them laid out like that. I felt like I had to escape. Escape from myself. I felt as if I should be there with them. I can't explain it."

"You don't have to," Jack said. "But if you want to try I'm happy to listen."

"Are you going to ask me the same questions again? Try and see what I remember?"

Jack nodded.

"We'll get to that," he said. "I've been kind of busy these last few days talking to people."

"People?"

"Someone who knew Stiglitz, years ago. I wanted to find out what kind of person he was. And a New York City fire chief who's got a theory on the fire. I spoke to Henry's father just last night, and Chrissie too. You know she's been waiting here in the building for you?"

Connor seemed to deflate slightly at the mention of her name. "They told me. I told them to tell her to go home."

"Well, it would have taken a lot to keep her away, because she was as determined as hell to see you when I met her. Listen," Jack said, leaning in. "Like I said before, I'm not going to pretend things are going to be easy for you. But if you're honest about what happened in the fire, and in the days leading up to it, then we can help you. I know you might want to protect Henry, I know you might think you're doing the right thing, but believe me when I say there are much wider issues at stake here. There are other factors, suspicions around Stiglitz, what he might have been doing, who he might have been doing it for, there are other things that are going to be taken into account."

"What kind of suspicions about Stiglitz?"

"I think you already know. The things Henry told you about. His fear that Stiglitz was making people sick. Now, what I'm going to do is tell you what we think we know about the fire. I want you to think carefully on it, and then I want you tell me what happened, ok?"

"I already told you . . ."

"I know what you told me. You heard yelling and pipes banging. You ran to the generator cabin. You struggled to open the door and you found the two bodies inside. Thing is Connor, it didn't happen that way."

He looked at Connor for a moment, waiting to see what his reaction would be.

"The photo I showed you had two bodies in it, Stiglitz and Henry," Jack continued. "But Henry was not much more than a pile of ash. Stiglitz on the other hand was lying on his back, arms and legs in the air. There's no logical explanation for why a fire would almost incinerate one body but not the other if they were both in there for the same amount of time. It doesn't make sense, not in a confined space." He paused and looked at Connor, trying to see his eyes through the dressings. Connor lay still. "The expert I spoke to said it wasn't possible that the two bodies burned in the same fire."

"What would they know?" Connor replied.

"Quite a lot, as it happens. They've seen a lot of fires. They said it didn't make sense. Couldn't have happened the way you described."

Jack paused, taking his time.

"He gave us quite a conundrum. He also gave us a possible explanation. What do you think that explanation might have been?"

Connor shrugged.

"Come on, Connor," Jack said.

"I don't know what he said," Connor replied. "How could I?"

"Alright. Makes no difference either way whether I say it or you say it. I was just hoping you might start talking. The expert suggested that the reason one of the bodies was still holding onto human form even after all that heat and fire, is because it was . . ."

"Frozen," Connor interrupted.

"That's right. But, of course, if that was the case, it would mean Stiglitz was dead before the fire started. And that would mean he wasn't killed in the fire. And that would mean either he died in an accident, maybe he got lost when he was outside in the storm and froze to death, or he was deliberately locked outside and froze to death. It would also mean either you or Henry set his body on fire."

Jack took his packet of cigarettes out of his coat pocket. He flicked one out but he didn't light it.

"From what I've heard, no one is exactly mourning Stiglitz," he continued. "In fact, if he was still around it's likely he would be under investigation for the very things Henry accused him of. So, if you have something to tell me, now's the time to speak. Because if you don't speak, we've got no way of knowing whether there was an accident, or whether you or Henry killed him."

He tapped the cigarette on the side table, put it to his lips.

"Hell, we've got no way of knowing whether you killed them both, Henry and Stiglitz. All we do know is that you're lying about what happened. Didn't go down the way you described. They didn't try and fix the generator. Not possible. Not unless Henry carried Stiglitz's frozen body all the way to the cabin."

Connor didn't say anything. His head sank so that his chin was on his chest.

"So, what happened?" Jack asked. "What happened to the three of you while you were trapped out there under the ice?"

Connor pointed at the juice. "Please," he whispered. Jack passed it to him. Connor held the cup clumsily between bandaged hands and took a sip. Then he nodded. His words came out slow.

31

Walter Reed Army Medical Center
January 1, 10:00 A.M.

Henry was a good guy," he said eventually. "A decent man. A leader. You could trust him, but when it was just the three of us trapped out there, I don't know, he changed. The plane that was meant to pick us up made three passes, tried to set down each time but couldn't. We watched it, all packed up and ready to go. You could see the lights on the wing tips moving all over the place as it came down, like a kid waving a flashlight. Almost flipped over on the third attempt. Henry was standing next to me, he was cussing. Getting more and more irate each time. In the end it bounced a couple of times on the ice then took off again and flew away. That was it.

"I had a shortwave radio pack I was using to talk to the pilot. It only worked within a couple of miles range. Less with the storm. The pilot was sorry. He said he'd come back. We just stood there for a few moments. He didn't come back. I guess he meant when the storm was over. The winds were getting even stronger. Whipping up around us so loud you had to shout.

"We dragged our gear back inside. It was dark in the base. Pitch black. The electricity was switched off. The only lights outside were for the runway, they were powered by a stack of batteries." Connor paused and shook his head. "And when I say runway, I mean half a mile of ice we cleared of drifting snow every time we needed to use it. I had a flashlight, so I led the way. It was damn tricky with all the junk we'd left in the base. No one was bothered what state we left the place in. It was going to disappear under the ice.

"I led us back down Park Avenue and through the tunnel to the rec room. That's where we set up. I left the flashlight on so we could at least see each other, but Stiglitz said that was dumb, we didn't know how long we'd be waiting so we should save the batteries. Henry disagreed. He said the storm would pass and they'd be back soon. That was their first argument. I played with the radio pack for a bit, but it was all static and I wanted to save the battery. Plus we were too far inside to get much signal. They'd packed up the antennas and the rest of the radio equipment from the comms room a couple of days before. The radio pack was all we had left.

"We sat like that, in the dark, for I don't know how long. Maybe an hour, maybe two. None of us really felt like speaking. Occasionally you could hear the metal or wood in the cabin make a cracking sound. It wasn't breaking, it was just getting colder. So were we. Funny thing, the colder you get, the harder it is to make decisions, so we just sat there telling ourselves they'd be back for us soon. We didn't know what the weather was doing, you couldn't hear anything from outside in there. The snow deadened all sound.

"Anyhow, I got tired of sitting around. For some reason the darkness made me feel dizzy, and the cold, it was coming in. As if the room was filling up with water. I didn't like it. I said I was going to power up the generator and get some light and heat on before we froze to death. I was joking. Not a very good joke. Gave me something to do anyway. I don't like sitting around.

"The generators were off the main tunnel. Before they put nuclear power into the base we had a whole series of them running continually. Tons of diesel stored to power them. They put the reactor in because of all the diesel we were going through. It wasn't practical to keep pulling hundreds of tons of fuel over the ice to the base. They'd left a couple of the older generators there. They tended to break down, no one was bothered about dragging them all the way back to Thule to ship to America. Lucky for us."

Connor took another careful sip of juice and drew a breath. The effort of talking was tiring him out.

"I rigged up a loop so we were only running power for three of the cabins: the kitchen, rec room, and one of the dorms. Any more than that and we'd go through the fuel too quickly. Took me a couple of hours and by the end of it my flashlight was barely working."

Jack nodded, listening carefully and making notes. "They were lucky you were there."

"They'd have got round to it eventually," Connor replied. "I went back to find the others. When I got back I could hear Henry and Stiglitz arguing. I don't know what it was about this time but they were still in the dark. I turned on the lights and told them to make me some dinner."

Connor lifted a bandaged hand to his face and touched gently at the dressings.

"Are you ok? Do you want a rest?" Jack asked.

"No, it's ok. I mean, it feels like something's stuck to my face. The doc told me the blood vessels are only just starting to connect to the new skin. It's like growing into a bandage."

"I take it there was still some food there?" Jack said.

"Plenty. Tins of stew, soup, tinned fruit. Hardtack. Half a ton of flour. Cartons of long-life milk. Like I said, the cleanup wasn't too precious. Sometimes it's like that. If it's not worth the cost of transportation then we leave it in place. They weren't going to fill a plane full of fuel and fly it out there in winter just to carry some tins of food back. I forget what we ate that first night. The stoves had gone, so it would have just been something cold out of a tin. We didn't have any bedding so we slept in our clothes. The floor was cold. I remember that." Connor became quiet, his shoulders dropped a little.

"I didn't sleep well," he said. "Just the three of us lying there, in the dark. In the cold. And Henry called out a couple of times. He didn't know he was doing it, but it woke me. Don't know if Stiglitz heard it too. If he did, he didn't mention it.

"I must've got some sleep because I woke about five A.M. and Henry and Stiglitz were both gone. Henry came back covered in snow. He said there was no let up in the storm. It was worse than the day before. We ate some biscuits for breakfast. Drank water. The pipes hadn't frozen yet; they were well insulated. Stiglitz came back after a while. Henry wanted to know where he'd been. Stiglitz was cagey. Said he'd just been doing some checks. *What kind of checks?* Henry said. Stiglitz just gave him one of those looks that said he didn't have to explain himself to anyone.

"There was nothing much to do but wait. Henry said he wanted to check the ventilation shafts. There were twelve. He didn't want them icing up. I offered to go with him, but he refused. I think he wanted some time alone. I wasn't too happy about it. The vents were spread out over the tunnels, an area of about four square kilometers above ground. You could easily get lost in a storm and not make it back. He told me he knew what he was doing. I guess he did. I couldn't stop him anyway. I was the lowest rank out of the three of us and even if I wasn't he'd have just done what he wanted.

"He was outside for almost an hour and when he came back he didn't look so good. He was pale and shaking. His lips had started to turn blue. At first I thought it was because he'd just come in from the cold but then he started burning up. I told him to rest. He didn't want to. I tried to get some water for him but nothing came out the faucet. Stiglitz had disappeared again so I couldn't get him to help. Henry was angry about that, asking where Stiglitz had gone. *What did it matter?* I said. He said he didn't trust him. He said I shouldn't trust him either. I told him to calm down and made a bed out of clothes. In the end he laid down for a while. I got suited up, went outside, and collected snow in containers. I left it to melt in our cabin. I have to say I would have appreciated a little help from Stiglitz. God knows what he was doing. I think he used to go for runs, do training. He came across as a little obsessive like that. He didn't bother to eat with me and Henry but he drank the water I'd collect. Henry told him to get his own. I said it didn't matter.

"Once Henry started getting worse Stiglitz seemed to be around a lot more. He'd sit there watching him. I found a chess set buried in the back of one of the cupboards and asked him to play. Stiglitz was pretty good. We played a couple of games to pass the time."

Jack looked up from his notes.

"Really?" he said, remembering what he'd read in Henry's file, Stiglitz's childish refusal to play again once he'd been beaten by Connor. Maybe the boredom of waiting for the storm to end had changed his mind.

"He beat me," Connor said. "He always beat me. I was distracted by Henry. I was really starting to worry for him. The fever wouldn't break. And he was having these dreams at night and during the day. He'd point across the room, say he could see someone, someone there, watching him. It was scary to witness. It sounded like he was having a relapse, the thing he had back in January last year. I mean, I'm no doctor. I don't know if getting ill like that could bring it on again, but I didn't like to leave him on his own.

"Thing is, someone had to go outside and check the vents. Stiglitz didn't offer to help. When he wasn't watching Henry, he did his usual disappearing act. Off into the tunnels. I don't know how he could stand it, walking those tunnels on his own. That place was silent.

"It must have been, I don't know, three or four days in. The fever finally broke. Henry seemed a little better. I gave him water and tinned fruit. He sat up. Began talking normally. Asking how long we'd been there. Saying he was sorry for not being able to help. Sorry for causing so much trouble. That was just like him, apologizing for not sharing the work. I said the storm couldn't last much longer. They'd send a plane for us any day now. We talked a bit about families, what we'd do when we got home. He was looking forward to seeing some daylight. I said I was, too, hell yes.

"Everything seemed normal. Normal given where we were. And then . . . he started saying someone was outside the room. I said of course they were. Stiglitz was off doing whatever it was he did. He was talking in a normal voice. No fever, just the same reasonable tone he'd been using to tell me about his family.

"He was saying someone was knocking on the door, wanting to come in. I listened, there was no sound coming from the door. It was just the two of us in there. No one outside. *Can't you hear it?* he said. I said no, there was nothing to hear. He started to look at me a little strange. He was shaking his head, saying, *No, Connor, don't tell me you're with them.* I asked him who exactly he thought I was with, given we were both sitting in the same room in the same damn base in the middle of an arctic storm. He wasn't listening to me, he was just staring at the door. He got up, he was still a bit shaky, and started pulling whatever bits of furniture he could find across the room and putting them in front of the door. I told him to go easy. It was like he couldn't hear me.

"Then Stiglitz turned up. Started pushing at the door and yelling to be let in. Henry looked absolutely terrified, I've never seen an expression like it. He just covered his ears. Asked me to make it stop. I said it was just Stiglitz. Henry was screaming, standing there in the middle of the room, hands over his ears, yelling like he was fit to burst. I was starting to feel a little afraid for myself. Henry was a big guy. I mean, I can take care of myself, don't get me wrong, but he was looking wild about the eyes, he was . . ." Connor paused. "He was capable of doing some damage. To me, to Stiglitz, hell, to the room we were sleeping in."

"And did he?" Jack asked. "Did he hurt you or Stiglitz?"

"No," Connor whispered. "Not that time. Stiglitz managed to push open the door and came in, asked what was going on. Henry just sat back down on the floor, hugging his knees close to him, staring ahead. *Don't let him in*, he said. *Don't let him in*."

The door to the recovery room opened. Connor stopped talking and looked up. The chief medical officer strode across the room. He cast a glance over Connor, placed a hand on his head and turned it gently, inspecting the dressings. Then he turned to Jack.

"Time's up, Mr. Miller," he said. "You've had your half an hour. In fact, you've had more, almost an hour. My patient needs rest."

Jack looked at Connor. He felt shortchanged, but didn't want to pull rank and insist on staying, not now Connor was being cooperative. He got up.

"I'll be back later," he said. "You get some rest. Anything I can bring you?"

"Cold beer would be good, if you can get it past this guy," he said, gesturing with one of his bandaged hands at the CMO.

"I'll do my best," Jack replied.

32

Walter Reed Army Medical Center
January 1, 12:00 P.M.

Jack pulled the CMO to one side as he left the room.

"He seems to be recovering well," he said.

"You mean he's cooperating with you," the doctor replied.

"No, I mean there's a change in his outlook. I'm wondering if his reaction to the photograph might've been beneficial in some way, a form of catharsis. It allowed him to focus on and react to the trauma he'd experienced in a way he hadn't been able to before."

The doctor stared at him coldly. "Well, it's not a procedure I'd recommend. Generally speaking it's best if patients don't try and pull off the skin we've just grafted because they're being questioned by a government agent about the deaths of their colleagues."

Jack stepped out into the winter sun. It hung behind the lime trees that circled the hospital grounds, their fine, bare branches spread fishbone shadows across the grass. Frank was leaning against the car, watching him. He pulled up the collar of his coat.

"You want to go back and brief Coty?" he said.

Jack shook his head. "Not yet. I'm going to talk to Connor again later. He's cooperating. I need coffee," he said. Frank was looking across the street. A woman on the opposite side had stopped under the awning of a café. She was standing in shadow.

"What is it?" Jack said.

"Get in the car," Frank replied, not taking his eyes off the woman. Jack got in. Frank slid into the front seat and started the engine. "Someone's watching you, trying not to be seen. Under that awning." He spun the car around in the parking lot and drove onto Georgia Avenue.

Jack stared through the window.

"There, you see her?" Frank said as they drove past. Jack twisted his neck.

The woman wore a woolen hat pulled over her ears and had turned her back to read the menu. The hem of her dress was poking out under the coat and there was a large leather suitcase at her feet.

"It's Chrissie," Jack said. "Connor's fiancée. Pull over, would you?" Frank cast a glance in the rearview mirror then pulled over. Jack got out.

"Hey!" he called after her. The woman had turned and was hurrying away, not looking at him, the heavy bag slung over her shoulder. "Chrissie, it's me, Dr. Miller." He ran toward her, placed a hand on her shoulder.

She spun defensively and said, "You can't make me leave. It's a public sidewalk. I'm perfectly within my rights to be here. I can be anywhere I like outside of that hospital."

Her blue eyes stared fiercely at him.

"I'm not going to make you leave anywhere."

"Oh, really?" Chrissie replied. "After I was thrown out of the hospital?"

Jack lifted his hands, his palms open.

"I don't know anything about that, wasn't me. Connor's been in and out of surgery. I just spoke to him."

Chrissie's lip trembled and she let the bag slip to the sidewalk. It sat there, crumpled.

Jack reached down and picked it up.

"Join me for a coffee," he said. "I'm going back to see him later today. I can pass on any messages."

"Does this mean he'll look like Connor again?"

Jack looked away. "No, he's going to look different. You'll have to get used to it. So will he. Come, let's get a coffee."

"Is he with you?" Chrissie said, gesturing at Frank, who was doing his best to look inconspicuous, studying the window of Lady's Fashions.

Jack turned and looked at Frank. So much for being discreet.

"He'll wait in the car."

They sat at a table near the back of the café. Jack ordered a coffee, Chrissie ordered a chocolate milkshake. "You saw Connor just now?" Chrissie asked, taking a sip of her shake.

"I did," Jack replied. "They brought him round yesterday."

"Did he mention me?" Chrissie asked.

"He needs time. He's got to process what he's been through," Jack replied, not answering the question.

"What has he been through? You told me there was a fire, he couldn't help the people he was with."

"It's more complicated than that. He was trapped at the base in difficult circumstances for seven days, with two men who . . . well, put it this way, it would have been easier if it was just him. They weren't exactly a help."

Chrissie chewed the tip of the straw, then took it out of the shake and placed it on a saucer.

"Any good?" Jack asked.

"Not bad. Not as good as the ones back home. A little too thick." She picked the straw up again and stirred the shake. "Did those other men hurt him?"

"No, I don't think so. They were difficult, though, for different reasons."

"Connor isn't a fighter. But he's smart. Super smart. And if anyone could survive being trapped out there in the ice it would be him. One time his pa caught him taking apart his console. They had a big old Magnavox. Connor had taken it apart to see how it worked, cleaned it up a bit so it sounded better, but his pa went crazy. Took a belt to him then threw him out. He wasn't no more than ten and it was midwinter. Midwinter in Wyoming is cold as hell, and their farm was about five miles from anywhere. You'd be cold-drunk in ten minutes. That's what happens. You go all sleepy and strange and freeze all over. Connor hid in the cattle shed for three days, sleeping with the cows to keep warm. Who would do that to their own child?"

"Sounds like his father wasn't fit to look after him."

"No, and the police wouldn't do anything when they found out. He told them he was disciplining the boy. No harm done. *No harm done!* He was lucky Connor lived. God knows what really happened to his mother. Died in childbirth, his father said," Chrissie stopped. She stared at the table. "He's strong. Inside. A survivor. He had to be. And I miss him. And I don't understand why he won't see me. It's not like him. Not like him at all. We've been together since high school. We tell each other everything."

"I'll tell him you're still here," Jack said. "Where've you been staying?"

"Downtown," Chrissie said, looking away.

"Don't they let you leave your bag at the hotel?" he said. Chrissie put her arms protectively around the bag.

"Of course they do. I just like to have it with me."

"Sounds like a nice place," he said, expecting a spiky retort. She didn't make one, she was too tired. "Listen," he said. "I can claim expenses. Talking to you is part of my work, so if you've got a receipt for the hotel I'll put it through the system. And if you want to stay somewhere where it's safe enough to leave your bag in the room, then change hotels." He took two twenty dollar bills out of his wallet and slid them across the table.

She stared at the money, then back at him, as if he'd insulted her.

"It's not charity and it's a not a gift. It's a legitimate business expense I can claim on your behalf. Find a decent hotel near the hospital. You know, if you were married the army might even pay for you to stay nearby so you could see Connor."

"Well, we're not. Because Connor was too damn busy making plans. And I don't take money from anyone, thank you very much," she said.

"You think I'm paying out of my own pocket to stay in Washington while I talk to Connor? Of course not. I can claim for the coffee and chocolate shake too. Come on, take it. The army should be putting you up anyhow."

She looked at the money, then back at Jack. He wasn't sure she believed him, but she must have appreciated the effort he was going to not to make her feel bad, because her fingers closed over the bills and she slipped them into her purse.

"I'm going to talk to Connor this evening," he continued. "You can call me at the Willard tonight and I'll tell you whether or not he wants to see you. Here." He took a card out of his wallet and scrawled the name of the hotel on it.

"I'll do that," she said, taking the card. Jack checked his watch.

"That's good. I better go. You take care," he said.

He left the café. He liked Chrissie. She was naïve but street smart, and she knew what she knew. She knew she was the best thing for Connor, and that was all there was to it. It was going to be a long and difficult recovery process for him, and he would need support adjusting to the world. He evidently had no family to help him. Jack stopped. A patrol car had parked in front of Frank's Ford, the red light on top spinning lazily, the engine still running. One officer was standing on the street, thumbs hooked over his belt, the other was leaning in at Frank's window.

"Everything alright, officer?" Jack asked as he approached the car. The policeman saw him and stood up straight, then walked round the car and stood in the way of the door.

"This your driver?" The policeman asked.

"He is."

"You need to move on. You can't stop here. What's your name?"

"Dr. Jack Miller."

"I need to see some ID."

Jack wanted to argue, but the day was too short. He took out his badge and showed it to the officer, who took it off him and peered closely at it. He read the ID number out loud, and the other cop wrote it down in his notebook.

"You can't stop here," he said.

"We're on official business," Jack replied.

"Oh yeah? What kind of business is that?"

"It's not something we can talk about."

"No," the policeman replied. "I can see that. I can see what kind of business you're doing. Taking out a young woman and buying her milkshakes." He turned to the other officer. "Apparently these two men are on official business. Something they can't talk about." The other officer nodded. "Official business for these guys is taking out a woman half their age. Maybe I should book you for soliciting. Come to think of it, maybe I should book her." He pointed at Chrissie, who had just left the café and was walking quickly in the opposite direction, bag slung over her shoulder.

"Maybe you should read up on probable cause before you do," Jack said. He didn't want to argue, it was like poking a barking dog with a stick, but he couldn't help himself.

"You're telling me how to do my job?"

"Someone needs to. Give it up, officer, or you'll be licking stamps and taking thumb prints for the next twenty years." He reached out and whipped his ID out of the officer's hand. Then got into the car and slammed the door.

Frank started the engine. The officer banged on the roof with his fist, then walked round to Frank's window.

"I see you again I'm booking you. I don't care if you're waiting for the goddamn president," he said.

Frank pulled away. Revving the engine.

"What the hell was that about?" Jack said.

"They're from the same department as the detective who pulled you in for questioning. Just trying to make life difficult."

"Really? They're still sore?"

Frank turned and cast Jack a sardonic look. "You never met a cop before?" he said.

33

Washington, DC
January 1, 5:00 P.M.

They drove downtown and stopped for a sandwich. Jack bought a six-pack of beer too. Connor wouldn't be able to drink but he might appreciate the gesture, and Jack wanted him to stay onside, to keep talking. They were back at Walter Reed in the early evening. The sun had slunk behind the trees that edged the parking lot and the Corinthian columns and white plaster portico that hung over the entrance were turning a tired shade of gray.

Jack showed his badge. Waited for them to call the CMO. Waited for him to arrive once he'd been called. He took longer this time. Spoke at length to two other doctors who happened to be passing. Then he turned to Jack and confirmed he could go and talk to Connor for no more than thirty minutes and that, once again, he would send someone to check on him when that time had passed.

He didn't accompany Jack to the elevator, so Jack made his own way to the recovery room. He peered through the doors of a couple of wards on his way. As wells as burn victims there were a number of amputees.

If he'd had more time he'd have liked to talk to one of the doctors about how they made it back from the battlefield with that kind of wound.

A doctor was in Connor's room, leaning over him, talking softly. He turned quickly as Jack entered, said a curt *good evening* and left. Jack watched him go. He was in a hurry.

"I brought you a present," Jack said, taking the six-pack out and holding it up for Connor to see. Connor eased himself up so he was sitting straighter and peered at it. The room was dark, just one small lamp on the side table that gave off a weak yellow light.

"Thank you," Connor said. Jack pulled a chair across the floor so he was closer to the bed. It made a scraping sound.

"You had some lunch?" Jack asked.

Connor nodded. "Food here's ok. Same as the military."

"Better than eating tins of cold ham and fruit salad I bet?"

Connor nodded. "And hardtack. There were boxes of the stuff. You dream of fresh bread."

"Before I left you were saying Henry wasn't well. He'd recovered from the fever but he was acting strangely." Jack checked his notepad. "You said he told you he thought someone was banging on the door when no one was there, and then he had a strange reaction when Stiglitz came in the room. He sort of crumpled and backed away."

"That's right. Weird thing is, I think Stiglitz kind of enjoyed it. It was like he had this power, like when someone's trained an animal."

"What did he do?"

"He didn't do anything much. Just watched him. But you could tell it pleased him to see Henry squirm. The poor guy. He had this look, like a child, like he didn't understand what was going on. *What's the matter, Henry?* Stiglitz would say. *Not feeling so good? I thought you seemed better.*

"Henry spent a day or so all curled up, just sleeping on the floor. Barely ate anything. I tried to talk to him, but I couldn't get much out of him. He was mumbling. No temperature anymore but he kept saying he didn't want him to come back. I don't know if he was talking about Stiglitz or if this was something only he could see.

"I just wanted the damn plane to come and pick us up. I mean, how long can a storm last? In the end I took the radio pack and went outside to see if I could send a signal, make contact, anything to hear a voice from the outside world. There was nothing. Just static. The wind was whipping snow in every direction. I went out further. I was desperate to hear someone. Sick of the place. I thought I was picking something up. Thought I could hear something. I don't know, maybe it was just that I wanted to hear someone, needed to hear someone, I was telling myself there was someone there. A distant voice, it seemed real. I tried talking but they didn't answer. So maybe there was no one there and it was all my imagination. Or maybe my signal was too weak to transmit to them.

"Anyway, I realized I'd gone further than I should've because when I turned round I couldn't see anything behind me other than the darkness and a thousand swirling flakes of snow. I had this sudden feeling of dizziness. I didn't know which direction I was facing, didn't know which way to go back. You can't use a compass out there. It's too close to the pole. I felt sick, you know that kind of panic, that feeling you've done something so stupid and it was the easiest thing in the world not to do and if you hadn't done it you wouldn't be in this mess? That's what I felt. Don't know how long it took me to realize I could still see my footprints, just about, leading back to the base."

Connor shook his head. "Pretty dumb, I know. But it gets to you. The darkness. The cold. I crawled back, face close to the ground. I was so scared of losing my way. I'd gone further than I thought. I was creeping back in the darkness and I couldn't shake the feeling that it would never end. I'd just keep crawling over the snow deeper into the endless night. Then I saw it. Or at least I felt it. The ground was slipping away from me. I was on the slope that led down to the entrance to the base. I felt happy. You know how I said I was dizzy before? Well, now I was dizzy with relief. I rolled over on the snow. Suddenly all that fear was gone. Everything was right again. The storm wouldn't last much longer. They'd pick us up soon, and maybe I even had heard something outside. Maybe there was someone nearby and they were already on their way.

"Those feelings didn't last long, because when I got back inside Henry was gone. I waited a while, thinking he'd gone to the toilet or something. Then I waited some more. It sounds bad but part of me just felt relief. Relief I didn't have to listen to him or look at him all curled up on the floor. He'd made his clothes into a kind of nest. I even helped him, giving him a couple of sweaters to make a pillow. That was how he'd been sleeping the last few days. I knew that I should go and look for him. But I kept putting off that thought. I was still warming up. I needed to eat something. He'd be back soon anyway."

Connor paused and turned his head toward Jack. "Do you think you could open one of those beers? Just a sip. That's all I want. It's hot in here."

Jack reached down and took out a bottle. He placed the cap over the edge of the bedside table and hit it so the top came off. He poured a small amount into a glass and passed it to Connor. Connor sipped slowly, then passed it back to him.

"I want you to know that Henry wasn't a bad person," he said.

"I know that, you already told me. And I've read his files. I know he wasn't."

"It's just that, what he did next, I mean. He wasn't well. I don't want to embarrass his family. Henry worshipped his father."

"I appreciate that. But for your sake, you need to tell me what happened," Jack said. "It's your life you need to worry about. Not Henry's reputation. Not how his parents will feel."

"Sure. Ok, well, I lay down for a bit. Guess I was tired. The cold sapped my energy and after coming back into the warm I just wanted to lie down, so I settled into my corner of the room, made myself as comfortable as possible. Told myself I'd just shut my eyes for a moment, then go check on Henry.

"I fell asleep. Not for long, only an hour or so. I was woken by Henry coming back. He seemed different. More purposeful, I guess. Striding into the room. I asked him how he was feeling. He just sort of laughed to himself. *Much better*, he said. He was blowing into his hands trying to warm them. He had some snow on his hair. I asked him if he'd been outside. All I got was a little nod. Said he was starving and went to get some food from the kitchen. I didn't know whether to feel relieved or worried. He asked me if I wanted anything to eat. I said, *Why don't we wait for Stiglitz, sit and eat together*. I was hoping they might be able to sort things out before we got picked up. No point carrying all that bad feeling back home.

"Henry shook his head. He said no, he wasn't going to wait for Stiglitz. I asked why. He said there was no point. At first all I thought he meant was he didn't care about the man, so why wait for him to get there so we could eat together? But he had a funny look about him. I said I was glad he was feeling better and maybe now would be a good time to try and sort things out. He said I didn't need to worry, he had sorted things out. I was worried, I can tell you. Henry was so calm.

"*Where is he?* I said. *Where's Stiglitz?* Henry just looked at me. *He's fine. You don't need to worry about him. We don't need to worry about him anymore.* I asked him what he meant. He said he meant what he said. We didn't need to worry about him. He laughed, then got on with making his dinner, scraping meat paste all over hardtack. I said I was going to find Stiglitz. This was getting ridiculous. They needed to sit down and talk it out. He dropped his food and came and stood between me and the door. Told me I wasn't going to look for Stiglitz and to sit back down.

"*You don't need to worry about him,* he said again. I asked him why, I asked him what he was talking about. He smiled again, that strange little smile he'd been doing and said, *He went outside.*

"I wasn't sure what to say. There was something about the way he said it. There was more to it. *What do you mean he went outside?* I said. *What's he doing out there?* Henry just shrugged and said how should he know? But there was something in his eyes, a kind of smirk, a secret. I didn't like it. I told him to get out of my way, I was going to find Stiglitz. He didn't move.

"I went to push past him and he pushed back and the next thing I knew I was out cold. Didn't even see his fist it was so quick. That's if it was his fist. It felt a lot harder. He must've had something heavy in his hand.

"When I came to he said he was sorry, kept saying how bad he felt and asking if I was ok. He'd even made a cold press for my head from ice in the tunnel wall.

"I said I felt alright. He blamed his illness, and being cooped up inside. Said he couldn't stand it here. He looked really sorry. Really upset. He kept saying I was his friend, and he shouldn't have done that.

"I didn't realize how late it was but it was already close to midnight. I'd been out cold for a few hours. My head felt like it was splitting. He got me a cloth and a jug of water. I washed the blood off my face and neck. Then he got me some food. More meat paste on crackers. I was so sick of it. Kept asking if I was ok every five minutes. I said I was fine. I wasn't fine. And the fact that Stiglitz still hadn't come back wasn't making me feel any better.

"I asked where he was. He said we should rest. We could look for him in the morning. I didn't like that. Not if Stiglitz had gone outside. If he was out there in the storm we needed to get out there, we could put on the runway lights, something that would help him. I don't know why I was saying all that. I guess I just didn't want to face up to what was happening. If he'd been outside since before Henry knocked me out, well, there wouldn't be much point in looking for him.

"In the end he agreed. Think he got tired of listening to me going on. We got suited up. Found a couple of extra flashlights. Went out through the main doors. We used rope to stay connected to each other. I led the way. Henry's line went all the way back to the base so we had an anchor. The lights from the runway glowed under the snow. You know how some kids read under the cover with a flashlight? I used to do that, comics mainly. But it looked like that. It was good to see them switched on. Made me think a plane would be coming in. Someone would get us.

"Stiglitz wasn't anywhere near the entrance. We swept the area with our flashlights, out to about half a mile. I suggested we try the escape hatches. There were eight of them. They came up from the tunnels. I thought maybe he'd tried to get in again through one of those. Henry wasn't keen. They were spread out over the site and they were almost impossible to see. I said we had to. We couldn't leave him. We doubled back toward the base, into the wind. You had to keep your head down, your eyes almost closed. You could feel the wind trying to find a way through your coat, pulling at the seams with cold fingers, pressing against your eyes.

"We didn't have to go far. My flashlight picked up a shape, a bump in the snow. I ran toward it. Tried to anyway. I crouched down. Reached out. There was a little black piece of material peeking through the snow. I brushed the snow off. Stiglitz was all curled up like a baby. He must have been desperate to try and conserve heat. He had no chance. He was like a block of ice, solid.

"I just wanted to get him back inside. My brain kept saying he'd be ok. We just needed to warm him up. It was like moving a piece of furniture. He didn't even have shoes on. Wasn't wearing a coat either.

"I started shouting at Henry, trying to make him hear me over the wind. What the hell had happened? Why was he outside without any shoes on? Without any gloves? Not even wearing a goddamn coat? How long was he out there?"

Connor paused. He was breathing deeply. His shoulders rose and fell with each breath.

"You ok?" Jack said. "Want a drink or something?"

Connor shook his head, staring straight ahead. He continued. "We laid him out in the main tunnel. Henry just looked at the body like it was nothing, not a person. And then he smiled. Not at me. He was smiling at Stiglitz. He was happy. Happy to see him curled up like that, happy to see how he'd died, his body all clenched up, face twisted, his eyes frozen shut.

"It scared me, the way he looked at him. We stood there in the tunnel looking over this body. *We need to tidy this up*, he said. His voice was calm. Sounded like he was asking me to help him get dinner ready or clean up the yard.

"I asked him what he meant when he said 'tidy up.' He just frowned, crouched down, and tried to get his hands under Stiglitz's arms. Told me to pick up the legs. He said they'd be here soon, and we didn't want anyone seeing the body. *No way we can explain this.* He shook his head and kind of laughed. Kept saying 'we'. I didn't like that. Far as he was concerned we were in it together. I don't know how he figured that.

"I bent down to lift Stiglitz, and we picked up his frozen body once more. I figured Henry was just planning to hide him in a tunnel somewhere. We carried him through the base, and you know what? Henry was whistling. He was whistling like we were strolling through the park on a summer day. I asked where we were going, he said not to worry. I'd find out soon enough.

"I keep going over in my head why I went along with it. Why I just carried the body. Why I didn't stop Henry. Make him listen to me.

Hell, I could've pulled a gun and told him to go back to the rec room and sit and wait till we were picked up. Truth is I knew there was no reasoning with him. I knew that any confrontation would turn ugly. I knew I didn't have it in me to pull the trigger. And I still didn't want to believe it was actually happening. It was like a dream. All those days trapped underground and now this.

"We carried that body to the cabin with the generator. Almost half a mile through the ice tunnels. We set it down inside. Henry was still in his own world. Spring in his step. No regrets. I could see everything he was doing made perfect sense to him. I guess I knew by then what he wanted to do.

"Henry dragged Stiglitz toward the generator. Then he opened a jerry can and threw diesel about. I was staring at the body, like some kind of idiot. I was there but I didn't feel like I was there. Didn't feel real. I remember thinking I liked the smell of diesel. That was the thought that ran through my brain. Crazy."

Connor paused. Drew a breath.

"I turned to face Henry, and he was pointing a gun at me. *Sorry, Connor,* he said. *You got to stay here too. You got to stay with him.* His eyes were welling up. *Otherwise they'll know. They'll know it's not right.* He had a lighter in his hand. He flicked it open.

"I yelled back at him to drop the gun. I was screaming all sorts. He took a step toward the door, gun still aimed at me, and dropped the lighter.

"*You got to stay here. I'm sorry. I am. Why couldn't you leave it? Why couldn't you just leave him outside?* I don't know what was going on in that brain of his, but it was misfiring something crazy. He was crying too. Crying as the fuel came to life, turned into a blue flame sliding all over the place." Connor shook his head.

"Whatever had been holding me back was gone. Something snapped. Suddenly it wasn't all happening to someone else. It was happening to me, and there was no way I was going to be trapped in that room and burn up with damn Stiglitz. I lunged for him, he was only a couple of yards away. He wasn't expecting it. He fired, but I was moving quick and I was already on him when he pulled the trigger. He fell back. The shot went wide. There was a whoosh, I turned, and it felt like something had stripped the skin from my face. The fire was everywhere. All over my hands. They were in the blue flames on the floor. I was scrabbling to my feet, trying to get up. I just wanted to get out. I could feel the heat all around me. I tripped over, fell through the door and onto the boards on the ice. The pain in my hands and on my face, I can't describe it. I was pressing them into the ice wall of the tunnel, trying to cool them.

"I looked over my shoulder, thinking Henry would follow. I picked up an ice pick in case he came for me. He didn't. He must have knocked his head when he went down. I tried to get closer to the cabin, see if I could pull him out. I couldn't get near. It was white hot. Went up like a furnace. I fell back, tried to get as far away as I could, crawling down the tunnel. Didn't make it very far."

Connor paused and looked at Jack. His breath coming thick and fast. "That's all I got," he said. "After that I passed out. Woke up in this place three weeks later."

His head fell back against the pillow. Jack stood and placed a hand on his shoulder.

"You did good," he said. "You did what you could."

"No one's going to believe me. It's my word against Henry. Farm boy from Wyoming versus a war hero son of a general. And I'm the only one alive. They're not going to want to hear my story. They're going to say it didn't happen that way. That's why I lied, why I said it was just an accident. The two of them caught in a fire, trying to fix the generator. I thought it would be best. Easiest. Doesn't matter anymore, does it? Both of them are dead. I didn't stop it. Couldn't."

"I wouldn't be so sure about them not believing you," Jack said. "And you mustn't blame yourself for what happened. I know how it feels." Jack paused, looked at Connor lying in bed, the bandages on his skin.

"How can you know?" Connor spoke in a harsh whisper.

"I know what it feels like to blame yourself for the way things turned out. When my wife died I couldn't let it go. The idea I was in some way responsible. But you have to, you have to learn to live with it and not let it get to you. And when it comes at you, because it will, you just have to think on something else. Something good. Something real. Don't let it drown you."

"What happened to your wife?"

Jack hesitated, uncertain how much of his own life to reveal. Connor stared past him, he looked helpless. "Car crash. Some dumb kid drove straight at us. I'd had a fight with him in a bar earlier. I know it was all on him, his decision, his hate, but it's hard. Because things would've turned out differently if I didn't act the way I did. If I hadn't knocked him down."

Jack stopped, aware Connor was now staring at him. For a second he thought he caught something in his eyes, a strange look, almost like a look of pleasure. Then it vanished. Connor nodded.

"Thank you," he said.

"There was nothing else you could have done. You rest now." Jack looked at him a moment longer, wondering whether to tell him that Chrissie was still in Washington, hoping to see him. He decided he should.

"Chrissie is still in town," he said.

Connor looked up.

"Is she? I told them not to let her into the hospital. I thought she'd go home. She should just go home."

"It might help if you saw her."

Connor shook his head.

"I don't want her to have to deal with this, with me in this state, with whatever investigation they're going to do once you hand in your report."

"Don't worry about the investigation. For what it's worth, I think it would be beneficial for you to see her."

"No," Connor said, shaking his head. "I don't want *this* for her." He held up his hands, as if that was enough to explain what he meant.

34

Langley, Block B basement
January 1, 10:00 P.M.

Jack didn't go back to the hotel, instead he asked Frank to drive him to Langley. He wanted to type up his report while it was still fresh in his head.

He took off his jacket and hung it over the chair, then took out his notes. He was feeling better than he had in days. His head lighter. It wasn't just the fact that he'd be able to get back to his normal life, or because he'd finally got the truth out of Connor, it was because he felt as if Connor had made progress as a patient. And it felt good to be part of that.

He placed his hand under the lamp on his desk and let the warmth from the bulb warm it up, before massaging it and beginning his lop-sided typing. He could understand why Connor had lied, firstly about not being able to remember and then spinning a story about an accident.

As he'd told Connor, what had happened in the seven days they were trapped under the ice was part of a much bigger jigsaw. There was more to it than Connor could see. There was more to it than Jack could see, but it was now up to Coty to investigate Stiglitz and determine what he'd been doing, and who he'd been doing it for.

He wrote his report, set out everything Connor had told him. Cross-referenced it with his interviews with Reverend Peterson, Archie Bell, and Peter Mendelson. In his opinion Stiglitz had administered some form of psycho active drug on four of the soldiers stationed at the base in December last year, with the goal of studying the extent to which such substances could be controlled and potentially weaponized.

Of the four, Henry was the only one who had returned to the base. He had set aside his suspicions about Stiglitz, presumably out of concern for his own career. But it was clear from Connor's testimony that he had suffered a reoccurrence of those hallucinations during the storm. It may be that he grew suspicious of Stiglitz, his disappearances, and Stiglitz poisoned him as a form of preemptive action. It may be that the stress of being trapped under the ice brought those fears back to the surface without any outside intervention. Or it may be that Stiglitz poisoned him for sport, to watch him fall apart. Jack couldn't discount it.

He finished typing at three in the morning, sealed the file and marked it for Coty's attention, then went back to the hotel, ordered a fine single malt on room service, and slept better than he had done in days.

The next day he woke at eight, showered, and took breakfast in the hotel's French brasserie, Frank still watching from another table. A fresh pot of coffee and blueberry pancakes to start the day. He doubted whether anyone in France had ever eaten blueberry pancakes for breakfast but having tasted them he decided they probably should. Chrissie had called the hotel and left her number. He went back to his room to return the call. It wasn't easy. She kept saying she couldn't understand why Connor was being like this. It wasn't like him. He tried to reassure her, told her Connor had made good progress. She said she had to see him. He should at least have the decency to tell her he didn't want to see her himself, after she'd been waiting for him all this time. And not just in Washington. The years she'd put on hold. She sounded determined. She said she was going to go to the hospital again. Try and make him see sense. He told her there was no point, Connor needed more time. But even as he told her he realized nothing he said would make any difference.

Frank drove him to Langley for a debrief with Gill and Coty. It was ten in the morning by the time they got there. Coty and Gill were working through stacks of papers, spread out over a conference table in Gill's office. Pages from flip charts were tacked to the walls with names, dates, and locations written on them. Stiglitz's name at the center. Arrows pointing outward, red lines looping hopefully across the pages.

It looked like they'd been at it some time, sleeves rolled up, collars loose. The room was stale with smoke and a crippled cigarette trailed its final breath over the side of an ashtray. They barely acknowledged his arrival.

"You look busy," Jack said.

Coty and Gill exchanged a glance. Coty said, "I read your report first thing. Good you got Connor talking. Finally. We've been collating the projects Stiglitz has worked on or been involved with since he joined the military. It'll need a specialized team to go through it. Ring-fenced. We're working out how much damage he might have done during his career. Never mind what he did at the base in Greenland."

"Have you told the military?" Jack asked.

"Not yet," Gill said, standing up straight and stretching out his back. He placed his hands on his hips. "We'll keep it quiet a while. We'll have a better shot at working out how far this goes without their interference."

Jack nodded slowly. This wasn't his world, this place of second guesses and obfuscation. It was enough for him to get to some kind of truth and hope the patient could use it to move forward.

"Is Connor in any danger?" Jack said.

"No, we're going to put the word out through the embassy channels," Gill said. He picked up the cigarette that was hanging over the side of the ashtray and stubbed it out. He flicked the last one out of his packet and lit it impatiently.

Jack stared at him, not comprehending what he meant by *embassy channels*.

"The chaplain was part of a clean-up job," Coty said by way of clarification. "They were tying up loose ends. Trying to delay us finding out Stiglitz was one of them. So were the soldiers at the asylum. Cover up what Stiglitz was doing. But there are certain diplomatic channels we can use to make clear that this is no longer necessary. I've already set that in motion."

"So what, you just talk to someone at the Russian embassy and tell them to back off?" Jack said.

Coty sniffed impatiently.

"Not in those words, but yes, that's how it goes down," he said.

"They took out two servicemen, maybe three if they've found Archie, and a former army chaplain, all to protect Stiglitz?"

"He was a key asset," Gill replied.

"Even after he was dead?"

Gill turned his back and walked to the window, puffing on his cigarette. Coty ran a hand through his hair, he looked half-apologetic, half-irritated.

"Once a spy is uncovered, you question everything they worked on. You check everyone they worked with. Doesn't matter if they're alive or dead," Coty said. "You rebuild systems and introduce new passwords and security. Stiglitz's handler would have wanted to protect him for as long as possible, that way the intelligence he passed on would stay live. That's why they've been following you, trying to work out where you're going, who you're talking to."

"And the work he did for them at the base, the drugs he gave the soldiers. You're not going to tell the army?"

"No. Not yet. We need to understand what else might be compromised. Stiglitz was a law unto himself. Based on your interviews with Mendelson, Archie, and Connor, and the transcript of the interview with Henry, I'd say he probably enjoyed this part of his work a little too much."

"And the dogs."

"Yeah, that is pretty fucked up," Coty replied. "I don't know how he got through his psych assessments. You'd think someone would have picked up that he wasn't quite right in the head."

"He got through them because he knew how to manipulate people, how to play a part. He was smart. Dangerous too," Jack said. "If it's ok with you I'd liked to be involved in Connor's follow-up treatment. As far as possible. We've built up a degree of trust that would lay a good foundation for future therapy. And he's going to need a lot of help."

Coty stared at him blankly. It occurred to Jack that follow-up psychiatric treatment for Connor was nowhere on his radar.

"We'll see," Coty said, doubtfully. "Here." He reached for a file and handed it to Jack. "The autopsy on Stiglitz. Came in last night. He was buried upstate. The ground's cold so he was in pretty much the same condition as when they brought him back from Greenland. I had a quick look through it. I can't understand most of it but it supports Connor's testimony. Identifies enlarged cell spaces within subcutaneous tissue. Which they say could indicate he was frozen before the fire started. They also examined the lungs for evidence of smoke inhalation. The left lung was too damaged to reveal anything conclusive, but the right lung was more or less clean, which is consistent with him being unconscious before he was burned. Taking those two elements together, they've concluded he was dead before the fire started, and acknowledge that there is cell damage consistent with the effects of freezing on human tissue."

"As we thought," Jack said, scanning the summary.

"That's your copy," Coty said. "If you still want it."

Jack slipped it into his briefcase.

"I do. I'd like to see how they ran the tests. I'm going to pick up my things from the hotel and then head back to New York. I take it you don't need me anymore?"

Coty and Gill had returned to the papers they'd laid out on the table. Their attention already focused on finding out how much damage Stiglitz had done in the course of his career. Coty looked up as Jack left.

"We'll be in touch if we do," he said.

35

Langley, Virgina
January 2, 10:30 A.M.

Jack left them to·their clouds of smoke and files. He was pleased to shut the door on them, to leave it all behind. His work was over. It looked as if theirs was only just beginning. Frank drove him to the airport from the hotel. He was quiet most of the way. It was the same look of concentration he'd had when they drove back from Ithaca.

"You've set something in motion here," he said as they pulled onto the highway. "They had their suspicions but what Connor said has confirmed it. It'll take months for them to work through it. They have to unpick everything. Everything Stiglitz touched. And then there's the fact that he was running a live clinical trial for the Russians using US servicemen as guinea pigs. It looks bad for the army. So bad I can see why Coty and Gill don't want to tell them. But it's not so great for the Agency either. The soldiers evacuated from the base were killed on US soil at the institution in Kentucky. Archie, too, unless he's managed to get the guy first. And the chaplain."

"Didn't Coty send someone to check on him?"

"He did but Archie was gone."

Jack shook his head and lit a cigarette. He breathed in the smoke, then wound down the window and flicked it onto the tarmac. He didn't want it after all.

"Yeah," he said. "Not good."

"You don't know the half of it. The moment you present a report that indicates a serious failing in another department you might as well prepare yourself for war. Except that war with a nation state is probably shorter and less messy."

He pulled up outside the airport.

"Coty's pleased with your work," he said. "Did he tell you?"

Jack thought for a moment.

"Not in so many words," he said.

"He's pleased. So is Gill. I just thought I'd let you know as it probably wasn't obvious from their faces."

Jack had a row to himself on the flight back. He took off his jacket and stowed it in the locker. He opened his briefcase and took out the autopsy report. It was only three pages. He was interested to find out how they'd measured the cell size to determine the extent of the tissue damage, and how this compared with tissue that wasn't frozen.

The first page summarized the state of the body. He skimmed it and read the report on the cell damage and lung toxicity. As Coty had said, the electron microscope had shown enlarged spaces between the cell walls. They'd included two cross-section diagrams. Referenced a number of other studies. It was good work, thorough but concise.

Cause of death was stated as unknown. Other than the burns, there was no sign of trauma, no damage to the skeletal structure.

Jack decided he needed to buy Nate a beer. Or several. He was the one who'd come up with the theory that one of the bodies had been frozen, and he'd taken it on himself to do the background work, reviewing the fire investigation reports.

The plane taxied onto the runway, the propellers spinning, the engines loud. The sky was low and overcast. He found himself thinking about Chrissie. It would take time for Connor to adjust to his injuries. He hoped they could find a way through it, and if he didn't want Chrissie to be a part of his life he hoped he'd find the courage to tell her himself.

He was about to put the file back in his briefcase when his eye caught one of the details in the description of the body on the first page. The report listed the size, weight, and approximate age of the victim, noting that the amount of damage made it difficult to give precise figures. Next to "height" they'd written *approx 6 ft 1 inch*.

Jack read the line again. *Approx 6 ft 1 inch*. Tall. Stiglitz hadn't struck him as tall. He closed his eyes and tried to remember the photograph . . . he was outside the labs at Cornell with Mendelson. If anything, he was smaller than Mendelson. How tall was Mendelson? He didn't remember looking up to him when he stood on his doorstep. Come to think of it, Mendelson was slightly shorter than him. Couple of inches at least. Maybe six foot. Which meant, as far as he could remember from the photograph, that Stiglitz was under six foot. Unless Mendelson was standing on a step. He couldn't remember reading anything that described Stiglitz's height. And the autopsy only said *approximately* six foot one. It could be off by an inch or two, given the state of the body.

The plane taxied to the start of the runway. He could feel the wings shudder as the cross wind got under them. He read through the second page more closely. It described where they had taken tissue samples. It stated that the right shoulder had provided a useful place for harvesting tissue, due to the thickness of the deltoid muscle. The report noted that this was typical in both infantry men and athletes, particularly football players, who tended to build up significant muscle mass in this area.

Jack stopped reading. Stiglitz was no infantry man and he was no athlete. He was a noncommissioned officer. He hadn't been carrying a rifle around the parade ground for the last five years, or through the Vietnamese jungle. He didn't have well-developed shoulders. He was a slight man. He was a slight man who was under six feet tall and was used to working in a lab or at a desk.

But that wasn't what the autopsy said.

Jack blinked, trying to take it in, to keep up with the conclusions his brain was racing toward.

Who was it? It sounded like Henry. Was it Henry?

The physical description matched him. But that didn't make sense. Henry was the other body. The body that was hardly there. Burned away to ash and bone. None of it made any sense. He read it again. And again.

The plane was getting ready to take off. The props spinning. Jack tried to stand, hands on the arms of the seat, pushing himself up. He didn't know where he was going, barely knew what he was doing. He just knew he needed to get up, to move. Get some air. He couldn't. The seatbelt. It was holding him down. He pulled at it to release it and felt the plane shudder as the engines dug deep and raced to takeoff. The plane lurched forward, accelerating along the runway, the movement pushed him back into the chair. The world outside blurred, spinning past.

Then the strange surge forward as its wheels left the ground, the feeling that there was nothing solid beneath him, that he was in another place now, pushing his way through air that pushed back at him, resisted him, flowed under and over him, thick as water.

It wasn't Stiglitz. The body that had been frozen, the body that was dead before the fire started, it wasn't Stiglitz. What had Connor told him? Henry had killed Stiglitz. He had shut him outside. Let him freeze to death. Carried him into the generator cabin and set fire to him.

It wasn't true. It wasn't Stiglitz. Stiglitz wasn't frozen.

His chest was tight. He was struggling to breathe. Struggling to think what that meant. What it meant for everything Connor had said.

The plane climbed higher, leaving Washington far behind, leveling out above the gray clouds. He felt as if he was sinking.

"Is everything ok, sir?" The stewardess appeared beside him. She looked concerned. Jack took a handkerchief from his pocket and dabbed at his forehead. His eyes were struggling to focus. He looked across at her. All he saw was the blue of her uniform, a dash of pale pink in the scarf around her neck. He wanted to speak. Couldn't find words.

"First time in the air?" she asked, passing him a glass of water.

Jack took it and drank a few sips. He shook his head dumbly, passed the glass back to her.

"Would you like me to see if there's a doctor on board?"

"I am a doctor," he said weakly.

"Well, if you need anything just let me know."

Jack nodded, cleared his throat. "Ok," he muttered. When she'd gone he stared blankly at the file. He raised his hand, which seemed to be made of lead, and placed it on the report, under the section he'd just read. He focused on his forefinger. The world was reforming, the words disentangling. His forefinger had a small cut running across the top knuckle. He hadn't noticed that before.

He read the words again, and they said the same things they'd already said to him. The frozen body wasn't Stiglitz.

36

En route to New York City
January 2, 12:00 P.M.

The plane stayed in the air while the world beneath him fell apart. He was flying back to New York but he might as well have been flying to a different country. He stared at his watch. The hand that counted the seconds seemed to get stuck on each movement, reluctant to give way to the next.

Jack tried thinking, but his mind was fogged. If that body wasn't Stiglitz, it must be Henry, and the other body was Stiglitz, and the whole story Connor had told him was nonsense. More lies. Why? Why would Connor lie? He'd sat there and he'd told him in detail everything that had happened, from Henry getting ill to shutting Stiglitz out in the cold. Carrying Stiglitz's body through the tunnels. The gunshot. The fire. He'd even torn off the bandages, torn at the skin on his face when he showed him the photograph of what the fire did.

His face.

Burned and torn and ruined by the fire. Unrecognizable.

In the confusion of his mind, a thought started to form. Something solid. Something he could hold on to. He could hear Chrissie's voice. The clear crystal ring of her logic.

I don't understand why he won't see me. It's not like him. Connor would never do that.

Connor would never do that. What Jack had taken for denial, Chrissie's inability to accept that Connor didn't want to see her, was simply the truth she knew in her heart.

Connor would never do that. He wouldn't say he didn't want to see her. That's because the man in the hospital wasn't Connor.

Stiglitz.

The thought fizzed and cracked like a flashbulb, leaving a darkness thicker than night. Had he really been talking to Stiglitz all this time, not Connor?

The scale of the deception loomed in front of him like a great precipice. He could just about bring himself to look over the edge, but he couldn't see the bottom. And every time he picked a nice solid thought and threw it over he heard no sound, it just fell and fell and never connected with something solid, something real.

Stiglitz.

He'd known liars, plenty of liars, at least half his patients were either lying to him or lying to themselves. But he got to the truth. And he helped them get to the truth, too, whatever it might be, whatever meaning it had for them. Not this time. This time someone else had let him figure out the answer, they'd fed him what he wanted to hear. Stiglitz was ahead of him every step of the way. He knew exactly where he wanted the conversation to go. He knew exactly how to do it. First, he refused to talk, then he presented a weak story about how there'd been an accident, then he'd appeared to cave and tell him the whole story, pretending he'd been afraid to speak in case he incriminated his friend Henry.

Bullshit. It was all bullshit. Hide a lie inside another lie. Make someone work for it. They'll want to believe it's true because they feel as if they're uncovering it for themselves.

Jack stared at the seat in front of him. Gray leather headrest. A plastic tray. He fought the urge to punch it.

He was on his feet as soon as they landed, pushing his way down the aisle past the other passengers. The door opened and he ran down the steps, didn't notice the sharp bite of the easterly wind, the snow banked up on the sides of the runway. He was through the glass doors, along corridors, out the arrivals gate, still running. The phone booths, his hand in his pocket digging out quarters. He almost threw them into the slot. Called Coty. Waited. The line hummed. The operator put him through.

Coty was in a meeting and not to be disturbed, his secretary said. Jack said he knew that but it was urgent. Didn't matter, the voice on the other end of the line replied, Coty had left specific instructions that no one was to interrupt him. No messages whatsoever, unless his house was on fire and his wife and children were inside. And even then, he'd said it better be a big fire.

"Is his house on fire?" the secretary asked.

Jack tried not to hit the wall with the receiver.

"Listen, you need to go into that room and tell him to check the height of the body in the autopsy against the medical records for Owen Stiglitz. Have you got that? It changes everything. Tell him that. He's not going to ball you out, he'll be grateful. My name's Dr. Jack Miller. You tell him what I said and that I'm waiting for his call. He can reach me on this number. Please. Just do this. He's still in with Gill, isn't he? I was with them this morning. It changes everything they're working on. Please. Just do it."

"He said no . . ."

"He meant nothing irrelevant," Jack interrupted. "He needs to know this. It's what he's working on."

"Alright," the voice replied. "But I can't promise he'll call you back. Except to tell you to go away."

Jack replaced the receiver. The other phones were all taken and a man in a business suit waved impatiently at him to move on. Jack folded his arms and leaned back against the phone.

Something in his expression made it clear to the man there was no point arguing. Jack lit a cigarette and was halfway through it when the phone rang.

"Coty?" he said.

"Five nine," Coty replied. "Stiglitz is five foot fucking nine. Jesus Jack. The bastard stitched us up. He's . . ." Coty paused. There was something approaching awe in his voice.

"He's very smart and very dangerous," Jack said, finishing his sentence. "Borderline sociopath. Or rather psychopath, given the enjoyment he seems to take in manipulating others. Have you called the hospital?"

"I've sent Frank and a couple of other agents down there. Can you come back to Washington? You can have the pleasure of helping us with our interrogation."

"I'm on the next flight," Jack said.

Coty and Frank met him at Dulles airport. Jack was surprised to see them both.

"This way," Coty said, leading Jack toward the car. The wind was up. It had been snowing heavily since he left. They got in. Engine on, heaters up.

"What have you done with Stiglitz? Are you guarding him at the hospital or is he somewhere more secure?" Jack asked.

Coty glanced at Frank.

"We sent a team to the hospital straight after your call. Stiglitz was gone," he said.

Frank pulled out from under the concrete canopy that covered the entrance to the airport. A flurry of snow hit the windscreen. The wipers did their best to clear it but it landed thickly, insistently.

"Gone?" Jack replied. "What do you mean *gone*? He can't have just gone. He needs medical help. Ongoing care. And when I saw him he could hardly move. How could he just walk out of there?"

"He had help," Coty replied. "A team moved in to take him. Same cell who've been doing the cleanup. He's a high-value asset. They wanted to get him out. And it's not that hard really. Once he's out of that room he's just another patient on a trolley. I expect they simply wheeled him to the doors and loaded him into an ambulance. If you look like you're meant to be somewhere, no one asks whether you're meant to be there."

"My God," Jack said quietly. He thought back to the last time he'd been to the hospital, the doctor he'd seen talking to Connor. The man who'd slipped out when he'd arrived without introducing himself. Was it that easy? You took it for granted that places were safe. They were secure. They were protected. But they weren't. How could you protect against an enemy that looked the same as you, dressed like you, sounded like you? Someone who looked like they belonged as much as you did—maybe even more?

"There was someone with him last time I saw him," Jack said. "Not the CMO. Another doctor. At least I assumed he was a doctor. I don't know. There was something about him. He was talking to Connor. Stiglitz, I should say. He was leaning over, close to him, whispering to him. Didn't introduce himself. Then he left. It looked strange. I hadn't seen him before. I should have stopped him. Questioned him."

Coty shrugged.

"Don't beat yourself up about it. If you had spoken to him he'd have made you think everything was fine. They'll have needed at least a three-man team for this. And that won't be the only time they met with him. They had to work out when to move him. To let him know what they were planning. This was his get-out. I think his reaction to the photograph, pulling at his bandages, pulling at the skin grafts, the damage he did, it was all part of the show. Maybe they told him they needed more time, maybe he thought he'd get that by picking at the work they'd done on his face."

Jack was listening, but he could scarcely take it in. He spoke softly. "Back at the base in Greenland. The burns he suffered. He must have done that to himself. He must have done it so that he could pretend to be Connor, then he swapped the tags around, put his tag on Henry. Can you imagine what it takes to pour the gas onto your skin, to let yourself burn?"

"No," Coty said. "But Stiglitz would've worked it all out. The precise amount of fuel. How to put it out. And you can bet he'll only have done it once he knew a plane was on the way."

"So he killed the other two," Jack said.

"Maybe they were onto him," Coty said.

Frank had pulled onto the highway but the traffic had ground to a standstill in the snowstorm.

Coty twisted in his seat. "There's something else," he said. "Connor's fiancée. She couldn't keep away from the hospital. I don't know what you told her but she came down this morning."

Jack felt sick to his stomach.

"I told her Connor didn't want to see her."

Coty continued. "She got to the hospital around nine thirty. The CMO took her to Connor's room, stayed a few minutes, then left them to it."

"And?" Jack said weakly.

"He carried on with his rounds. Returned after an hour or so and they were gone."

"Stiglitz took her? Why?" Jack asked. "Why would he take her?"

Coty didn't reply.

"In case we catch him before he can leave the country. In case he needs something to bargain with," Frank said.

"And if we don't catch him, if he gets to a port or on a private plane or however it is they're planning to get him out of the country, what will they do with her?"

Frank and Coty were silent. Then Coty said, "He's not going anywhere for the moment. The snow's been coming down thick all afternoon. They'll be in a safe house somewhere close to Washington, waiting for their chance to get away. He needs to hold on to her."

"For now," Jack said grimly.

37

Langley, Virginia
January 2, 5:00 P.M.

They pulled off the highway and drove through the suburbs to Langley. The daylight was dulled by the snowstorm, and they made slow progress. Security guards checked their badges and waved them through, stamping their feet to keep warm.

Frank pulled into the parking lot. Coty had the door open while the tires were still rolling. Out of the car, his impatient footsteps loud on the concrete floor. He turned and glanced over his shoulder at Jack and Frank.

"Come on," he yelled, calling the elevator.

Jack followed Coty along a series of corridors until he'd lost all sense of direction. Considering how out of shape he looked, Coty moved surprisingly quickly, and he talked and talked without pausing to take a breath.

"Soon as we heard Stiglitz was gone we set up an ops room," he said. "Finding him takes precedence over anything. Whatever we need—Fed support, police—we've got it. That team isn't leaving the US. Not with Stiglitz."

He pushed through a set of double doors without pausing. Steps led down to a large room, almost the size of two basketball courts. A windowless bunker. Four long tables were laid out, each one surrounded by five or six intelligence officers. Telephones were spaced evenly along the tables. Some of the officers were on calls. Some were reading through files, heads down. Others pored over plans of buildings and maps. There was a low hum of voices, cigarette smoke clouded the air.

On the far wall a large board showed a map of the city with all roads out of it marked in yellow pen. A circle had been drawn around the hospital in red. All airports, private airfields, and ports were marked too.

"That's the distance they could have traveled since this morning," Frank said, waving his hand, following the outline of the circle. "Taking into account the weather. The CMO saw them at the hospital at 9:30. If they left straightaway they'd have had an hour before the snow got too heavy. They can't take a passenger flight and all freight is being checked. Two cargo planes left this morning from Dulles. There was nothing on the manifest capable of containing a bed or chair with Stiglitz in it. No large crates. In any case, we've alerted the authorities and told them to check."

"What about private airfields?" Jack said.

"Closed because of the weather. And none were close enough for them to get out this morning. The nearest port is Baltimore," Coty said. "But if they're headed that way we'll get them. They won't have got there yet in the storm."

Gill was leaning over one of the tables, going through papers, talking to the team around him. There was a list of district police stations next to the map, each had a phone number alongside it. The alert had gone out. He looked up when he heard Coty's voice.

"What's he doing here?" he said, pointing at Jack.

"Helping us."

"Not in here. We've got handlers speaking to their agents. Goddamn it, Coty." He turned to talk to someone, then changed his mind and spun round. "You know what? Just send him home. He's done enough."

Coty turned to Jack, held up his hands and gave him a long-suffering look.

"Let's go before he asks me to arrest you," he said with a half smile. Once they were out of the room he turned to Jack. "Gill's like this when he's under pressure."

"And when's he not," Jack said. "Listen, Coty, I know he's doing all he can to find Stiglitz and the girl. I'm sure he's got everyone following every procedure you've got, calling every agent who might know something about the cell working in Washington." Jack paused. "But the last time Stiglitz was cornered he killed Connor and Henry, then poured gas on himself and burned half his face off so he could impersonate Connor. And not only did he pretend to be Connor, he sat there pretending to be a version of Connor that was telling lies, making up stories, because he wanted to protect a friend. He set up a complex character, doing the wrong thing but for the right reasons, and waited for me to uncover it, thinking I was helping him, thinking I was getting to the truth. And he managed to maintain this cover whilst coming out of an induced coma pumped full of drugs."

"I know. I get it. He's smart. So what?" Coty said.

"I'm saying he's not going to be reading the same manual as Gill when it comes to making his escape. The CIA handbook for running down a rogue agent isn't going to work. He won't be trying to get to an airport or a port. He won't be doing whatever Gill or your analysts would expect him to do. They won't be driving him in a truck along the highway, straight into a police ambush."

"You think he's still in the city?"

"I think he's either here in DC or close by. I think he'll sit it out for a few days. Maybe even longer," Jack said. "He'll enjoy the thought of us spending hours trying to track him, mobilizing half the country to shut off roads and check freight."

Coty leaned against the wall.

"I get it. But I'm not about to go and tell Gill he's got it all wrong. And I wouldn't recommend you tell him either. The man doesn't have another handbook." Coty reached into the pocket of his jacket and took out a pack of cigarettes. He ripped open the wrapper and flicked one out, and offered it to Jack. Jack took it. "If you were Stiglitz, where would you hide? Just out of interest. Seeing as you've spent the most time with him."

Jack shrugged.

"Couldn't even begin to guess," he said.

"Oh, that's swell. Why didn't you say so at the start of your little speech?" Coty said, flicking cigarette ash on the floor.

"But I know someone we can ask," Jack replied.

38

Langley, Virginia
January 2, 6:30 P.M.

Coty leaned back against the wall. His eyes narrowed, trying to work out who Jack was talking about. "Come on then, stop trying to prove how much smarter you are and give it up," he said eventually.

"Detective Hayes, the one who brought me in for questioning," Jack said. "You said yourself there was no way he could have found me without a tip-off. Someone saw me the night I met with Reverend Peterson, followed me back to my hotel, followed me to the hospital the next day. Watched me have breakfast at the café with Chrissie. They told the police where I was and they told them I'd met with Peterson. Police brought me in for questioning and they went through my things, including my notebook with Mendelson's name in it. Then guess what? Mendelson gets a visit before I even get a chance to talk to him. I'm not saying that the detective is a part of it, but one of his contacts is either part of the cell that's taken Stiglitz or knows them."

Coty stared at the end of his cigarette.

"You could go see him," he said, thinking it over. "But I don't think he'll talk."

"He might if I get him on our side."

"He's not on our side, he's on his own side. I'll find out if he's at the precinct tonight. If not, I'll get his home address. Take Frank with you. If Hayes doesn't feel like opening up you'll need Frank to persuade him."

Frank and Jack drove from Langley along the highway north of the city. The roads were quiet, snow piling up quickly in the fields and coating the trees, large flakes sticky with cold. They'd taken a Jeep pickup from the pool fitted with snow tires. Frank was staying low in the gears and pulling past anyone else still out on the beltway.

They took the exit at Montgomery and rolled into the suburb of Rockville. The darkness here was softer, warmed by streetlights and the glow from within the long, low houses. Realtor signs hung outside every third or fourth property. A new development.

Frank drove to the end of the street then turned the car slowly and doubled back on himself.

"All these roads look the same," he said.

"It's this one," Jack said, squinting at the number on the mailbox. Frank pulled up. Jack opened the door, Frank didn't move. He switched off the engine and stayed still for a moment. Then he took the key out of the ignition and slipped it into his pocket.

"He isn't going to want to talk to us, and he isn't going to want to come with us, you know that don't you?" Frank said.

Jack shrugged. "Let's see."

"He has a wife and kid. They'll be having dinner around now."

"Which means he's more likely to behave himself."

"No, no he won't," Frank replied. "Coty told me to make him talk. Do you know what that means?"

Jack frowned.

"I'm guessing it means you'll do the same thing to him he does to the suspects he picks up each day?"

Frank shrugged. "And then some."

They walked up the path to the front door, past a large automobile covered in snow.

"Lincoln Continental," Frank said. "On what he makes?"

Jack pressed the bell, a cozy sign above it said "bless this house." He could hear a child's voice laughing, the muffled sound of music from the show on their TV. It felt as if they were about to break something.

Footsteps. The door opened and a woman stood in front of them. She was around thirty. Her dark hair cut in a neat bob, olive skin, a clear complexion, and the kind of carefree expression that sets in after two strong martinis. It started to fade the moment she saw Jack and Frank, their large frames crowding the doorway. She looked them up and down.

"You're not selling anything are you? Because you can move right along if you think I'm going to buy dictionaries or vacuum cleaners or anything else."

"We're not selling," Jack said. Frank took out his security badge and showed it to her. She looked at it, frowned.

"Who is it, Martha?" a voice called out from inside. Martha looked at the badge one more time.

"We're here to see your husband," Frank said. He was about to tell her to go and get him when Detective Hayes appeared in the hallway, a boy of about five following him. The boy wore a Mickey Mouse bathrobe, the hood up. He hid behind his father's leg, Mickey's ears poking around the side.

"Good evening, Detective," Frank said. "We need to talk, in private. Do you have a room we can use?"

The detective marched forward and stood in front of his wife. Mickey Mouse followed him.

"What the hell do you think you're doing coming up here?" He stabbed his finger at Frank. "Turning up at a man's home at dinner time. You want to talk to me you call at the station."

"Is there somewhere we can talk?" Frank said again, his tone was soft. "It's a matter of national security." He glanced uneasily at Martha, then shifted his foot forward so they couldn't close the door.

"The hell it is," Detective Hayes replied. "You're just sore because my boys caught you yesterday. Martha, these fine gentlemen here were attempting to solicit the services of a young woman. They think they can get away with it because they work for the government. Now they're here, harassing me at my home."

He looked like it was all he could do not to spit in Frank's face. His wife took a step back, looking down, concerned for her son.

The detective reached forward to shut the door. "This is my property and you're leaving," he said.

Frank put his hand on the door. He sighed. It was a deep sigh. A sigh that was filled with inevitability, a sigh that saw the way this was going to end and didn't relish the thought of having to provide the last word.

The detective turned to his wife. "Martha, go back inside. Take Billy upstairs. I don't want him to hear the kind of language his pa is about to use."

Jack and Frank watched as she scooped up the boy from the hallway. The boy's face flicked from intrigue to anger as he balled his fists and began hammering on his mother's back and yelling to be put down as she carried him away.

As soon as she was gone the detective turned back to Frank and leaned in close.

"What is this bullshit?" he said. "If you think I'm going to talk to you without a subpoena compelling me to do so then you're out of your fucking mind. I've been through this before. I know how investigations work. Get a warrant first." He stared at Frank. "Now fuck off. Both of you, or so help me God every time we see your car, every time you enter the city we'll fine you, we'll bust you, you won't be able to order a goddamn cheeseburger without someone . . ."

He didn't get any further. Before he'd finished the sentence, he was lying on his back in the snow, next to his Lincoln. Jack wasn't sure how exactly Frank had done it. Nor was Detective Hayes. He'd been aware of a sort of low scoop onto Frank's shoulders and the ground swapping places with the sky, but that was all. He tried to get to his feet, but he'd landed badly and his back was hurt. He rolled onto his front, shook himself off like a dog, then stood. He wasn't wearing any shoes, and the snow soaked through his socks. Frank stood between him and the house.

"A few questions. And no more threats. Please. It makes you seem guilty. And you don't want to give that impression to us. Not with what we're investigating. If you don't want to talk in the house you can get in the truck." Frank pointed at the Jeep.

"The hell I will," the detective muttered. "You've just assaulted a law enforcement officer. Do you know what the penalty is for that?" He lunged before he'd finished his sentence, a surprise right hook, his whole weight behind it. But it was too slow and too obvious for Frank, who dodged to one side. The detective followed it with an ambitious uppercut but Frank saw that coming too. He twisted and blocked it, then he hit the man hard in the center of his chest with the palm of his hand and watched as he collapsed backward, winded, once more landing in the snow.

"I can do this all night," Frank said, reaching down and yanking Hayes up onto his feet. "But we have a situation you need to help us with." He pulled the winded detective to the car, opened the door, and threw him into the back seat. Jack glanced over his shoulder at the house. In the upstairs window the curtain was pulled back. He could just make out the face of the boy watching as they took his father away.

39

Rockville, Maryland
January 2, 8:00 P.M.

This is bullshit," Hayes said as Frank put the Jeep in gear and pulled away from the curb. "I've got no shoes. No coat. You're out of your mind."

Frank drove to the junction, then took the road that led to the highway. The snow was starting to settle.

"It would be easier if you were willing to talk to us," he said, shaking his head.

"For you, yeah," the detective replied.

Frank focused on the road ahead, staring into the flurries of snow that whipped against the windscreen.

"About ten minutes north of here there's a track that leads up to the creek. One of those little streams that joins the Potomac. Forms a small lake. There are no houses built up there yet but I guess the developers will get round to it soon. It's nice and quiet."

"What are you going to do, drown me like you did Peterson?"

Frank didn't reply. He opened his window. Ice-cold air filled the cabin.

"Do you really think it was us who threw Peterson into the river?" he said. The detective shrugged.

"Wouldn't put it past you," he said. "God knows what the Agency gets up to. Apart from stopping us from doing our jobs."

"Who told you where I was?" Jack asked. "The morning you came to arrest me. Who gave you the tip-off?"

"No one," the detective replied.

"Come on," said Frank. "Play ball."

"You want me to give that up, you'll need a subpoena."

"You already said that. We don't have time," Frank replied. He turned down a side road. The snow was thicker. The Jeep crawled along over the uneven ground.

"We're going to get stuck out here if you go much further," the detective said.

"Yeah," Frank replied. "I think you're right. We can walk from here." He stopped the car but left the engine running and the lights on. Snowflakes swirled in front of them, making their way into the open window.

"I'm going to give you two choices," Frank said. "Either you talk to Jack here in this nice comfy car or I take you down that track to the creek in your socks and shirtsleeves and you and me will have ourselves a little conversation on the riverbank."

"You wouldn't," the detective said, but some of the certainty had gone from his voice. He was shivering. Jack opened his door and got in the back seat next to him. He took out a packet of cigarettes and offered one to the detective, who shook his head. Jack took one for himself and put them back in his pocket.

"Who was it?" Jack asked. "Had to be someone you knew. Someone you trusted. You acted pretty quick."

Detective Hayes stared ahead. Frank sniffed and twisted in his seat; he was growing impatient.

Jack continued. "You were about your kid's age during the last war, weren't you? Maybe five or six when it got going. I guess you don't remember much about it. When a war ends there is a lot of drinking and parties and homecoming celebrations, and then you know what happens? Another war starts. Sometimes straightaway, sometimes after a few years. But as sure as night follows day, men will find a reason to start killing each other again. The war that started between us and the USSR began pretty much as soon as the last war ended. It's mostly hidden, but sometimes it pops up unexpectedly right here. Like a mine in the ocean. You're sailing along just fine and then this thing surfaces in front of your boat and blows everything to pieces. That's what happened to Reverend Peterson. It's also what's happened to Chrissie, the woman I was talking to when you picked me up. They've taken her. The problem for you," Jack tried to keep his voice calm, but he could feel it tighten at thought of Chrissie, "the problem for you is that whoever gave you the tip-off about me is on the wrong side. They're not with us. Which puts you on their side too. And that is not a good place to be. And I want to find that woman, because I like her and she's good and she's got nothing to do with any of this."

Frank spoke. "What Jack's trying to tell you is that you're in a whole load of shit. Up to the neck. Don't see us as a threat. See us as a lifeline. This is your chance to save yourself."

"What you say next is going to determine the rest of your life." Jack spoke quietly, his words carried gently on a cloud of cigarette smoke. "I want you to know that. Sometimes it's not obvious that a little decision is going to change everything. You don't realize till it's passed, and then there's nothing you can do about it. But this is different. Because we're on the same side. We have to be on the same side. If we're not, and you're on the other side, then you can say goodbye to that house, that kid, that wife of yours. Martha, wasn't it?"

The detective stared at his socks. His shivering had turned into shudders and he clasped his arms around his chest. Frank reached forward and closed the window.

"What happened to the girl?" the detective said at last.

"They took her. They're holding on to her. We think they'll use her as collateral to get a very bad man out of the country," Jack said.

The detective shook his head and spoke in a quiet voice. "The guy who gave me the tip-off about you and Peterson . . . it's not possible."

"Who is he?" Jack asked.

The detective stared out the window. He shook his head.

"Just a mechanic. Guy called Marek. Owns the garage over on Pennsylvania Avenue, intersection with Fourth Street SE. Has a gas station and a workshop."

"By the Capitol?" Jack said.

"Pretty much."

"How did you meet him?" Frank said.

"He reported a couple of stolen automobiles that had passed through his garage. Turned out to be a big operation, across state lines. This was four years ago or so. I cracked it, thanks to him. It helped my career. I was grateful. He asked if I could recommend his garage to service the cop cars. So I did."

"With a little kickback on the side?" Frank said.

The detective shook his head dismissively.

"He gives me a discount on new cars. That's all. Not even a big one. Main thing for me is he has eyes on the street. He's not some wino making up stories trying to wheedle a few dollars out of a cop, like most of them, he's . . ." The detective frowned.

"He's a nice guy. Always buys a drink. Makes you laugh. Good company," Frank said.

The detective looked confused.

"He has a family. They go to church. He's American. Same as you and me."

"And after you brought me in he asked to go through my briefcase?"

"He said he'd seen you take something from Peterson. Thought it might be important. He went through it with me. He was just helping. He didn't take anything. He just read the damn notebook you had. Hardly anything written in it anyway."

Frank put the Jeep in reverse and drove backward down the road.

"Where are you taking me?"

"His garage," Frank replied through gritted teeth.

They drove back to Washington in heavy snow. Down Wisconsin Avenue, through Georgetown. The detective was silent, so was the city.

The garage was a part of a large corner plot overlooking Seward Square. Frank drove past. There were gas pumps and an empty parking lot out front. Behind that a large workshop took up the ground floor of a three-story building. The sign outside the workshop said Abernathy's Automobiles.

"Abernathy?" Jack said, reading the sign.

"He went with Abernathy for the business," the detective said. "Said it sounded like a good, Irish-American name."

"I must have driven past this place a thousand times," Frank said. "Looks like the workshop's closed but they've still got someone on the gas pumps. Lights on in the parking lot."

He pulled onto Fourth Street SE, turned the Jeep around, then parked so they had a clear view of the garage. "I don't think they're going to get many customers tonight. How many people usually work there, other than your friend Marek?"

"There's four of them in the workshop and one out front."

"Did you ever speak to them?" Frank said.

The detective shook his head. "Not really. They changed quite a lot. Marek said they were mainly extended family. Sometimes there are a couple of American boys too. I think he even gave a job to the commissioner's son one summer."

"I'll bet he did. I'm going to take a look round," Frank said.

"Aren't you going to call Coty?" Jack asked.

"Not yet. Looks like the only person here is the kid selling gas. He's about fourteen. If there's anything out of the ordinary we'll let Coty know, and they can send a team down to check the place over."

Frank got out of the car. Jack watched him walk toward the garage, shoulders hunched against the cold, snow glowing orange in the light from the parking lot. A truck rolled by, heavy-engined but the sound softened. Jack followed its taillights in the rearview mirror until it disappeared. He didn't like it. The quiet. The waiting.

When he looked up again he could no longer see Frank. A car rolled into the gas station. A large black Cadillac. A government car. The kid ran out of the little office and started to fill it up. Jack blew into his hands to try and warm them, massaged his knuckles. The dull ache of his arthritis was getting worse with the cold. As if he was always holding something cold and heavy. He waited. The detective reached forward and turned the heat up. The Cadillac paid and pulled away. It drove past them. They waited some more. It was a large site. Jack checked his watch. Half past eight. Frank had been gone about ten minutes. He tried not to think about Chrissie. About what must have been going through her mind that morning. The discovery it wasn't Connor in the hospital bed. How had she found out? Did they tell her straightaway when they took her? Did they wait? Had she known as soon as she saw him lying there? Had she guessed it? He hoped to God she was ok.

He took out his packet of cigarettes. One left.

"I'm going to get some smokes from the drugstore. Want anything?"

"Pair of shoes and a coat," the detective replied.

Jack crossed the street. He ran quickly, collar up. Pushed open the door of the little store. A bell rang. It was bright and warmer than the car. He asked the teller for a packet of Lucky Strikes.

"Not much business for you tonight," he said. The man behind the counter was elderly with bloodshot eyes. He was sat on a stool hunched at the counter, reading a paper. "I'm surprised you're still open."

"Sign says we close at eleven and that's when I close, not a moment before," he said. "You never know what folks might need." He reached behind him, took a packet of cigarettes from the shelves, and placed them on the counter. "Anything else?" he asked.

"That's all, thanks." Jack paid and put the packet in his pocket. "Have they been busy today?" he asked, gesturing toward Abernathy's Automobiles. The teller glanced awkwardly over his shoulder through the window, wanting to return to his paper.

He shrugged. "Busy time of year for them. Lots more accidents on the roads." He looked up and frowned. "But come to think on it, no. Not today. Usually the boys come in for a soda or whatnot. Just one truck earlier. Think maybe the workshop closed early."

Jack nodded. The sickness had come back to his stomach. Frank still hadn't come back. Through the shop window he saw a man walking from the garage toward the Jeep. He felt relief. Frank coming back. He stared a moment longer. It looked as if the man was wearing a black leather motorcycle jacket. Not Frank. The man walked quickly. Hands by his sides, no gloves.

The man stopped and peered briefly inside the car, then turned, took something from inside his coat. Jack heard the crack of the car window shattering. The dull thud of a silenced gun. A second shot. The man turned back toward the garage and flashed a light. Jack stared at the Jeep, the silhouette of the detective slumped forward.

The killer got inside. The engine fired. The whole thing can't have lasted more than a few seconds but Jack felt as if time had slowed to a standstill. He watched the car drive toward the garage. The workshop doors opened and the car drove inside.

"You know that fella?" the man behind the counter asked. "Because he just drove away in your Jeep."

Jack shook his head, slowly.

"Yeah, I saw." He looked over at the workshop. "Do you have a gun?" he asked.

"Do I have a what now?"

Jack had already reached over the counter, feeling along the underside. He pulled at something heavy and metal taped there and found himself holding an old revolver.

"Now just you hold on," the man said. He grabbed the sleeve of Jack's coat but Jack pulled away too quickly.

"Does it work?" Jack asked, looking down the barrel, opening the chamber, and checking it was loaded.

"Of course it works. What's the point of keeping a gun that doesn't work?"

"Good. Do you have a phone?"

"No."

"Where's the nearest one?"

"There's a booth four blocks south."

"How far?"

"About a fifteen-minute walk."

Jack opened the door. Looked up at the building. Fifteen minutes was too long. Anything could happen in that time.

The traffic lights that hung over the center of the intersection changed from green to red, but there were no cars to stop. Jack ran quickly to the other side of the road, kept close to the buildings. He was out of any line of sight from the workshop.

He wanted to call Coty, but it would mean leaving the street where the workshop was, and what if they left? He wouldn't see where they went, wouldn't get the license of the vehicles they were in. He couldn't risk it. They'd be getting ready to go now. They'd been found. They'd have to move to another location. Another hiding place, and he'd be back to square one.

And Frank. And the detective. They wouldn't take them with them. *Shit.*

How many of them were there? At least four, based on what the detective had said. The odds weren't in his favor. He had no knowledge of the layout of the building. No idea where they were positioned. He had a lousy old revolver that had been taped to the underside of a counter in a drugstore for about forty years. He looked across at the gas station in front of the workshop. Put his hand into his jacket pocket and took out the cigarette lighter. There were two pumps. And underneath them was thousands of gallons of gasoline. He flicked the lid off the Zippo and ran his thumb over the flint wheel, turning it slowly. Stiglitz thought fire would be his escape. Well, it wasn't. Not this time. This time it was going to trap him.

40

Fourth Street SE, Washington, DC
January 2, 9:30 P.M.

Hey," Jack said, opening the door to the booth by the gas pumps. "I need a jerry can of fuel. Car's run out a couple of blocks away."

"Sure," the kid behind the counter replied. "You're lucky, I was about to close up." He was no more than seventeen, his skin marked with acne and a fuzz of mustache on his top lip. He went outside to fill a can from the pump. Jack followed. Watched him as he carefully unscrewed the cap, put the nozzle inside. When he was done he handed it to Jack.

"Two dollars for the gas. You can return the can once you've filled up. Unless you want to keep it, then it's two dollars fifty."

"Thanks," Jack said. "Now I need you to run to the nearest phone booth and call the police and the fire department."

"Say what?" The kid looked confused. He stepped back.

"I'm going to set fire to this place," Jack said. He took out the revolver and pointed it at him. The boy stared back.

"So you'll need to call the fire department and the police. Go on, run, get out of here!" The kid shook his head, not understanding what he was seeing. He turned and started to jog, glancing over his shoulder.

Jack extended his arm, aiming the revolver at the boy. He ran faster, slipped on the pavement, got up, and sped off. Jack ran to the entrance of the workshop. He emptied the can along the bottom of the wooden doors, soaking them in fuel. Then he bent down, flicked the flint wheel, and held the blue flame of the Zippo against the door. He watched, making sure the gasoline caught. Hungry flames ate up the wooden panels. He ran back to the pumps. Crouched behind them, waiting, wondering how long it would be before whoever was inside caught the smell of burning. And how many of them would come to put it out.

The fire did its job. The flames quickly took to the doors. The wind was strong, and it pulled the fire up, sending smoke swirling around the building.

The doors to the workshop slid open, moving apart like sheets of flame. Two men appeared with fire extinguishers. Dark figures silhouetted against the bright light. Jack could make out two more figures inside, hanging back, watching what was going on. They sprayed CO_2 on the doors but the flames were slippery, skidding away from the gas, further up the door, up the sides of the building.

One of the extinguishers stopped working. The man holding it threw it down and ran back inside.

Jack gently eased the nozzle of the gas pump out of its holder and stepped out from behind the pump. He squeezed the handle, holding it away from him, then lit the gas.

An arc of fire leapt forward. A clumsy, heavy spray, like blue paint flung from a can. It caught the man who was standing by the door, trying to put out the fire. Lit his clothing. In a second, he was burning, diving into the snow, rolling over.

Gunshots came from inside. Jack ducked behind the pump, let go of the handle, and shook off the flaming drips of gas. Glass shattered. Metal tore. He felt the pump shake as bullets hit it. And heard the screams of the man on the ground. He peered around the side, still holding on to the fuel hose.

He saw two figures crouched over the man he'd set on fire, rolling him over. Jack opened the Zippo, angled it so it caught the nozzle of the pump, and flicked fire at the three men once more, catching them with a shower of burning rain. They spun away. Human torches, trying to shake it off. One ran across the parking lot, toward the snow on the sidewalk. Dived to the ground. The other was tearing off his jacket.

Jack dropped the hose, took out the revolver. Hoped to God it worked. He fired low, two shots aimed at the legs of the man taking off his jacket. One of them caught him, he toppled forward. Masonry cracked on the other side of the street. Silenced shots fired from the doorway of the workshop, like stones smacking rocks. Jack didn't duck, he didn't even flinch. He walked toward the burning doors, holding the revolver with arms outstretched, and fired twice into the wooden wall. Exactly where he thought the shots had been fired from. Something slumped forward. Staggered, like it was carrying a heavy load. The figure lifted its arm, fired twice more. Wild shots. Glass shattered. Jack ran forward, kicked the gun from his hand. Grabbed him by the lapels of his coat.

"Where are they?" he asked. "Where's the girl? Where's Stiglitz?" The man mumbled something. He was middle-aged. Gray hair. A pair of glasses, now broken, hung from his nose. His eyes looked lost, afraid. He looked more like a librarian than a mechanic. The coat was damp. The damp was warm. Jack smelled the soft, metallic tang of blood.

"Where are they?" he asked again.

The man shook his head. He opened his lips, bubbles of spit were all that came out. Jack dropped him back onto the tarmac. The heat from the burning doors scorched his face. He held up his hand to protect himself. The fire was starting to eat up the walls. Jack looked behind him. The three men he'd set alight had managed to put out the flames. Two of them were still moving, crawling back to the workshop. The other one was still.

Inside.

No lights. Dull shapes. He could make out two police cars at the far end. The black-and-white panels standing out in the dark. The wind was blowing smoke inside. He coughed. New life was in the fire as it tasted dry wood and paint in the sign over the workshop. It crackled as it ate them up. Jack knew that if it managed to get a grip on the inside the building would be gone. There were tanks of gas used for welding up against the wall, the smell of engine oil, just waiting for a friendly flame to bring it all together.

Forward, quickly. His breathing was tight. The Jeep was parked to one side. He peered in. The detective wasn't there. They must've moved him. A van was next to it. He pressed himself against the side, moved cautiously around it. The back doors were open. A hospital trolley was inside.

They were getting ready to move Stiglitz.

Where was he? And where were Frank and Detective Hayes? Where was Chrissie?

He called their names; the smoke was getting thicker.

There was a wooden staircase at the back of the workshop. He ran up the steps. He could hear the roar of the fire outside, louder now. His shoes slipped. Something dark underfoot, greasy. Oil or blood. A sudden bang and the step in front of him split. Two more shots sailed past him. He ducked, turned. In the entrance way, leaning heavily against the door, was the silhouette of a man, arm raised. He fired again as he staggered toward the van.

Jack ran. One bullet. He had one bullet left in the chamber. There was a corridor at the top of the stairs. Two doors leading off it. He pushed at the first. A storeroom. Car parts. Boxes. He tried another, flipped the switch. The light flickered. Filing cabinets. Shelves. More boxes. He ran up another flight of stairs, taking them three at a time, heart racing. Desperate now. He could hear sirens outside. The wail of fire trucks and police cars. The smoke choking him.

Another door. Light underneath it. He reached out, turned the handle. Pushed it open. Then threw himself back against the wall. No one came out. Light spilled into the corridor, doing a strange swirling dance with the thick smoke. He glanced round the doorway into the room. A quick movement. No guns went off. No bullets fired. He looked again. A desk had been shunted to one side. In the middle of the room was a chair, and sitting on that chair with a drip hooked up to his arm was Stiglitz.

"Where are the others?" Jack asked, grabbing Stiglitz and yanking him up.

"You?" Stiglitz whispered. "What are you doing here?"

"Where are the others?" Jack asked again. "Where's the girl? Where's Chrissie?"

Stiglitz shook his head. Jack pulled at the furniture, dragging it out of the way, looking behind it. The cupboards, the desk. No Chrissie. He turned and left.

"Don't just leave me," Stiglitz called out after him. "You can't just leave me."

Jack kicked open another door. He heard an engine fire up in the workshop. Tires spun and squealed as it revved awkwardly, the gears too high. Then the sound of metal crumpling against concrete and the quick shatter of glass. Someone trying to escape. Someone injured who could barely drive.

Sirens too. Getting closer. Rising and falling in the night air.

"Chrissie!" he yelled. He ran up the next set of stairs. "Chrissie!" Top floor. The corridors thick with smoke now, he pulled his scarf over his mouth. Heard something. He was in an attic room. A quiet voice.

Muffled. Gagged. At the back of the room, under the eaves a hooded figure. He recognized the cotton dress and the pumps. Jack reached down and pulled off the hood.

"Chrissie!" he said.

Her mouth was taped, hands and legs bound tightly. Jack pulled off the tape as gently as he could. A cloth was stuffed behind it, he pulled it out. Chrissie coughed, started to choke.

"You ok? Think you can walk?" he said, as he struggled to undo the ropes around her legs.

She gasped. Eyes wide.

"It's me, Jack, Dr. Miller. It's going to be ok. I'll get you out."

"I can't feel my legs," she whispered, her voice hoarse.

"You're just stiff, you'll be ok."

He couldn't make his hand work. Couldn't get it to undo the rope. The smoke was filling the room. Jack took out his lighter. Held the flame under the rope, singeing the chords—burning his hand as he did so. He didn't care. Didn't feel it. At last, he broke the rope.

He helped her to her feet, through the smoke, one arm round her waist, both of them coughing. A man loomed in front of them, flashlight blinding them. Jack raised the gun. A firefighter, helmet on, mask over his face.

"How many in the building?" he yelled when he saw them.

"One on the floor below and two others, somewhere. I don't know where," Jack shouted.

He felt as if they were tumbling down the stairs. Two, three, four firefighters with them. He was aware of black-coated figures in masks moving through the smoke. They were carrying something. A chair, Stiglitz, two on either side.

Down the stairs. Across the workshop.

"Check the pit," Jack said, trying to shout, his lungs filled with smoke. "Under the car." He turned, frantically pointing at the pit. It was the only place he could think of where they might have dumped Frank and the detective.

He heard a voice call out, "There's someone down here. Two people. I need help."

Jack was outside, breathing in a lungful of cold air. Chrissie next to him, bent double, retching. She fell down, hands in the snow. There were ambulances and fire engines parked across the street. They looked haphazard, like discarded toys.

Jack saw a firefighter emerge from the workshop, a body over his shoulders. He moved slowly, knees bent under the weight of it, to one of the ambulances. He set the body down gently on a stretcher.

Another firefighter came out from inside. Another body.

Jack ran toward them.

A voice was shouting over a bullhorn. "Everybody back, move back. Away from the building."

"Are they ok?" he asked.

The fireman was out of breath.

"I don't know. I think this one's breathing," he replied, pointing at Frank. "Just. Face is all bust up. What the hell happened here?"

Jack didn't answer. The workshop was up in flames. They were moving everyone back, ambulances, police cars, just the fire trucks remained. He saw the van on the other side of the street, crumpled against the corner of the Bank of America. There was no one inside it. Either they'd tried to run or they'd already been taken away in an ambulance.

He watched a paramedic talk to Chrissie, who was crouched on the sidewalk. She stood up stiffly, shaking, he put a blanket around her.

Stiglitz was still in his chair. They'd put him down in the middle of the road, as if he was a relic rescued from a museum. A medic was fussing over him.

Jack walked to him, the roar of the fire, the rush of water from the hoses, the shouts of firefighters filling the air. The sounds merged together as one. Distant, pushed back by the noise of the thoughts in his head. White snow and black ash fell around him, caught in the spinning lights of the police cars and ambulances and fire trucks. He felt an uncomfortable level of violence turning over within him. His fists were clenched. He unclenched them. Rubbed the knuckles on his bad hand.

"Looks like we both enjoy starting fires," Stiglitz said softly as he approached. He twisted awkwardly to look at Jack, then said, "I imagine you're feeling a mixture of emotions. Don't blame yourself for not working it out sooner. Who I am, I mean." He lifted a hand wearily, speaking with a casual superiority. "You weren't to know. Well, technically, you were supposed to know. You could have got there sooner. When they gave me a transfusion and got the wrong blood type, gave me Connor's type and I reacted badly, that should have indicated something wasn't right. But the human capacity to ignore what's in front of their eyes never ceases to amaze me. And if someone tells you their name you tend to assume they're not lying. Even though you probably should, shouldn't you?"

Jack looked at Stiglitz as he spoke. Stiglitz stared back, watching Jack's reaction, waiting to see if he'd needled him. There were a thousand things Jack wanted to say, to call him, to accuse him of. But he didn't play into Stiglitz's hands. Instead he just said, "It's over for you."

Stiglitz shook his head.

"Is it? I don't think so. You don't know how these things work." His voice still casual. As if he was making small talk at a cocktail party. Explaining a matter of etiquette to an out-of-towner.

"Is that right?" Jack replied.

"I'll cut a deal. Tell them how sleeper cells are organized in American cities. It's impressive. All these ordinary people doing ordinary jobs. Waiting. Watching. Part of our society. Coty has no idea."

He said Coty's name slowly and deliberately, to show Jack he knew who he worked for. To impress him. To make him feel small. Jack didn't feel impressed, he felt weary.

"You mean the guy who ran the garage?" he said.

Stiglitz nodded. "And others like him. Did you kill him?"

Jack shrugged. "Maybe," he said. "Or maybe the wall did." He pointed at the other side of the street, where the van had hit the Bank of America.

Stiglitz made a little laughing sound.

"You're a most unusual doctor. I think you'd enjoy reading the research I carried out at the base."

"I don't think I would."

"You know the Agency is also researching the influence of psycho-active drugs? Extremely limited applications, in my view. Not so much a blunt instrument as a blunt instrument attached to a rocket that could fire in any direction. Still, it was useful. Quite an oppor-tunity. And I'd be happy to share it with the Agency. Save them some legwork."

"You killed Connor and Henry. They won't do a deal with you."

Stiglitz shrugged.

"Did I? I don't think you know anything about what happened in the arctic. Not really. You only have Connor's testimony, and I think you'd struggle to get that admitted as evidence, don't you?" Stiglitz laughed, a gentle sound, staring into the fire. "If it suits them I'm sure they'll keep the official line that the fire was an accident—not like the one you set under this place. Means they can spirit me away. No need for a big hoo-ha. No need for any embarrassment. Senior military leaders do hate to be embarrassed."

Jack turned away. He didn't want Stiglitz to see how he was getting under his skin. He could feel the old revolver heavy in his pocket. One bullet left.

"What is it, Dr. Miller? You look like you've got something in your mouth you don't want to swallow. Spit it out. Say what's on your mind. Isn't that what you advise your patients?"

Jack turned to face him. "Alright. Let me tell you something about the kind of man you are, Owen Stiglitz, because in all of this I get the impression you think you're just about the smartest man who ever lived. And maybe you have got this all sewn up. And maybe you'll cut a deal. And maybe they'll try and cover the whole thing up and pretend nothing ever happened. But, to paraphrase Elisabeth Mendelson, it's not hard to be smart if you're born clever, the trick is not being an asshole. And you're an asshole."

Stiglitz laughed. "Elisabeth said that? I must have made quite an impression, all those years ago. Although I'm not sure how well that diagnosis sits with more traditional psychiatric evaluations."

Jack ignored him and continued. "You know what stands out for me? When you were pretending to be Connor, you said you beat him at chess."

Stiglitz stared back at him.

"I said a lot of things, and you wrote them down like a good little shrink. I could have said anything. Beat him, lost to him, what does it matter?"

"No," Jack shook his head. "It was more than that. Not all lies are equal. You were settling a score. You lost to him. He beat you."

"What makes you think we even played chess?" Stiglitz said. "I was making up the whole thing."

"You played. He won. In real life. In the rec room at the base. You played again. He won. And again. You couldn't beat him and you hated it," Jack said. "And you're so small and so deluded, you had to settle the score in your made-up story. When you played the part of Connor you had him admit you were a better chess player. You did that because he beat you. That's who you are. You didn't need to mention chess. But you chose to. Do you know how small that makes you?"

Stiglitz was silent for a moment, then shook his head and smiled. "You make it sound as if I'm controlled by some bizarre inner turmoil. I can assure you that's not the case. I'm not the one being held captive in some dark prison of the mind. Connor was always so desperate to prove himself, so keen to show he was more than just a farmer's son. If anyone is held captive, I'd say it's him." Stiglitz stared hard at him, holding his gaze. A challenging look.

"He worked you out, didn't he?" Jack said. "He figured out what you were doing. Challenged you on it. The radio transmissions, the testing. He beat you at more than just chess, didn't he? He got you. While you we're trapped out there. He worked it out, so you killed him and you killed Henry."

"Did I, Dr. Miller? You're trying very hard to make a story fit your theory. Remember what happened the last time you did that? You were convinced I was Connor and Henry had killed me. That was also very wrong. Maybe it's time you found a new profession. Don't blame yourself. That's what you said to me, isn't it? I know you have some strategies to avoid feeling guilt, even when something is your fault—like your poor wife's death. Let me give you a word of advice, don't bring up your personal life when talking to a patient. It's very unprofessional. At least this time you saved the girl," he nodded at Chrissie, "just about."

Stiglitz smiled. Jack turned away. Hands in his pockets to keep them from grabbing Stiglitz's throat and choking the life out of him. He'd heard enough. He asked a police officer to put a call through to the Agency to let Coty know what was going on, then he walked over to Chrissie and put an arm round her. She was in shock, still wrapped in her blanket, crouched on the ground.

41

Langley, Block B
January 3, 1968, 2:00 A.M.

After the fire there was a formal debrief. It started the same night and went on into the morning. It continued through the morning to the afternoon. And on into the evening. Jack answered endless questions. The same questions, over and over. Why had Frank gone into the garage on his own? Why did the detective wait in the car? Why didn't he have shoes and a coat? Why did Jack go and buy cigarettes at that precise point in time? How long was it before he saw someone shoot into the car. When did the fire start?

The decisions made on the spur of the moment were held up to the light, analyzed, noted, and cross-referenced. The questions repeated. Recorded. Played back.

And then they talked to him about the interviews he'd carried out with Stiglitz, back when Stiglitz was Connor. They asked him to tell them everything Stiglitz had said. They reviewed that against the reports he'd written. They asked why his suspicions weren't aroused sooner. Why he didn't realize he was talking to someone else, not

Connor. He asked them the same question. Especially after Stiglitz rejected the blood transfusion. He felt as if he was the one being investigated. He was right.

Gill wasn't there all the time, only when he felt particularly angry about something. When he was there he stood with his arms folded, and told Jack it was a massive fuckup. It was going to make it harder for his department to get things done. Put a lot of other projects in jeopardy. Somehow Jack had trouble believing it was all his fault, which was what Gill seemed to be suggesting over endless cigarettes and cups of coffee gone cold.

Jack asked what they were going to do with Stiglitz. He got no answer. He asked what they would do about Chrissie, but, again, he got no answer.

And then they'd had enough and said he could go. It was almost twenty-four hours later. He didn't see Coty before he left. He spoke to him once, briefly, when he called the hotel. All Coty said was they'd be in touch again soon and would he be so good as to not leave New York for the next few weeks.

Jack returned to his apartment. He opened all the windows, let the cold air flow through the place. There was a careless swipe of blood he'd left on the wall. He tried to clean it off. He fell asleep on his sofa, then got up and fell asleep in his bed. He slept for a day, went for a steak dinner, and then slept some more. Jack went back to work.

He read through the follow-up notes the other doctors had provided on his patients. He caught up on correspondence. And over the next few days he began to see patients again. But he couldn't get Connor out of his head. Or rather, the Connor that Stiglitz had portrayed. Because he knew there was something of Connor in Stiglitz's performance. That's how Stiglitz worked. And Jack had opened up to him, told him about his past, about his wife's death. He'd wanted to help him, for personal reasons as much as professional ones. It made him feel the loss of Connor, in a strange, secondhand way. And he knew Stiglitz would've gotten a kick out of copying him, the way he spoke, the stories he'd told. Acting the part. And he knew Stiglitz would have enjoyed the fact that he'd fooled Jack. He would have chalked it up on his mental scoreboard. Stiglitz versus the world.

And Chrissie. He thought about Chrissie and the way she carried her hope around in a suitcase and wouldn't put it down, sleeping at the hospital, refusing to accept that Connor didn't want to see her. Because that wasn't Connor, that wasn't what he'd say. And she was right. But now she had to let go. She couldn't keep carrying that bag around the rest of her life.

And Archie Bell, who sat opposite him drinking coffee in his trailer in Holden, talking about how he'd sent a rocket into the night sky and ran around on the ice till he got frostbite, thinking he was being chased by some figure in black. Archie Bell, who ran away from the asylum, swam across a freezing lake, and fled hundreds of miles cross-country. He hoped he'd gotten away before they came for him. They still hadn't had word from his uncle.

And Reverend Peterson. Who seemed defeated, even before Jack had met him. Kicked out of the army due to his drinking. But he'd done the right thing. He'd known something was wrong, he'd known talking about it would put him in danger. He'd stared at danger with the same grim determination he'd stared at the full bottles of whisky in the backroom of his church.

And Detective Hayes. His son watching from the upstairs window as they drove away.

And General Carvell, in a coat that had grown a size too big.

One less father. One less son.

It was all because of Stiglitz, who would make a deal and walk away from the deaths as easily as a cat that's killed a couple of sparrows in the garden. And as much as he tried not to think about it, to get on with work, to see his patients, when he did the thought made him angry, angrier than he'd ever been since that stupid drunk kid drove him and his wife off the road, exploding their life and his happiness.

So, he read through case notes and saw patients and reviewed journals and case histories and kept himself busy, and two weeks later, when Coty called him back for a follow-up interview, Jack told him he wasn't going to Langley. He wasn't going to spend another day cooped up in a windowless room answering the same questions over and over again from every different angle. Which is why on February 7 he was sitting on a bench near the Lincoln Memorial, watching an elderly woman scatter birdseed from a plastic cup as the wood pigeons, gray doves, and sparrows scuttled and hopped and flapped their wings to try and grab some grain.

By his side was his wife's copy of *Tender Is the Night*. He flicked through the pages as he waited, not reading the story but reading the phrases she'd underlined, remembering her questions, her curiosity, her delight as he tried to explain what they meant. He looked across the park, saw Coty from a distance, getting out of the back of his Agency car. His short, squat figure hurrying along the path, past the couples out walking, the women pushing strollers. The daytime detour of the elderly, escaping the drone of the TV. Jack could hear Frank's voice in his head. *Assume everyone is a threat.* He decided to assume everyone was out for a walk instead, getting some exercise on a cold, bright Washington morning.

Coty waved, arm extending in a brief, almost violent, motion. Under his other arm he was carrying a newspaper. He shook Jack's hand as if he hadn't seen him for twenty years, then sat his large frame down on the bench. The bench creaked. He placed the newspaper next to him.

"I would have preferred one of the clubs, somewhere warm with a decent slug of brandy in the coffee," Coty said.

Jack stared ahead. "The cold will help you keep to the point."

"They were pretty tough on you in the debrief, weren't they? Always are. If it's any consolation I got treated the same. Probably worse. Because I let you go and see the detective without telling Gill. But we're out the other side now. Analysis complete and you're smelling of roses. They appreciate your efforts. Gill does. He's come round. Understands we'd be in a worse position without you. Stiglitz would've played Connor for a couple of months, then sailed out of the country to work his magic in Moscow. We'd look like fools. That's if we ever worked out we'd been made to look like fools."

"What's happening to Stiglitz now?"

Coty shifted uncomfortably and frowned.

"Gill wants to make a deal. Stiglitz has a lot to bargain with. He says the fire at the base was an accident."

"Bullshit! Gill knows it's bullshit. Come on, Coty."

"Stiglitz has a lot to bargain with," Coty repeated softly. "The sleeper cells. How they're organized. We need to know how they're organized."

Jack shook his head.

"Did you at least give General Carvell the body of his son? I assume Henry hasn't gone back in the ground with Stiglitz's gravestone overhead. Because I think even Gill would have to agree that's a pretty shitty way to treat a soldier."

"He's had a proper burial. Full military honors. General Carvell returned the container that has Connor's ashes in it. Connor doesn't have any family. I asked Chrissie if she wanted it but she said no, she doesn't believe he's dead. Still can't accept it."

Jack nodded, then said, "I'll speak to her. The least I can do is try and help her understand what's happened. Did you get a death certificate confirming it's Connor in that box? Might help. Sometimes it becomes real for people once they see it written down."

"Not yet. I'll get the coroner to take a look then send on the certificate."

"Not to her. Send it to me," Jack said quickly. "I'll take it to her and we'll talk. Don't simply send her the damn thing."

"Of course, I didn't mean . . ."

"How's Frank?" Jack interrupted.

Coty flicked open a packet of cigarettes and lit one, staring through the smoke at the woman with the birdseed.

"Getting there. They shot him twice, shoulder and hip. He lost a lot of blood, but he's on the mend. Tough old bastard. The detective didn't make it."

"I didn't think he would."

"It was a head shot. Gill's had meetings with the chief of police. Those conversations are not easy. The official line is that it was revenge for the part he played in uncovering a stolen car syndicate back in '63. They'll hold a ceremony. We got the four men who helped Stiglitz escape, though. Two had gunshot wounds, two suffered third-degree burns over most of their bodies. They wouldn't have lasted the night. I take it that was all you?"

Jack stared into the distance. He nodded, an almost imperceptible movement. He hadn't thought about them. He wasn't going to think about them.

Coty took a drag on his cigarette.

"You always did run toward the fight," he said. "I wish you'd joined the Agency. You know how rare it is to find someone who can think and fight at the same time?"

Jack shook his head. "Don't start that again. I've got enough consequences to live with without piling up more."

Coty picked up the newspaper he'd brought with him and passed it to Jack. "Thought you might want to see this. Page four," he said.

Jack opened the paper. It was a copy of the *Bangor Reporter*. There was a story about a hunter who'd been found in the snow, three miles outside of Bangor. Gunshot wound in the leg. Appeared to have walked some distance before collapsing. Long-range hunting rifle next to him. There was no ID, and it wasn't possible to be certain how long the body had been lying there. Based on the depth of snow covering it, they estimated at least one week. A grainy headshot was printed below the article with a note asking for help identifying the man. The face was edged in crystals. Hair framed by white snow. Jack stared at the picture—the insulation salesman he'd spoken to at the hotel.

"Did Archie do this?" Jack said.

Coty nodded. "We picked him up at a drop-in clinic. He had a flesh wound in his shoulder where he'd been winged by a .33 bullet. Same caliber as the rifle this man was carrying." Coty jabbed a finger at the photograph in the paper. "The wound was infected. He was burning up. He'd left it as long as possible before getting treatment."

"Is he ok?"

"He's fine now. And he knows he doesn't have to run anymore. No more AWOL charges or people taking shots at him with hunting rifles. He seemed keen to return to the army. I got the impression he preferred soldiering to fixing cars."

Jack nodded.

"Look, are we still good?" Coty said. "I mean work-wise. Can I still send you psych assessments? There's no one I trust more."

Jack frowned. "Just make sure you send me the coroner's report on Connor and set up a meeting with Chrissie," he said. "Once that's done you can send me whatever files have piled up on your desk. But if you really value my insight, don't employ Stiglitz. Lock him up where no one can see him and no one can hear him. He's dangerous. I don't mean because he betrayed his country. I mean as a human being.

He wants to get inside your head without you noticing, move things around, watch you as you flounder, trying to work out why nothing makes sense anymore. That's what he did to Henry, to the other boys, too, and it's what he did to me."

"I know, I get it," Coty said, taking a drag on his cigarette.

"I don't think you do," Jack replied softly.

42

Waverly Place, Manhattan
February 14, 12:30 P.M.

Jack returned to his apartment, his clinic, his life. It was another week before he heard from Coty again. It was Valentine's Day and he was sitting at his desk reading through the notes for the patients he was seeing that afternoon. A fine gray drizzle was falling and most of the snow had slunk away, apart from a few clumps of dirty slush piled up in gutters and on windowsills. He'd bought Martina the largest cactus he could find and tied a pink bow around it, the spikes poking through the silk ribbon. He left it on her desk while she was out having lunch. He did the same every year—apart from when he forgot.

Martina usually reciprocated with the ugliest tie she could find, something synthetic with the kind of colors that had never, could never, exist in nature. Or a belt made for a man with a waist twice the size of his. She then attached a note with a receipt claiming expenses to cover it, made sure it was at least a day late. The warped domesticity suited them both. Jack didn't analyze why, although sometimes he thought he should.

He skimmed through the referral notes for the patients he was due to see that afternoon, then he checked the in tray to see what else had come in. There were two medical journals he subscribed to, invoices, and sales materials. He flicked through the papers, noticed a Washington postmark on one of the envelopes. He opened it. It contained another envelope, which slipped smoothly onto his blotter. This one was addressed to Coty at Langley. It hadn't been opened. On the outside of the envelope Coty had scrawled a note. *Coroner's report for Connor Murphy. Best, Coty.*

Jack slid his letter opener under the fold. Inside was a one-page document. He read it quickly. The coroner had provided a statement confirming that they could not sign a death certificate for Connor Murphy based on the remains sent to them. Jack sighed. *So much for using a death certificate to give Chrissie some kind of closure*, he thought.

He cast his eyes over the form. The coroner had asked a forensic pathologist to review the remains. The pathologist, having carefully considered the fragments of bone, teeth, and the small amount of charred soft tissue that was left, would not confirm that the body belonged to Connor Murphy. They went further and said they would not be prepared to confirm that the remains themselves were human. Jack read the line again. *Not human?*

Some of the dental fragments were of an unusual shape and the amount of debris was far less than you would expect from a full-grown man.

The report concluded that it was not possible to give any further information about the deceased or provide any view on their identity without full disclosure of the circumstances surrounding the death. The report was signed by a Dr. Paul Franklin.

Jack picked up the phone. Sometimes medical professionals gave you slightly different answers when you talked to them in person, as opposed to when they were drafting an opinion for a formal legal record.

He dialed the number on the report and waited. An impatient voice answered. Male, in his fifties, sounded like he hadn't had lunch yet, Jack thought. He told the doctor he was calling about the report on Connor Murphy.

"Who?" the doctor replied irritably.

"Connor Murphy. The request would have come from Paul Coty via Langley. We sent you his remains last week. I wanted to ask you about the report. It's very circumspect. I wanted your opinion off the record."

"I don't give opinions off the record," the doctor replied.

"Ok, well, how about context? Is there any more context you can give? You can see what we're working with here."

"Not really. It could have been anyone, given the state the remains were in. If you know it's this Connor Murphy fellow then why bother sending it at all?" Dr. Franklin replied.

"In your report you wouldn't confirm whether the remains were human."

"No. They're only fragments. Could be a dog, given the shape of some of the teeth fragments, could be anything. You gave us no context when you asked for the report. And those remains would only equate to about half a body, if that. Where's the rest of him? We usually have statements, photographs, background information. We can't work like this. I won't simply tick a box because someone needs a death certificate for an army pension, or whatever it is you want."

Jack could tell the man was still speaking, because his voice kept coming down the telephone line, but after he'd mentioned the fact that it could be a dog, he couldn't take in any more information. Could only hear sounds, not words.

"What kind of dog?" he asked, dumbly.

"What are you talking about?" the doctor replied.

"You said it could be a dog."

"Just an example. I meant I'm not certain it's human."

"But you said it could be a dog. Why did you say that?"

"First thing that came to mind when I thought of an animal."

"Your report talks about the shape of the teeth."

"Yes."

"Same as you'd find in a dog?"

"Same as you'd find in lots of animals. But not like you'd find in a human. Although, again, this is based on reviewing fragments that have almost been incinerated."

Jack paused, then said, "If I'd sent you the report, and said it was a dog, a husky, for example. Would that have made more sense?"

The doctor was silent.

"Possibly. The amount of debris is certainly consistent with what I'd expect from a medium to large dog. Although I've never been asked to carry out an autopsy on a dog and I'd have referred you to a vet."

"Just for the sake of it, and this isn't going in any report, would you say there's a higher chance that it's a dog or a human? Based purely on what you've seen, forget that it came from us with a name attached to it."

The doctor was silent for a while, then said, "If you'd asked me cold to identify what was in that box, then based on the amount of ash and shape of the teeth I'd say it was more likely to be a dog than a person." He paused. "But that doesn't mean it is. Even if it's not human, it might not be canine."

"Thank you, Dr. Franklin." Jack put the phone down. He felt numb. He called Coty.

"I'm guessing you didn't read that report before you sent it to me," Jack said. "Given it was still in the envelope."

"No. I sent it straight to you. Like you said. I can get my secretary to give you Chrissie's number if you want to arrange a meeting with her."

"I don't want to arrange a meeting. Not yet. I want you to go and ask Stiglitz what he did with Connor Murphy, because those remains are the husky Stiglitz killed. The one he and Henry had a fight over. I'd bet my life on it. He dug up a frozen dog and burned it and that little shit is laughing at us. God knows what he did to Connor but he didn't burn him with Henry."

"Wait, roll back a minute. The autopsy said it was a dog?"

"Not exactly. In the report they wouldn't confirm if it was human. But I spoke to the pathologist, he said it was more likely to be canine than human."

"But he couldn't say for certain?"

"Go get Stiglitz and ask him what he did with Connor. We don't have a body. We have unidentifiable remains that are more dog than human."

Jack thought back to what Stiglitz had said when he accused him of losing at chess to Connor, *If anyone is held captive, I'd say it's him.* He hadn't paid it much attention at the time. He should have. Stiglitz got a kick out of telling you what he'd done, and watching as you failed to work it out.

"I think he trapped him somewhere in the base," Jack continued. "Trapped him there and just left him. The last thing he said to me was this allusion to Connor being held captive. He used the term figuratively, said because he was always so desperate to prove himself he was the one who was held captive. But with Stiglitz, everything matters. He only said it because he wanted to tell me what he'd done and watch me not work it out. Well, too bad for him. I've worked it out. And we need to go to Greenland, to the base. We have to search it. To find Connor."

"Come on, Jack. You're emotional. I get it. Stiglitz played you. Played all of us. He got inside your head. He's a manipulative bastard. But there's no point flying out there. There are miles of tunnels. He could have hidden the body anywhere. We'll never find it. That's if it's even inside. It could be out in the snow, buried under ice. Impossible to locate."

Jack's hand gripped the receiver.

He could hear Stiglitz's voice in his head. *If anyone is held captive, I'd say it's him.*

Present tense. He'd used the present tense.

"I'm not looking for a body," Jack said.

Silence from Coty, and then, "You're looking for Connor but you're not looking for a body. What are you talking about?"

"I mean I think Connor could be alive. At least, I think he was alive when Stiglitz was rescued. He locks him in some room, takes his name, and leaves two bodies so no one will ever look for him. It's perfect."

"Alive where? How? It's not possible. Doesn't make any sense. Why would he do that?" Coty replied. "Why not just kill him?"

"You're not thinking like him. You have to imagine what he'd do. Even if it makes no sense to you. Stiglitz likes to take people apart from the inside. That's how he wins. It's his game. The things that hold the mind together, the walls that hold back the nightmares. He wins when he breaks those down. Stiglitz wins when he shuts Connor in an empty space, in darkness, where the only thing he can see is the inside of his own head and there's no chance of anyone ever coming for him. Not when he kills him." Jack realized his hand was shaking. He drew a breath, put the receiver in the other hand. "You wanted my considered professional opinion. Well that's it. That's what he'd do. Based on what he told me that's what he's done."

"It's a theory," Coty said quietly. "I need more than that if I'm going to persuade Gill to let me send a team to Greenland to search the base."

"Yeah? Well I don't. Connor worked out what Stiglitz was doing. I'm sure of it. We know Henry spoke to him about Stiglitz. We know he had suspicions about him, it's all in the interview with Henry. Connor worked it out and this was how Stiglitz dealt with him. Showed him he was nothing. Showed him Stiglitz always wins. Locked him in a room while the rescue team came and took Stiglitz home. Dug up a damn dog and burned it so there were two bodies."

He heard the line hum. Coty said nothing.

"Are you still there?" Jack said.

"It's off the chart," Coty replied.

"It's off your chart. This is where his brain derives pleasure, gets its satisfaction. This is how he lives. This is why he killed Mendelson's little mongrel and the husky. To hurt people. To see them suffer. He's done the same to Connor. I know it, damn it, I know him. I can feel it. And he's won. If we don't go out there and look for Connor he's won."

"The base will be in darkness," Coty said. "Minus God knows what outside and not much warmer in the tunnels. The doors to the cabins might be frozen shut. Pipes will have burst. Gases could've built up. The ice is unstable. Tunnel walls might've collapsed. And Connor could be anywhere. Look, I know you want him to be alive but that doesn't mean he will be. Even if Stiglitz left him alive he'll have died by now. It's not a field trip to Maine or Ithaca. It's the goddamn arctic. Most likely outcome is you dead and no Connor. Gill won't sign it off."

"Don't hide behind Gill," Jack replied. "Give me a couple of soldiers who've worked in the arctic." He thought for a moment, then said, "Or better still, give me Archie Bell. He knows the base and he knows how to take care of himself in the cold. He'll know where to look, where to go."

"Archie?" A pause from Coty. "He's recovering. And even if he were strong enough I doubt he'd want to go back there."

"If he knew why we were going he would. If he thought we were looking for Connor and there was a chance he was alive, he'd want to help. You couldn't stop him. He's that kind of person. You can't leave it like this, Coty."

The line hummed.

"Ok," Coty said eventually.

"Make it happen," Jack said.

43

Andrews Air Force Base, Maryland
February 21, 10:00 A.M.

It took a week of planning. A week of calls. Conversations with Archie Bell, with his doctor. With the base commander at Thule. Archie and Coty planned the trip from an ops room in Andrews Air Force Base, Maryland. Jack joined them the day before they were due to fly out. Archie looked better than when Jack had last seen him, but he wasn't going to win best-in-show on the parade ground. His hair was long and his beard skimmed his chest. The haunted look had disappeared from his eyes, but he was still drained from fighting off the infection.

During prep for the trip Archie had inspected each piece of gear, slowly, methodically. He packed the ropes, the knives, the coats, the sleeping bags. He checked everything, then he checked it again. They took an oxy-torch for cutting metal. Axes in case they needed to break down the doors between the tunnels. Archie talked him through the layout of the base. Jack learned it by heart, counting the number of passageways that led off from the main tunnel, the cabins in each tunnel, from the rec room to the library to the fuel storage tanks. It would be dark inside; the power couldn't be switched on.

Archie circled the areas he thought gases could have built up, the water wells, the holes sunk deep into the ice to dispose of waste—human and chemical. He planned the route through the base as if they were a set of caves. They'd make a camp. Give themselves three days. Progress would be slow.

"The outside temperature is minus seventy-five at this time of year," he told Jack and Coty. "The winds usually whip around at about eighty miles an hour. It's 140 miles east of Thule, and the entrance to the base will be covered in snow. We'll have to dig it out before we can get in. They can't leave us there until they know we can get in, otherwise they might as well just drop us in the middle of nowhere and let us freeze to death. We'll need help to open it up."

"I'll brief the commander at Thule," Coty said. "Do you really think there's a chance Connor could have survived, trapped in one of these rooms in darkness?"

"With the right clothes, food, and water, then yes. Physically he could stay alive. But the cold, it drains you. Everything is an effort. You'd just want to sleep. And mentally you'd have to build yourself a whole world, a routine. Divide your time into night and day. Mark it somehow. Even then," Archie shook his head and stared ahead, "he'd need to believe someone was coming back. He'd have to tell himself each day that today could be the day he's rescued, knowing that it probably won't be, but believing it could be. The Inuits who helped us site the base have a word for it, for the feeling the night will never end. The fear that comes over you. The gradual inability to distinguish your dreams and nightmares from reality. They call it the dark that doesn't sleep. They say it's like a sickness."

"What's the cure?" Coty asked.

"Dawn," Archie replied.

"He'll have to make his own sunrise, each day," Jack said. "Inside his head. He'll need a serious capacity for self-delusion to get through this." He corrected himself. "Hope. Not self-delusion. Hope's a balance of fantasy and pragmatism. People who suffer delusions don't know the difference. Do you think he can do that?"

Archie shrugged.

"I'd give Connor a better chance than anyone," he said. "But who knows. He might have just laid down and given up. It's what most people would do. It's what your body would tell you to do. It's your fastest way out of the endless darkness. And it's been well over two months. Just close your eyes and join it."

Archie and Jack flew on a cargo plane to the military base at Thule on February 22, almost three months after the fire Stiglitz had started.

It was cold and noisy in the plane, a Lockheed Starlifter. After the first few attempts at a kind of shouted conversation they gave up and let the sound of the jet engines win. They sat for over six hours on the narrow red benches that ran the length of the fuselage. The cargo was stacked about three inches from their knee caps, and when the plane juddered and shook through a patch of cold air the heavy crates rattled against them.

They landed at Thule as the sun was rising. The dark sky giving way to pale gray. It wasn't until they'd unloaded their gear that Jack realized the sun was going to take at least a month to get any higher in the sky. The pale dawn he could see in the distance was simply the slow end of a winter night.

Two enormous hangars loomed over the runway. Their floodlights cast layers of overlapping shadows across the snow, so that every shape was in three places at once. Including Jack. Including Archie. The Lockheed taxied into a hangar, already skimmed with a layer of snow. A giant turning awkwardly, seeking shelter.

Jack pulled the hood of his parka up and tightened the cords so it held his head tightly. The muffled warmth made the cold on his face even more intense. He looked around, turning his whole body, his sight restricted by the hood. He'd forgotten the scale the military worked on. The vast expanse of runway. The enormous fuel tanks. The strange emptiness of the outpost. Everything entirely practical, functional. Accommodation for soldiers consisted of prefabricated cabins. They looked like large cardboard boxes strewn about in the snow. The gear Jack and Archie had bought was unloaded from the plane and stacked against the wall of the hangar. A member of the ground crew took them to meet the Air Force commander.

"You ever felt a cold like this?" Archie said as they walked through the snow to the commander's hut on the west side of the base.

Jack shook his head. "Wind's got teeth," he said.

They flew out later that afternoon on a twin-engine plane that had a pair of short, wide skis looped under the wheels. The skis made it feel as if they were never going to get off the ground, but once they turned into the headwind the plane leaped upward. There were six on board, including the pilot. Three members of ground crew had been sent with shovels to help dig out the entrance to the camp. Even with the extra weight in the plane they were thrown about like a bumblebee in a storm. Archie was silent, his hands tight on the arms of his seat. Jack felt his stomach lurch with each dive and swoop of the little plane. The base commander had described it as the edge of the world. And that's what it was. The insignificance of the tiny plane in the vast sky played on his mind.

"How long will it take to get there?" Jack asked the pilot.

"About an hour," the pilot replied. "Maybe less now that the wind's behind us. Won't be easy to find though. And this time of year, end of winter, you've got about three feet of snow above the permafrost."

"Is it hard to land on?" Jack asked.

"Nah, it's a very forgiving surface. Smoother than tarmac. Absorbs some of the bumps. Just takes a little longer to get off the ground."

The plane banked and the pilot switched on the landing lights. The beams raked the ground.

"Should be near here," he said. "But I don't want to set down till I've found it." He turned another circle, pointing the plane toward the ground. Circles of white appeared below them, as if they were looking through binoculars at the blur of white snow. Jack couldn't see anything other than flat ground. The pilot lifted the plane again and banked in a wider circle, then pointed the nose downward.

"There," he said. "You see that indentation?" Jack stared at where he was pointing. The lights cast a fleeting shadow over a broad trench. It grew as they sped toward it then burst back into darkness as they flew past. "That's the slope that leads down to the entrance. We'll have to do some digging. Hard to say how much. Maybe four feet."

He banked the plane once more then put it down as close to the entrance as he could get.

"You've got a hell of a sense of direction," Jack said. "Like a human gyroscope. Don't think I could remember which way we're pointing or how far into a turn we've gone."

"Done a lot of night flying," the pilot replied. "Wouldn't be much use out here if I hadn't."

The plane lights caught the slope that led down to the doors. Even though they'd stopped moving, the plane shook as the wind tried to pick them up and throw them back into the sky.

"First we dig out the entrance, then we unload the gear," the pilot said. The three members of ground crew and the pilot fastened snowshoes to their boots, then made their way awkwardly out of the small cabin, down the steps, and onto the snow. Jack followed, Archie behind him. The heavy parkas restricted their movement, and reduced their field of vision by half. They trooped toward the slope—sliding, crunching over snow—swinging the flashlight wide, looking for the broad channel that swooped down to the entrance.

The slope dipped down to a depth of about three meters. They walked down it, toward a wall of corrugated metal that stretched eight meters across.

"This is the entrance," Archie said, tapping a gloved hand on the metal. "We're standing about halfway up the main doors. There's a smaller opening set into them. We need to dig down another two meters to get to that. It's in the left-hand door." He took his shovel and dragged it over the snow, marking out a rectangle. "We clear this space. It'll give us a chance to open the door and get inside."

The rest of them nodded. Talking took effort, meant you had to draw in a lungful of painfully cold air and raise your voice to be heard above the wind. They set to work, digging out the snow, piling it on either side, clearing a path that sloped down to the entrance. The pilot moved the plane so the lights were shining directly at them. The yellow-white light gave an unearthly phosphorescence to the crystals in the snow.

Down and down they went, the shovels cutting away blocks of snow, which grew grittier and more brittle the deeper they went.

They cleared a big enough space to open the small door set into the main doors. It had taken just over an hour; it felt longer. Jack was hot with effort in his thick clothes. The sweat on his forehead stung in the cold.

"Feels like someone's taken a layer of skin off, doesn't it?" Archie said. "Move slowly. You don't want to get hot. You don't want to sweat. The wind'll freeze the moisture and you'll get an ice burn." He reached into his pocket and passed Jack a handkerchief. Jack pressed it to his forehead.

Archie turned and shuffled to the door, using the handle of his shovel to yank it open. He pulled it outward, the hinges reluctantly giving way. A rectangle of darkness opened up like the entrance to a tomb. Jack stared into it. The entrance to the tunnels under the ice. Somehow he was more afraid of going in there then he was of standing outside. He felt as if he was about to step into someone else's nightmare. Archie stared at him.

"What is it?" he asked.

"Nothing," Jack answered quickly.

"Let's unload your gear, get it inside," the pilot said. He walked back to the plane, up the slope. The others followed. Slowly, as if encumbered by old age, they unloaded the lamps, the generator, the cans of fuel, the heaters, the oxy cutter, the tent, the field telephone, and the food. They piled it onto a sled and slid it down to the entrance of the base.

"We'll be back in three days," the pilot said. "That's if the weather's ok. If it's not, you'll just have to hunker down and wait for us. Watch the fuel doesn't freeze. Here." The pilot reached into his pocket and took out a hip flask. "I want it back, so don't get lost in there." He stared at the entrance. "Good luck."

"Thank you." Archie took the flask.

Jack had a sickening feeling of dread as he watched the pilot and his crew head back up the slope toward the plane. He didn't wait to watch them take off.

"Best get inside," he said.

44

Greenland, abandoned US military base
February 22, 8:00 P.M.

They pulled the sled through the door, hefting it over the sill and onto the duckboards inside. Jack flicked his flashlight over the walls and the ceiling. A high arch above them, made from huge, curved sheets of metal. After the noise of the wind outside, the air was still and quiet. It waited for them to make a sound, then mimicked it with faltering echoes. Jack found it unsettling. More than that, he felt a raw and primal fear.

"Let's get the generator fired up," Archie said. "I'll run the pipes outside for the fumes. We'll set up camp in the offices off the main tunnel. It'll be quieter." Jack helped unravel the cables, making his way down the main tunnel and into a side tunnel. His breath clouded in front of him. The silence was vast.

The generator ticked over then started to chug away. Jack was grateful for the noise. He tried the door of a cabin. It wouldn't move. He gave it a shove with his shoulder, and it opened. Archie followed, rigging up lights and a heater. Jack looked around. The cabin was small. A noticeboard was still tacked to the wall, a timetable pinned to it.

A couple of broken chairs were stacked in a corner of the room and, in the yellow light of the lamps, Jack could see the outline of a cross on the wall, as if someone had drawn a line in dust around the religious ornament before taking it away.

"Was this the chaplain's office?" Jack said.

Archie looked around.

"Yeah, think so. You want to rest up a while?" Archie said. "Eat something?"

"No," Jack replied. "Let's bring our gear in here, set up the lights and heaters then get moving."

Jack followed Archie along the main tunnel. The ice walls glinted in the flashlight. Air still and un-breathed. It smelled of cold and metal. Something else too. Fuel. Charred wood. Jack checked the map. They passed the rec room. He shone the flashlight into the cabin, not sure what he was expecting to see. Not sure how much of what Stiglitz told him had been true. On the floor were three backpacks and clothes spread around.

Henry, Connor, and Stiglitz had slept here. Archie pushed past him into the room.

"Whisky," he said, picking up a bottle from the floor. It was half-full.

"Don't drink it," Jack replied. "It might have belonged to Stiglitz. We'll take it with us. I'll get it tested."

They had camped in this room, the three of them, while they waited to be rescued. That much of the story was true. And, in the corner of the room, clothes and a sleeping bag were spread out, making a rough circle, a nest, just as Stiglitz had described. Maybe Henry had lost it, Jack thought. A makeshift pillow still bore the impression of his head. He knelt and picked it up. Standard army-issue clothing: cargo pants, vests, and tees tied together with a sweater. Tied together carefully. Thoughtfully. He wondered if Connor had made it for Henry. Made him a pillow. A small act of kindness in the midst of the darkness. Rest your head until the nightmares subside.

He swept the floor with his flashlight. The beam picked out a black rook from a chess set lying on its side by the far wall.

They carried on their search. Back into the main tunnel, then down another of the side tunnels. Every so often Jack heard a rush of wind from deep inside the base, as if it was gasping for breath. The snow hadn't completely suffocated the place yet. They checked the chapel. There were rows of chairs facing forward, toward an empty wall. The altar had been removed. On the floor a couple of discarded hymnals. Back into the main tunnel. Then a turn to the left. Further into the base, to the kitchens. The ovens were gone. The sinks and pipe work remained. The pipes had split where the water had frozen. The floor was slippery, the base had laid a trap. They weren't welcome here. Jack made his way carefully over the ice and opened the door at the back of the kitchen cabin. Storage. Sacks of flour. Cans of meat and vegetables.

Back to the main tunnel. The smell of charred wood and fuel grew stronger. The air tasted bitter. They turned right, into another tunnel. Flashlight catching the burnt-out cabin. It had sunk into the floor as the fire burned and the hard-packed snow beneath it melted, and it now looked like a raft trapped in the ice. The wooden walls blackened and broken. The roof of the cabin burned away.

Above it the arched metal in the roof had sagged as the walls of the tunnel began to melt. Jack flicked his flashlight over them. Icicles had formed. Ice on the floor too. Pools of it. The light caught something metal, two curved poles sticking out of the ice floor.

He bent down to look at it. A sled.

"I bet Stiglitz used this to drag Henry's frozen body here," he said. "All the way to the cabin." Archie joined him, looked briefly at the sled.

"I still can't believe it." Archie shook his head. "Shutting him outside. Pouring gas on his body. Watching him burn." The metal roof creaked. A strange sound. "You think it's stable?" Archie asked. He flicked the beam of his flashlight over the walls and the collapsed tunnel roof.

"No," Jack said. "Let's move."

They checked the hangar where machinery had been stored. Rusting barrels were lined up against the wall and small pools of spilt oil traced an uneven path across the ice floor, like the footprints of a wounded animal. Sheets of tarpaulin lay discarded and crumpled in the middle of the vast space. Jack pulled at one of them to see what was underneath. The material was set hard as a sheet of metal, making his hands cold even in his gloves. Felt as if the tips of his fingers could snap off. Archie helped him lift it. Underneath lay nothing more than broken duckboards and stacks of corrugated steel.

"It's late," Archie said. "Almost midnight. I need to eat. And we should rest up a few hours."

Jack nodded. His lungs ached from the cold air and the effort of moving. They walked back to the office where they'd made their camp, slow progress, careful on the slippery floor. The generator rumbled away near the entrance to the tunnel. The room was warm, heaters on, lights on.

Archie lit the Primus stove. Jack struggled to open a couple of cans of meat stew. His arthritic hand felt numb and the sharp edge of the can opener was useless without force and direction. Archie took it off him and opened the can quickly, emptying the food into a pan.

Jack slumped onto the floor, his back against the wall. The electric bar heaters gave off a small circumference of warmth that felt as luxurious as a California sunrise. He pulled off his gloves, loosened his boots. The generator chugged away in the distance. Jack stared at the red bar of heat as if he was looking into a fire.

Fuel burned to drive an engine in a generator to make electricity to make heat. There was something not right about that equation, the inefficiency, the effort, but then there was something not quite right about people trying to survive in these conditions either.

"What was it like, living here?" Jack said, watching as Archie stirred the stew in a thin metal messtin on the flame.

Archie shrugged. "The place had a purpose. A mission. It was alive, alive with routines and shifts and people always busy. Ambition and energy. And we had a theater too. Movies occasionally. It didn't feel like this." He gestured with his fork at the space around them. "This strange emptiness. The cold always at your fingertips, waiting to draw you in. Put you to sleep."

Jack nodded.

"I wanted to see it," Jack said. "Ever since Stiglitz started talking I wanted to see it." He peered at the map. "We've still got the missile bays to search. The tunnel that held the reactor, too, and the waste tunnels. Also, the wells they sunk to melt water." Archie ladled out spoonfuls of the meat stew.

"Let's eat, then we can get some rest," he said. Above them they heard the creak of the roof. "Or at least try to. We'll look for the body tomorrow."

"You don't think he'll be alive?" Jack said.

Archie shrugged. "I don't think I would be. Even if Stiglitz left cans of food and water. Would you have the will to keep going, not just let yourself slip into the cold? All you have to do is stop eating and drinking and wait till you fall asleep."

Jack shrugged. "I'd wake up again. I'd want to believe someone would get here. I don't think I could give up on that idea, even if I wanted to. Some part of me would disagree."

45

Greenland, abandoned US military base
February 22, 10:00 P.M.

An exhausted darkness filled Jack's head and stilled his body. He slept for three hours. Then he woke with a jolt, unsure where he was. The flashlight lay beside his camp bed. He felt as if he was spinning, falling in the darkness. He grasped for it, flicked it on, spun the beam over the ceiling of the cabin, then over the floor. The world stopped spinning. Still again. He could hear water dripping. The low rumble of the generator. The empty quiet. Something else too. He listened. A creaking sound. Metal on metal. The frame of the cabin retracting.

He rolled onto his side. Tried to sleep. The noise continued. There was something about it. It was more of a scrape, metal running over metal. Not a creak. And it was consistent. A scrape, a pause, more scraping. Another pause.

"Archie," he whispered. There was no response. "Archie," he repeated. This time a muffled *"What?"*

"Can you hear that?" Jack said. Archie listened.

"S'nothing," he replied through his sleeping bag.

"Where's it coming from?"

"Go to sleep."

The scraping stopped. Then started again, different rhythm.

"That's not a random sound," Jack said. "Something's making it."

Archie pushed himself up on his shoulders. Tilted his head, pulled off his hat.

"It'll be the generator."

"It's not coming from the main tunnel," Jack said. "It's from somewhere deeper inside the base." He stood up.

"Wait," Archie replied. "You're not going anywhere on your own. It's too dangerous."

"Come with me then."

Archie cussed then threw back his cover.

"Waste of time," he said. "We should be resting. Ain't no point getting all worked up. You got to pace yourself in the cold."

Jack put on his boots and wrapped himself in the parka.

"The noise might stop if we wait. Come on."

They left the cabin, followed the main tunnel, Archie cussing and stumbling in his tiredness. Jack kept stopping to listen.

"It's this way," he said. Their flashlights flickered over the floor. "You must be able to hear it now."

Jack was awake. His senses alert. The ice crystals in the tunnel walls glistened. You could still see the horizontal lines where the plows had cut out the snow, no longer straight, but flexing with the gradual movement of the ice.

"Where are we now?" Jack said, taking the map out. Archie pointed at a section of tunnel.

"The cabins the scientists used are that way," he said, pointing at another tunnel. "It's not much further."

Jack's feet were cold and clumsy. The door to the tunnel was set into an ice wall and was shut fast. He tried to turn the handle with his gloved hand, but it wouldn't move. Instead he shoved it and shunted it with his shoulder.

"Ease up," Archie said. "There's no point rushing this, getting hot. We can come back in the morning and warm it up."

"No," Jack said. "We don't leave him a second longer than necessary. I'm going to get an axe."

"You don't even know if he's there . . ." Archie called after him as Jack stumbled back to their cabin. Archie sat by the door and waited, weary with cold. It took twenty minutes for Jack to come back. He had the axe tucked in his belt and was dragging the oxy-acetylene torch with him, the two tanks clinking together as he pulled it across the wooden floor.

"Why you've brought that?" Archie asked.

"In case we need it," Jack replied, leaning it up against the wall. He took a step back, then swung the axe into the door. The wood splintered. He hit it twice more. Kicked it open. Archie stood back, surprised at the level of force Jack exerted.

"Can you hear it?" Jack said. "I can't hear it anymore."

"I can't hear anything. I don't think I could hear much to begin with."

"It was coming from this tunnel."

They walked down the tunnel. The door to the first cabin was open, hanging off its hinges at an awkward angle. Jack pulled it outward to make room for them to pass, and the brittle metal hinges snapped. He lifted the door and put it to one side. They walked through darkness of the abandoned room, boots leaving a wet imprint on the linoleum floor. It was longer than the rec room. Filing cabinets lined one side. The air was stale and still smelled of cigarettes. Lights hung from the ceiling. A door at the end of the room. Jack opened it. Darkness stretched out in front of them. They shone their flashlights on the decking. Ahead of them was another cabin. Jack hefted the heavy equipment through the door.

"That's where Stiglitz worked," Archie said. "His lab." He waved his flashlight at it. Jack walked to the door. He kicked at it. It shuddered, but didn't give way. He hit it with the axe. The wood splintered. He kept smashing it, wrecking the layers of chipboard until there was almost no door left. He kicked again. What was left of the frame collapsed inward. Archie stood back, watching him.

"You imagining that's Stiglitz?" he asked.

Jack grunted, shone his flashlight through the broken door. The light caught the silver of the stainless-steel worktop. A broken glass beaker. Papers and pens. A blackboard covered in chalk notes, partly smudged.

"I read a transcript of an interview with Henry, from when he was getting treatment. He said Connor thought there was a room at the back. Or at least some kind of cupboard he couldn't get into. Henry made it sound like some kind of secret compartment," Jack said.

"Not secret," Archie replied, flicking the beam of his flashlight over a door set into the rear wall. "It's a storage unit. For samples and chemicals and whatever else he needed for his work. Henry's imagination ran away with him. This way," he said.

Jack walked through the cabin. He shone his flashlight at the door. There were two wheels that had to be turned to open it.

"An air lock, like you'd get on a submarine," Jack said. He put the flashlight down on the worktop, angled the beam so it pointed at the door, and tried twisting one of the wheels. It wouldn't budge. He ran a gloved hand around the mechanism, feeling a layer of ice that bulged around the surface. "It's frozen shut."

Archie leaned close, shone his flashlight on it. "You know what that means?"

"It's cold in here?" Jack replied.

"Someone poured water on it. No other way for ice to form like that. You'd get a fine layer of crystals on the metal as the air cools. Not a layer of ice. Someone poured water on that."

"Listen," Jack said. "You hear that?"

They heard the same noise they'd heard earlier. The same scraping.

"It's coming from inside. Get it open," Jack said. He reached behind him and dragged the oxy-cutter to the door, then banged on it.

"Connor, are you in there?"

He stood back to listen. No sound came from inside.

"It's air tight," Archie replied. "He can't be in there. He can't be alive."

"Open it," Jack said.

Archie pulled the tanks toward the door.

"I'll cut a hole. This thing's too hot to melt the ice without damaging the mechanism. Stand back. Don't look at the flame."

Jack held the flashlight so Archie could set the pressure levels for the gas tanks then stood back, watching as he applied the fierce blue flame to the metal door. The brightness burned red against the metal. The flame sinking through it in a roar of heat. He drew a slow rectangle. Angled his body away as sparks skimmed off the surface. A black line flowing behind the flame. The cabin filled with the smell of hot metal and smoke. Jack couldn't help but look, transfixed by the brightness of the light. When he turned away, the red line and blue flame stayed with him, imprinted on his retina.

At last the roar of the flame stopped. Archie switched off the gases, waved a hand to try and disperse some of the smoke. It smelled the same as the garage after the fire.

Jack walked up to the door.

"Connor? You in there?" he yelled. There was no answer. He raised his boot and kicked at the metal. The bottom section bent inward. The top clung on. He pushed it, shoved it with his shoulder, smashed it with his good hand. Smashed it with his bad hand. The panel gave in and fell onto the floor.

Jack grabbed his flashlight and stepped through the doorway. He was standing in a large room. A storage cupboard, made from stainless steel. The first thing that hit him was the smell, a sour odor of unwashed bodies and human waste so strong it almost pushed him backward. He coughed, fought the urge to retch, then raised a hand to cover his mouth and nose. Shelves lined the walls, stacked with tins and water containers. Jack's flashlight picked up shapes on the floor, clothing, buckets, containers. And in the corner of the room something else, cowering like a wounded animal. It shielded its eyes from the light, trying to make itself smaller, muttering soft, rasping sounds Jack couldn't quite make out.

He reached forward and placed a hand on the shoulder of the shaking figure.

"Hey, it's ok. We've come for you," he said. The man flinched and pulled away.

"*Not again, I'm not having this dream again. Go away,*" he whispered.

"You're not dreaming," Jack said, crouching down next to him. Slowly the man turned his face toward him. "We've come for you. We're going to take you home."

The man's eyes flickered. He frowned, trying to focus on Jack. Then he reached out a hand, as if he still didn't trust what he was seeing, and gripped Jack's arm tightly.

"You're real?"

"Sure am," Jack replied. "We're taking you home."

46

Greenland, abandoned US military base
February 23, 3:00 A.M.

They helped Connor back to their cabin. He didn't speak, but held onto them tightly, his hands clasped around their arms, his body shaking. Jack lifted him up the steps, kept talking. Telling him it would be alright. Explaining what they were doing, where they were going, when they would be picked up. Anything, just to give him the sound of a human voice.

Archie put on the lamps and turned up the heaters. Connor sat down on Jack's camp bed. He breathed deeply. His arm over his eyes, blocking out the light.

"Turn off a couple of the lights," Jack said.

"Thank you," Connor said, blinking.

"Good to see something. But it hurts. And it's blurred."

A single light remained. Archie angled it upward.

Connor appeared dazed, in a dreamlike state. He pulled off his woolen hat to reveal a mass of matted black hair and a forehead so pale it seemed to have been bleached white. Small scratches crisscrossed his skin and beneath the unkempt beard his lips were raw and cracked.

There were blisters on his fingers and black bruises under the broken nails, as if he'd been using them as tools. He gripped the edge of the camp bed, holding on to it, making sure it was real and not about to suddenly vaporize and return him to the locked darkness of the storeroom.

"Here," Jack said, passing him a water bottle.

Connor took it and drank. The world was starting to take shape. His breathing was beginning to slow.

He turned to Archie. Blinked, squinted. Rubbed his eyes.

"I know you, don't I?" Connor said, staring at him. The words caught in his throat.

"I'm Archie Bell. I was here last year. Didn't have the beard."

"That's right. Missile crew. But not you," he said, looking at Jack. "Who're you?"

"My name is Dr. Miller, I'm a psychiatrist. I practice in New York." As Jack said the words he realized how strange it must have sounded.

Connor's eyebrows went up. He looked around.

"We're not in New York. Unless I left my mind back in that storeroom."

Jack smiled.

"No. I was helping with, well, I was helping some people try and work out what the hell happened here."

"Just the two of you?" Connor said, looking round the room, his face confused. "Where's the rest of the rescue team?"

Archie spoke. "We are the rescue team. This man decided you were alive and that we should fly all the way out here, open up the base, smash through anything in our way, and bring you home."

Connor drew another deep breath and took a sip of water. "Well, thank you, sir. What made you think I was alive?"

"Stiglitz told me," Jack said.

"He did?" Connor coughed.

"Not in so many words, but I worked out what he meant."

"Where is he? I hope to God you've got that sorry son of a bitch in solitary."

Jack frowned. "He's being watched closely. It's complicated."

Connor stared ahead. "Give me some time alone with him and I'll un-complicate it for you." His hands were shaking as they gripped the camp bed. The knuckles white. He cleared his throat, breathed slowly, deeply. "What did Stiglitz say that made you realize he'd left me here?"

"Something about you being held captive. Always wanting to prove yourself."

Connor frowned. Shook his head. Then he started laughing. He laughed so hard he started coughing and rolled over on the bed.

"That's it? That's all he said?" His voice came through gasps of breath as he lay on his back. "And you came all the way out here?"

Jack nodded.

"It was the way he said it. Present tense. And by that stage, I had a good idea of what he was capable of."

Connor got his laughter under control, pulled back from hysteria. He sat up.

"Thank God. Henry worked him out before me. Henry had good instincts. Whatever they said about him, he got people. He could see right through them. Where is he? What did Stiglitz do to him?"

"He's dead. I'm sorry."

Connor sighed. Nodded slowly.

"How?"

"Stiglitz shut him outside, let him freeze to death. Can you tell us what happened? Only if you feel up to it. Otherwise rest. We've got plenty of time."

"I'd rather talk," Connor said. "Makes a change to have people here to listen." He took another sip of water, almost smiled. "First few days were ok. I set up the generator. Rigged up lights. Stiglitz and Henry argued about petty stuff. Stiglitz didn't help with anything, kept disappearing. Going off for walks through the tunnels. We didn't know what he was doing. Then on day four or five Henry caught him coming back in from outside. There was no reason for him to go out. It was dangerous. He gave us some bullshit about checking the vents. He'd never done anything helpful the whole time we were there. He wasn't checking any vents. And he had a rucksack on his back. Wouldn't show Henry what was in it. They had a fight. Well, you couldn't really call it a fight. Henry was bigger and stronger. Stiglitz was no match for him. Henry pulled the rucksack off him. Damn it if he didn't have a radio pack in there. Don't know where he got it from. Everything had been taken away. Henry started saying he knew what he was doing, knew who he'd been talking to. How it all made sense now. He wasn't going to get away with it. Stiglitz just ran off into the tunnels. We didn't see him the next day. Looked all over for him. Then in the evening we could feel it coming on. This awful sleep, this darkness. It soaked us up. Like we'd been necking bottles of bourbon."

"How did he do it?" Jack said. "How did he drug you?"

"Must've been the water. I used to collect snow to melt. We had a couple of containers. He must have put something in them. I went first. Henry was bigger and heavier. It took longer. I remember Stiglitz coming in the room, taking a look at us. Henry getting up. Staggering across the floor. Trying to get hold of him. Yelling at him, his voice all slurred. I could barely keep my eyes open. Stiglitz disappeared into the tunnel. Henry followed, lurching all over the place. Stiglitz was leading him somewhere. Taunting him. Henry didn't know what he was doing. He wasn't dressed for the cold. We were out of our minds. I couldn't stop him. He chased Stiglitz out into the darkness. I could hear the wind coming in. He would've frozen in a matter of minutes. Wouldn't have known where he was or which direction to turn." Connor's voice broke, his shoulders shook. "I should've guessed. Should've known Stiglitz would try something," he said.

"You couldn't have known what he'd do," Jack said. "Or what he was capable of."

Connor took another sip of water.

"What the hell did Stiglitz say when the rescue crew came? I was missing and Henry was dead, even he would struggle to explain that."

"He said he was you."

"He what?" Connor almost choked on the water.

"He put your tags on. Poured gas on his face and hands, burned himself beyond recognition. He was shipped back to Walter Reed, and when he woke up he told us he was you and that Henry had lost his mind and killed Stiglitz, then started a fire which he'd tried to stop."

Connor ran his hands through his hair.

"You thought he was me? Everyone thought he was me? What about Chrissie? She would've come for me. She would've insisted on seeing me. You can't stop her." His voice faltered at the mention of her name.

"I know," Jack said. "She was at the hospital, waiting for you every day. He kept saying he didn't want to see her. She kept saying you wouldn't say that, even if you were all burned up you wouldn't say you didn't want to see her."

"Course I wouldn't. I'd want her next to me."

"Well, she's waiting for you," Jack said. "She wouldn't accept that you were dead."

Connor sat very still. He covered his eyes with his hand. Jack sat next to him, put an arm around him.

"You got a drink or something?" Connor asked.

Jack passed him the hip flask.

Connor took a sip. Then another. He handed it back.

"I can't tell you how good it feels to see light," he said. "And people."

"We'll have you home soon. Plane's due to pick us up day after tomorrow. We'll call them, get them to come sooner."

Archie got up and started to prepare the radio equipment. As he did so he said, "How did you survive in there? If you don't mind me asking. Don't think I could've kept going."

Connor shrugged.

"I don't know. First few weeks it was real bad. I tried to set up a routine. Do some exercises. Push-ups. Star jumps. Anything I could remember. Sometimes I shouted at myself like a goddamn drill sergeant. I did that morning and evenings, same time each day. In the afternoons I went over all the books I ever read, every story I ever heard. Even ones from Sunday School, trying to bring back each page, each drawing, every last detail. And I built a house, one with a view out over the prairie for me and Chrissie, chose every piece of timber, hammered each tile onto the roof." He shook his head and paused. "But the time. There was so much of it. I kept telling myself someone was coming. Stiglitz left me food, cans of stuff. Half the time I had no idea what it was. Sweet, savory. Meat, fruit salads, biscuits. Gallons of water too. The room was insulated, always above freezing. I had gloves and a hat and thermals. He didn't want me dying, not before I'd had a chance to suffer. A few weeks in I found the ventilation shaft in the ceiling. I got the cover off, broke it up, and used it to cut away at the metal tube that went up through the ice, breaking off little pieces, digging out the snow around it so I could fit. I figured it would take about three or four months to get to the surface.

"I knew that even if I got out I'd die, but at least I'd die trying to get back to Thule. One-hundred-and-forty-mile trek westward. Ten miles a day. Two weeks. That's what I thought about. That's what kept me going. I had it all worked out. And those last few days, when I looked up through the shaft I was sure I could see something. Not the same black that surrounded me. A different tone, a lighter tone, a kind of gray. It kept me going. It was dawn. I knew it. Light was coming into the sky. The end of winter."

The plane picked them up the next day. They flew back to Thule, then joined a cargo flight to Andrews Air Force Base. During the flight Jack couldn't get the thought of Stiglitz out of his head. The scale of his cruelty, the fact that the Agency was going to do a deal with him. Well, now they had a witness to his crimes, surely they'd tear up whatever agreement they had. He needed to be locked away. He needed to suffer.

They landed on a bright February afternoon, sunlight sweeping across the runway, shadows long, air fresh and cold. Coty was there to meet them. So was Chrissie. Connor gripped the rail as he descended the steps, squinting, moving like a man not sure if he's awake or dreaming. An ambulance was waiting, ready to check him over. Chrissie broke away from Coty and ran toward Connor, before the medics could get anywhere near, and threw her arms around him, almost knocking him over.

Jack and Archie followed down the steps, past the embracing couple. They were spinning, like a planet, oblivious to anything else in their newly formed world.

Coty stepped forward and held out his hand to Archie in an oddly formal gesture. Archie took it. Coty told him he'd done a *fine job*, that he hoped it wasn't too cold out there. The words felt superfluous. Archie nodded awkwardly. Coty cast a glance at Connor.

"Is he ok?" he asked.

"He seems surprisingly well," Jack replied. "But I want to do his formal psych assessment myself. And I'm doing it before you start the debrief."

"Fine," Coty said. He took a step back, looked Jack up and down. "Something different about you, Jack. Can't quite put my finger on it."

Jack shrugged.

"That's why I'm the psychiatrist," he replied, fishing about in his coat pocket for a packet of cigarettes.

"If I didn't know you any better, I'd say you were happy. And not just T-bone steak and fries happy. But three-week vacation in Hawaii happy."

Jack grunted and lit the cigarette. More like Tokyo wedding day happy, he thought as he glanced at Connor and Chrissie. They had finally, reluctantly, withdrawn from each other so the medics could check Connor over. Stiglitz had come so close to winning. To ending Connor's life. To ruining Chrissie's. But this time Jack had turned the steering wheel in time. He'd got them out of the way of the oncoming truck.